VIPER

—————

THE HOLD ME SERIES
BOOK 3

ALY STILES

This novel was previously published under the pseudonym Alyson Santos and is a work of fiction intended for mature readers. Events and persons depicted are of a fictional nature and use language, make choices, and face situations inappropriate for younger readers.

Names, characters, places and events are the product of the author's imagination. Any resemblance to actual events, locations, organizations, or people, living or dead, is entirely coincidental and not intended by the author.

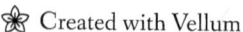 Created with Vellum

1

CLICHÉ

4:58.

A shiver of relief passes through me, an hour later than usual. Second day in a row. Fourth day this week. I'm on a roll.

I study the shadows in the hollows of my ceiling, those ghosts you see in the first seconds of consciousness. They're angry today. I guess they've been disgruntled lately—assholes. All I can do is wait until... There it is. The ceiling fan, evidence of recessed lighting.

5:03. *Shit.*

I push myself up on my elbows, reluctant to move until I make a definitive decision about Alicia. No, Alice. No... Dammit. I study the emerging silhouette of an early-twenties bartender. Gentle curves, smooth back still exposed because we never totally committed to what kind of night this would be. Yep, I got wasted and fucked a bartender. As if I'm not already a walking cliché. I should do breakfast for this one. It's the least I can do for all the free booze she fronted me.

I roll out of bed, pissed that I'm awake three hours after

ending the night. Not that it's new. It's become the norm over the last two weeks.

"Babe?" she mumbles into the darkness.

"Go back to bed. It's early."

"Then why are you up?"

"Can't sleep."

"Everything okay?"

"Great."

Why wouldn't things be great? I had everything. Now I have nothing except a stranger in my bed whose name I can't remember. I'm fucking great.

I squint into the blinding light and let it burn my eyes. For a moment, the stars spare me my reflection.

Funny how I used to admire the cocky SOB gazing back at me. Funny how quickly things can fall apart.

A knock at the door. *Seriously?*

"There's another bathroom down the hall." I think I do a pretty good job disguising my irritation.

"I know. Just checking to make sure you're good."

I grip the edge of the sink and force out an, "all good" instead of the curse running through my head.

"Okay. It's just I've never slept with a musician who gets up before eleven, let alone five. Is it me?"

I don't remember this part of her last night. Then again, I don't remember much after she followed me home.

"Yeah? You fuck a lot of musicians?"

Silence.

"Asshole."

Guess that answers my question about breakfast.

I DECIDE on a nice homebrew today, not feeling a trip to Tim Horton's. Alicia or Alice or whatever was gone when I ventured from the bathroom, and now a twinge of regret gnaws at my stomach. I don't know if I liked her, but she deserved better than what she got.

Still, my pain is more selfish. A few more hours with Alicia/Alice would have meant less time alone with my messed-up head. Some extra peace before the confrontation with my phone would've been nice. That stupid device never fails to highlight how my life has fallen apart.

With coffee brewing and island light blazing, I suck it up. Sure enough, several messages I don't want and none of the ones I do.

I scan the frantic texts from my manager and decide there's no way I'm listening to his voicemails. I get it: he's freaking out. Of course he is, but I have no answers for him. For any of them.

My phone buzzes and my eyes shoot to the screen like they do every time there's a chance it's Holland. But it isn't this time either. Why would it be? I've set new records on prick-level behavior toward the one person I care about beyond reason. Oh yeah, and completely shattered every single thing that mattered to me in the process. At least I'm efficient.

Nope, not my ex-best friend/bandmate when I check the e-mail. But there's a sale on deli items at the Superstore.

I shove my phone away and flinch at the shrill beep of the coffeemaker.

1. *Coffee.*
2. *Not looking at my phone.*

My to-do list now that I don't have music.

TODAY'S SCHEDULE of time-wasting is packed. It's a new talent, cramming my day with nothing and avoiding everything.

It's Friday, which means I watch TV for hours, work out even longer, and mess around on my guitar until I reach the threshold of what I can tolerate of my new life. That's when the bar comes in. Choosing which one among the network of choices in downtown Toronto has become the most stimulating part of my day.

I find myself at Stand and Stool for the second time this week, mostly because watching drunk hipsters muddle politics with angsty wrath has become my favorite distraction. Damn, and today I'm two hours earlier than yesterday, which was an hour earlier than the day before. Yes, the pattern registers on my brain as I take a seat, but it doesn't impact my conscience. I decide to compromise and go light for now.

"What do you have on draft?" I ask the bartender, a mercifully middle-aged man this time leaving zero chance of another Alicia/Alice regret.

"Amstel Light, Moosehead, Strong Bow, Heineken, Molson..."

"Any micros?"

"I have a Creemore Lager and Mill St. Tank House Ale."

"I'll take a pint of the lager."

"You got it."

Two tight-jeaned twenty-somethings on my left commiserate about an embargo imposed on a country they probably can't place on a map. Somehow this relates to elephants and a political dissident that isn't actually from said embargoed country. Also, pretty sure there are no elephants in that part of the world. What they lack in facts they more than make up for in passion and righteous scowling.

"What? No way! Wes?"

I turn toward the voice, my dark mood shifting into a smile. "Hannah Drake! Hey, sis."

"Oh my gosh, I can't believe you're here! Am I allowed to hug you even though you're fighting with my sister?"

"I'm not fighting with your sister," I say through her traitorous embrace.

"Uh, you quit the band."

"I didn't quit. She kicked me out."

She steps back, hands locked on my biceps to examine me like Grandma Wilkins used to do. "Well, can you blame her? You attacked her boyfriend. Twice, from what I understand."

"Attacked is a strong word."

"What word would you use?"

"Attacked."

She returns my grin and slides onto the stool next to me. "Luke's a good guy, you know."

"So everyone keeps telling me."

"People change. Look how much you've changed. You used to be a super-hot rock god. Now, you're just a schlub drowning his sorrows in a pint of broken dreams."

A snort rushes out. "Great, thanks. You're looking good too. Anyway, we're not broken up. Just on hiatus while we figure things out."

"A hiatus, huh? That sounds like a Label label."

"Hilarious. Hey, how's the job going? The boyfriend? What's his name again? Kirk Pastel-Tie?" At least this woman is used to my evasive subject changes.

"*Geoffrey* is fine. I'm living with him and his tie collection now. Job is okay too. I'm here to meet up with some coworkers."

"Yeah? Celebrating a big promotion?"

"More like the completion of another brutal week of lawyering."

I straighten for an exaggerated scan of the bar. "Yeah? Are any of them cute, single, and interested in a torrid affair with an ex-rockstar?"

"Depends what you mean by cute, torrid, and ex-rockstar."

I lean close, voice low. "I can be flexible."

She shoves me away. "Wow, so drowning your sorrows in booze and women? That's not cliché or anything."

"To be fair, they're pretty big sorrows."

"I always thought you were *creative*."

"Oh, I'm plenty creative, darling. Your friend won't be disappointed, I promise." I add a wink just to get a Hannah Drake eye roll. For old time's sake.

"Oh yeah? Like the time you drew my name in the Drake Family Gift Exchange and got me a Tim Horton's card?"

"You loved that gift card!"

"Sure, but I thought the debate was creativity not gift-giving capabilities."

I grunt and swallow another mouthful of Broken Dream lager.

"And anyway," she continues, "don't you think it's a little early in your retirement to consider yourself an ex-rockstar?"

"I have no clue. What's the timeframe on that?"

"Pretty sure it's not two weeks and at age twenty-nine."

I shrug and resume my fake scan of the floor. "Okay, then. Do you have any cute, single friends interested in a torrid affair with a rockstar on hiatus?"

Her radiant grin draws one from me. "I'll keep an eye out."

"Thanks."

"Speaking of which..." She waves over to a mixed-group of suits moving toward us. My crowd inspection becomes legitimate.

"What do you think?" she whispers, her conspiratorial glint sweeping over my face.

"Cute, but not so sure about the torrid-affair-with-a-rock-star angle."

"Yeah, sorry. They tend to prefer yachts to tats, but it's their loss."

I smirk and finish off the remnants of my drink. Yachts are pointless when you're on the road all the time. Maybe I should get a yacht now.

"You want to hang with us?" she asks. Great, a pity invite from my surrogate little sister. That's my life now.

"No, I'm fine. It was good to see you, though."

"You too." Her gaze turns serious. "We're going to miss having you around. I hope you patch things up with Holland soon."

I swallow. "Yeah, me too."

She squeezes my arm before leaving me alone with my empty glass.

TO SAY I'm affected by my encounter with Hannah would be an understatement. Rattled is more like it, and I find myself sifting through the veil of bar patrons more often than I'd like as the night wears on.

I catch a glimpse of her dark hair and formal business attire, grateful I turned down her invitation. I can't imagine how much I'd be hating whatever convo is making them chuckle into their martinis. Yeah, I don't get how Hannah Drake survives her own world.

Hannah has always been my favorite of Holland's sisters. She has an edge the others lack, a coarse wit that can grind through any bullshit, and heaven knows I'm caked in it. Holland has a similar quality, but she's softer somehow, too giving for a leech like me. Thankfully, we figured that out before locking ourselves into a marriage. But Hannah was never afraid to yank me off and toss me into the flames when I crossed a line she didn't like. A line like trying to fuck things up between her sister and her sister's boyfriend. I'd expected a slap, not a hug, the first time I saw her after the fall tour disaster. We'll chalk that one up to shock and her relief that it's Friday.

My phone buzzes. It's our manager, Jacob, again. Dammit. I ignore the call and drop it back on the bar.

"Ex-girlfriend?"

A polished woman stands too close not to be interested. Mid-forties, maybe. I look for a ring. No, thank god. I'm not into drama—except when it's necessary to protect the people I love. Which, let's be honest, is Holland Drake. She was my world for twenty years. Luke Craven better keep his shit together or I *will* kill him.

"Ex-girlfriend? I wish."

"Ex-wife, then?"

I grunt. "Definitely not."

"Current girlfriend?"

"Except I ignored the call."

"You could be a jerk."

I almost laugh and narrow my eyes for a fresh appraisal. "It's possible. Probably why I don't have a girlfriend."

"I'm Miranda."

"Wes."

She takes the seat beside me.

"What are you drinking?" she asks.

"Way more than I should be."

She signals the bartender. Gin and tonic for her. Another of what I'm having for me.

"You're buying me a drink?" I ask, eyeing her with renewed interest.

"You didn't stop me."

I shake my head, this time with a grin. "No, I guess I didn't."

"You have a nice smile. You should use it more often."

"Thanks. You have a nice ass."

She leans closer, fishing with bait even a teenage boy could recognize.

"What is it that you do, Wes?" she asks as the bartender slides her a glass. The stir stick raises to dark red lips, her tongue outlining the tip with enough aggression to hold my attention.

"I'm a musician." My game doesn't require more than that. My tattoos, the rigid definition pressing through lazy jeans and a fitted t-shirt. The air of not giving a fuck—which I don't. It's not even a game anymore.

"Oh, really? Do you play anywhere local?"

Now, *that's* always a fun question. Well, more specifically, their reaction to my answer.

"Sure, sometimes. We played the A.C.C. recently."

And there it is: the startled awe. The visions of ripping my clothes off in my posh rock god penthouse. Unabated lust to gush to her friends about the tryst with... She doesn't know who I am but it doesn't matter. I still haven't decided if she's going to find out.

"The A.C.C.? Really, wow."

I nod and drain my glass.

She wants to ask which band. It's all over her face but she's afraid of offending me, of hurting her chances at finding out what I look like stripped, sweaty, and pushing over her. I wait to see if she'll excuse herself to the bathroom to attempt an internet search. Yes, that's happened. Yes, it's always painfully obvious. I have a website, fan group, a few periodical covers, hundreds of images and promo shots. It's not hard.

Wes Alton, Tracing Holland. Well, formerly of Tracing Holland, but she won't discover that part yet. If Jacob has his way, no one will ever know because it's not happening. Over his dead body are we parting ways. For someone who's represented us for years, he still doesn't understand me at all.

"Hey, we're taking off," I hear behind me as a hand attaches to my shoulder. I turn and catch Hannah's grin. "I'd invite you, but I know lawyers aren't your thing." Her gaze flickers to Miranda before resting on me again.

"No, they're not. Just the one," I tease, enjoying her playful grimace.

"Sure, whatever. Hey, it was good to see you. You've still got my number, right? Stay in touch."

"Yeah. Same here."

Her fingers graze my neck before she disappears into the crowd behind her friends.

"She was cute."

She is, but describing Hannah Drake as "cute" feels wrong. She's my sister. Practically.

"Old friend."

"Really." The skepticism drips from her tone.

"Really."

Miranda studies the door, and my mood shifts. Defensive. It's been a quick transition for me lately.

"Girls don't look at 'friends' that way," she says, and now I'm just annoyed. All I know about this woman is her name and that she likes gin and chasing younger men.

I decide against being rude. She did buy me a drink after all. Two, I realize when the bartender shoves another beer toward me.

"What do you do?"

She adjusts closer at my renewed interest. "I'm an executive."

Hell yeah. I see it now. The power suit, the confidence. An attractive, experienced woman who knows what she wants never fails to get me hard. Her phone rattles on the bar, and my dick curses right along with her. She answers with an apologetic look. It's executive business stuff. Urgent. She's important.

Damn. Could have been an epic lay.

I'm fully prepared for her goodbye when she hangs up and asks for her check.

"I'm sorry, Wes. I have to run, but it was great to meet you."

I nod, watching her expression buckle at missing out on the opportunity to bed a rock god. But she'll get over it. The truth is Executive Miranda will probably be more interested in the fact that my father is Frederick Alton of Alton Media when she looks me up. Yep, that's out there for public consumption too. Wes Alton: poor rich boy.

"Here's my number, though. I'd love for you to use it," she says, scribbling on a napkin. Thick, dark eyelashes pound her message home.

"Thanks. Have a great night, Miranda," I say, studying her as she bites her lip and hesitates. I must be on point this evening if I'm giving Ms. Important Executive reason to pause when the office calls. Hannah would be proud.

Hannah.

Shit. Now I'm relieved that Miranda chose work over play. So not a rock god move. Classic schlub.

I GO HOME ALONE. No bartender, no horny executives, just me and my infuriating list of missed calls. I stretch out on the couch and finally return one, a terrible idea after a night of drinking, but that's my brand.

"Dammit, Wes. How long were you planning on ignoring me?"

"Thirteen days, apparently."

"Smartass. Wait, are you drunk?"

"Yes."

"Shit. I really need to talk to you."

I close my eyes but reopen them when the spinning makes my stomach churn. "So talk."

"But—"

"Talk, Jacob."

"Holland wants to negotiate. Work something out."

Silence.

"You there?"

"Huh?"

"I said Holland wants to negotiate."

Negotiate. That's what coworkers do. Business associates. Exes. Not lifelong best friends. I wouldn't have been able to respond to that sober.

"Hey, Wes. Hello?"

"Yeah?"

"Okay, so?"

"So, what?"

"I just told you Holland wants to keep the band together."

"Um, yeah. I heard you."

"You heard me? Dammit. Stop being a dick and just fix this already."

"Fix what?"

"Seriously? Unbelievable."

"She kicked me out. What am I supposed to do?"

"She didn't kick you out. She said she wants a different arrangement and formal contract between the two of you before you continue. You're on hiatus until you work it out, so let's do that and get you back on track."

My muscles contract, grip clenched on the phone until I fear for its warranty. Maybe it's the alcohol but this rage feels more universal.

"Come on every band goes through these growing pains. We'll—"

"*Every band?*"

"You know what I mean. It's a spat. It's—"

"You're talking about my best friend, Jacob! A band we started when we were teenagers. You're talking about something I gave up everything for. This is not some fucking business deal. This is my entire existence, everything that's important to me. So quit making it sound like a real estate transaction."

I gladly accept the silence on the other end. He doesn't get it. How could he? How could any of them? No one would except Holland, and she's done with me. I'm contract fodder now.

His voice is too calm for my temper when he continues. "You assaulted her boyfriend. You're lucky they didn't press charges and she's still willing to work anything out with you."

"Fuck you, Jacob," I say because he's absolutely right.

I hang up and turn off my phone so I don't have to ignore any more calls. I study the ceiling, letting my blurry mind take me to the moment I threw it all away. The moment my need to protect Holland shattered everything we'd built together. Was it stupid? Yes. Do I look like a jackass now that Luke's turning out to be a decent human being? Yes. Would I have done anything differently if I could go back? Hell no.

The nausea is beginning to climb from my stomach to my throat, and I force myself off the couch and stagger toward the bathroom. Four full meters. Impossible. Who designed this condo layout? I have to grip the wall for support as I inch toward safety.

New contract equals dissolved relationship.

I don't make it to the bathroom.

2

MIRANDA

I'm pretty sure rock bottom is a secluded alley with missing body parts, not the floor of your luxury condo, but it's not a place I'm proud to find myself the following morning.

I groan and force myself up, wincing from the blood throbbing through my head. I smell rotten, or is it the carpet? Probably both. Another proud moment for the new Wes Alton. I finish last night's failed journey to the bathroom and splash water over my face. The SOB doesn't look so cocky when he's staring into bloodshot eyes, wet streaks dripping down his cheeks onto a vomit-stained t-shirt.

I rid myself of the embarrassing reminder and run the shower. Forget my usual oasis in the master suite. I just need this shit off me as quickly as possible. I definitely need to ignore the fear that my disgust won't be erased by hot water and soap. It feels more permanent, a sickness that no amount of water can fix.

It's a short shower, ending with my head against the cold tile wall to catch my breath. I don't bother with a towel and shuffle back to my room. Perk of being alone. It drove one of my exes nuts, but then so did the way I folded my clothes, brushed my teeth, stacked the cabinets, and loaded the dishwasher. We lasted three weeks, which was still six days longer than any other relationship since Holland.

I throw on a pair of boxer-briefs and head to the kitchen to attempt coffee. My phone is still glaring at me from the table, but I'm not sure about that trial yet.

Dammit.

I wake the display, habit I guess, and wait grimly as it gathers evidence of everything I missed last night.

Jacob, check. And check. Oh, and check. C'mon, dude.

Shit. My sister too.

I click on that one.

"Wes!"

"Sophia!"

"Jerk. Hey, you're coming Friday, right? You never responded to the invitation."

"Friday?"

"Ugh, seriously? I hate you. My engagement party?"

Right. I sigh. "Depends. You still marrying that douche, Teddy?"

"Theodore, and stop being an ass. He's a good guy."

"So good he dumped you, what, three times if I recall?"

"It was complicated."

"By the fact that he thought he'd get a better offer from Lucy Vander-bitch."

"Wes, come on. That's in the past. We worked it out, okay? Please come. For *me?*"

That damn soft spot for my little sister.

"I don't suppose Dad will decide to sit this one out?"

"You two can be civil for three hours."

"Oh, I have no doubt he'll be *civil*."

"Please, Wes? Don't make me beg. Theodore is insisting on

all the rich people crap. Who's going to make fun of the stuffy linens and *canapés*?"

"Ah, yes. And the crudités. But of course," I add, horrible accent and all.

"Don't forget the catalog of aiolis."

"Truffle, for sure."

"Duck liver."

"Right. A zoo of livers."

"Unicorn tear cocktails."

I laugh. Damn, she's got me.

My breath escapes into the phone, and she squeals.

"You're coming?"

"I'll be there. But hey." This is important. "Only for you, got it? There will be no reconciliations, no interventions, and absolutely no references to Holland or any of the shit that went down."

Her hesitation doesn't inspire a lot of confidence. "Got it. Just you and your frowny face. But in return, you have to refrain from any backhanded insults to Theodore that he doesn't understand."

"Hmm... so I have to lower the reading level?"

"Stop it," she chuckles. "None at all. He's not as clueless as you think he is."

"But you admit he's still clueless."

"I'm hanging up now."

"Love you, sis."

"Love you too, jerk."

And yeah. Maybe I'm glad I called her back.

TODAY'S BAR couple is enraged about the lack of recycling regulations in the States. They don't compost. All that perfectly good worm food tossed carelessly among the environmental poison that is the trash-bag trash. I gulp whisky to distract my mouth from butting in with an explanation of our garbage situation on tour. God, their crafted man buns would explode.

"Fancy meeting you here."

Her familiar voice startles me from my musings. It's the only explanation for the sudden rush of adrenaline slicing through me.

"I could say the same. It's a Wednesday night. Shouldn't you be clocking hours? And where's *Geoffrey?*"

Hannah drops to the seat beside me, still all lawyered in a stuffy business costume. Decorative scarf and everything. I tug it with a smirk, and she smacks me away.

"I'm sorry. I don't remember asking your opinion," she quips while signaling the bartender.

"I didn't say a word. I mean, it's December. It's cold, eh?"

Yep, cuz that blue silky contraption is going to thwart minus twenty winds. I shouldn't laugh. It's just, I'll never not see the girl with black fingernails and a viper tattoo snaking up the left side of her torso. I thought her family was going to murder me after I took her to my artist for her ink. Holland bit my head off when she heard.

Now? Blue silk scarves and pencil skirts.

"It's called fashion. You should try it sometime."

There are too many easy strikes to choose just one so I settle on a twist of the lips.

The bartender pushes some fruity-looking thing in front of her.

"I think he forgot the little umbrella thingy," I say. "You drinking cosmos now like a good sorority girl?"

She shoves a shoulder into mine before taking a healthy gulp for my benefit. "I'll have you know that it happens to be delicious."

"Yeah? Did Emma introduce you to that concoction?" I ask, referencing her seventeen-year-old sister.

"Emma doesn't drink, asshole."

I grin.

"And what's the badass rocker drinking, huh?" My glass is legit wrenched from my fingers, and I almost lose my shit at the contorted look that spreads over her face.

"Whisky, ugh."

"What were you expecting?"

She shrugs. "I don't know. Troll blood."

I laugh. "Troll blood? That would have been better than whisky?"

"What you witnessed was shock, not disgust, genius."

"Oh, I see. Can I have my drink back now?"

My glass slides toward me, accompanied by an exaggerated huff.

"You know, Holland is pissed that you bowed out of the Bahamas charity thing at the end of your tour," Hannah informs me.

I grunt into my rippling reflection. "Why does everyone keep insisting that I'm the one who doesn't want me around?"

"Look, I don't want to get involved," she lies because this would be the first time ever. "But you both are acting like twelve-year-olds. Just apologize and fix the damn thing. There is no Wes without Holland or Holland without Wes."

"I did."

Her look is justifiably skeptical. "Like a real apology or a Wes Alton apology?"

"What's a Wes Alton apology?" I have to know.

Apparently, it comes with a Wes Alton smoosh-face. "'Hey, babe, so sorry that you're wrong about this. Hope you don't feel bad about how wrong you are.'"

I laugh so hard it hurts. "Wow. What's with the face? Is that how I look when I'm apologizing?"

"Oh, no. That's how you look all the time."

"Really," I say, leaning back for the fight.

She rolls her eyes. "I'm not going to tell you you're hot, so don't even bother."

"I knew it."

"Shut up. Don't start."

"Hey, that was your Freud-brain, not mine. Never even occurred to me you'd think that."

"Please."

I shrug back to casual whisky-drinking mode. "Just saying..."

Hannah stiffens at something behind me.

"Hey, there. I was hoping you'd show up again."

Shit.

"Hey. Miranda, right?" I'm polite as hell when I acknowledge the executive from Friday night on my other side. Hannah doesn't try quite as hard.

"Hey. Hannah here."

Their cool handshake sends my brain to spy movies and daring brush passes between agents and handlers.

"Miranda," Ms. Polished says, all confidence and possessiveness. "Wes Alton," she directs at me now that Hannah has been addressed and released. "Lead guitar and co-genius behind Canadian rock legends Tracing Holland."

"You looked me up."

"Of course. In the cab on the way to the office."

Hannah is securing her drink for an escape when I pull her back to the chair.

"Hannah is a good friend of mine," I say. "We've known each other almost our entire lives." I have no clue where I'm going with this, just that there's no chance that Miranda

Whatever gets to dismiss my almost-sister. It's that same protectiveness that ruined the most important relationship in my life.

"Oh, right. I remember you from Friday," Miranda says. Uh, huh. She remembers her competition from Friday.

I'm irritable tonight. She's got her work cut out for her.

"You were here with friends that night," the woman continues. Probes?

"Coworkers. I'm a lawyer," Hannah explains.

"Oh, how interesting. What kind of law?"

"Corporate."

"Oh? Which firm?"

"Regis, Whitlock & Sons."

"Wow, impressive."

"You know them?"

"Intimately. They represented our sister company in our merger two years ago."

"I wasn't with the firm then."

"No, I'd imagine not. You look too young."

Now, I'm the one who wants to escape.

"I am. Young and hungry, right?"

And here we go. I shoot Hannah a warning look, but she only returns her innocent "payback" face.

"Wes is very familiar with my enthusiasm. Aren't you?" Hannah says.

"Is that so?"

I'm sure Hannah is more than satisfied with Miranda's sudden scowl.

"You have a history?" Miranda asks me.

"He was engaged to my sister."

Apparently, that didn't show up in her research as she nearly chokes on her gin.

"Oh?"

"Yes, but as you know, it didn't work out," I remind the universe.

"No, I guess not," Miranda says. Is she disappointed or relieved?

Hannah's phone attracts her attention, and she glares at the screen.

"Who's that?" I ask.

She flinches before returning an unconvincing headshake. "Nothing. No one."

I lean in. "Just your boyfriend," I observe, and earn a shove.

"Mind your own business," she snaps, but still lets a smile escape with mine.

"Did he do something? Do I have to march over to Yonge Street?"

"No. You need to mind. Your. Own. Business." She finishes off her drink and leaves me with her tab.

"She's adorable."

Oh right. Miranda.

"She's like a little sister."

"It's obvious she likes you."

"Please. The woman hates me. That whole family hates me right now."

My analysis gives her the courage to frame a brave hand on my thigh. Okay, decision time.

"Well, their loss I'm sure."

I take a breath, sneak another glance, and warn, "Not really. I can be an asshole."

"Me too." Her purr complicates matters.

There's almost no space between us now. I'm afraid she'll lose her seat to another patron. Shit, then she'd be stuck on my lap all night.

I remove her hand from my leg and force a sly smile. Sly

because I'm not good at permanently closing doors to beautiful women.

"Do you actually think fucking a rockstar is a good career move?"

I've caught her off-guard. Not sure if it's the question itself or the directness of it. I find both fascinating and wait patiently. Follow up: does it make me an ass that I'm more interested in her answer than actually sleeping with her?

"This isn't a marriage proposal."

"Ah. Is that your speech for the board members?"

"Board members? It's not like I'll be posting in the company newsletter."

I stare at her for a moment. Maybe I've overestimated her cunning. "I'm Wes Alton of Tracing Holland. Everyone in Toronto knows everything I do with everyone."

I'm not being a prick. I'm actually being helpful. Starting to think this quick lay isn't worth the complications.

"We could be discreet."

"Like now?" I glance around the packed bar, and sure enough most eyes are trained on me. It's impossible to hide in your hometown. Now, the hard part—I suck at subtlety.

"Do you have a pen?" I ask.

Her confusion doesn't stop her from reaching into her purse.

I take it and grab a napkin. "Look," I say. "I'm doing you a favor, okay?"

I scribble my autograph and shove it back at her.

"You don't want this, Miranda. Trust me." And yeah, I don't either. I count out several bills and stick them under my glass. "Drinks are on me this time. Have a great night."

3

PRIVILEGED

It takes me a while to button a dress shirt and my nicest jeans on Friday night. Even longer to gather my wallet, phone, and keys. It takes an eternity to check the coffeemaker to make sure it's off.

Dammit, why did I agree to this?

I finally run out of excuses and catch a cab to my parents' house. The driver follows the speed limit the entire way, which is too fast for the first time ever. Every light is too green. Why doesn't this city invest in more stop signs? I should have made him take the 401 so we could stall in a rush-hour parking lot for an extra hour. *Sorry, Soph. The 401, eh?*

But we pull up third in line at the grand entrance of the Alton estate. My parents still insist on doing rich-people things like unloading guests in a parade of fancy vehicles. It's why I love taking cabs to their house. I'd ride a bicycle if it wasn't a fifteen-kilometer drive on the deadly GTA highway maze.

I get the looks I'd hoped for from the other guests as I pay my fare and thank the driver. A quick salute to security, then Alfred, the butler, and I'm inside. By the way, his name isn't

Alfred, but if you still have a butler in this century, you have to call him Alfred. He calls me Bruce, so it works. Double points because it pisses my parents off.

The foyer is as stale as it was the last time I saw it two years ago. Museum-white with a splash of red to celebrate this joyous occasion. It's also packed with guests. So many people I don't know, and too many I do. I'm the only man not in a tux, the only person who appears not to understand what's expected of an Alton guest. Sophia knows the mountain she scaled to pull me across that threshold. Who needs *Rolling Stone* critics when you have Frederick Alton for a father?

"Well, well. Wesley Alton has arrived after all. Looks like your sister wins the bet."

His voice alone has the power to make me cringe.

"Hey, Theo. Congratulations on joining the Alton cult." I grip the outstretched hand of my soon-to-be brother-in-law. He's not a hugger, which is the only thing I like about him.

"I couldn't be more thrilled."

"I bet. You sign your soul to the devil yet?"

"Who?"

"Frederick." He's still confused. My god. Only my promise to Sophia keeps me in this conversation. "I'm asking if you're working for my father yet." *Fifth-grade level, Wes. You can do this.*

"Ah!" He takes a sip of his drink and scans the hors d'oeuvre tray hovering beside us. Did he forget my question?

I try again. "How's the, uh, securities business these days?" There's a sentence I never wanted to say.

"Up and down, man. You know."

I don't.

He nibbles on a stuffed mushroom, and I've never loved my sister more than the moment she rescues me from her fiancé.

"Wes!" Sophia cries, all sweet charm in her pixie cocktail

dress. She throws her arms around my neck and drags me to safety.

"Congratulations, sis," I murmur against her short dark curls. "You cut your hair."

"Do you like it?" She twirls a shiny coil around her finger. "Mom freaked. Said I should have waited until after the wedding because now I've 'limited my options.'"

"No Roman goddess 'do for you?"

"Ugh. She wants me to look like Julia Harrington."

"Isn't Julia blonde?"

"Yeah, but her hair has the same texture as mine and she booked Aritese Robere for her entire wedding party."

"Huh?"

"Famous stylist." A dismissive hand wave and, "Anyway, he only works with hair over half a meter or whatever."

"Half a meter? There are people who have hair that long?"

"Lots of people! Everyone according to Mom."

"Well, I think you look great. You should wear your hair however you want."

"Aw, see that's why I love you."

She's looking over my shoulder, anxious eyes darting from my face to another target I can't see. "You got a chance to catch up with Theodore?"

"Um, yep. I believe we're all caught up."

"Did he tell you he's working for Dad now?"

"Yeah?"

Her teeth sink into her lip, and I kind of feel bad that I hate her boyfriend so much.

"Soph, if this is the life you really want, then I'm happy for you."

"I didn't want him to take the job, but you know how Dad is."

I stiffen as the answer to that question approaches with my mother in tow.

"Wesley. You came," the man I've managed to avoid for an entire year announces. He's correct.

"Dad. Mom."

"We heard about what's happening with Holland. So sorry, honey," my mother says.

"It's not a big deal. We almost have it worked out," I lie.

"I warned you not to go into business with your ex," my father says. "It never ends well."

I don't bother responding. I learned the futility of engaging my father in a discussion when I was old enough to talk.

"Do you need me to call my lawyers?"

"No, I'm good. Like I said, we're working it out."

"You lost your temper again, didn't you? My sources say this is your mess."

There's a coal in my chest that my father planted almost thirty years ago. An ember he has the power to ignite, simmer—explode—when he so chooses. "Maybe your sources should mind their own fucking business," I return to a wide range of gasps from surrounding guests.

"Wesley!"

"That kind of language may be appropriate *on the road*, but not in my house," Frederick Alton informs me.

Ah yes. "The Road." That dark abyss of debauchery that has claimed his youngest son.

"Fuck. Sorry."

"Wesley!" my mother repeats because after twenty-nine years she still hasn't learned that my full name doesn't scare me.

"You probably have more important guests to attend to. I can entertain myself. And don't worry, I wouldn't dream of disrupting the string quartet with my rock sacrilege."

I feel my father's glare burning into my back as I turn away, but it doesn't affect me like it used to. Not since they locked me out of the house for four days when I was a teenager because I chose music over their bullshit budget reports. They weren't accustomed to *nos* that can't be bought, manipulated, or extorted. I refused their blood money and became the only "no" in their universe. So they fired me like Alan the groundskeeper after he was caught pissing behind the north garage. Best day of my life, the day they stole their name back and told me to burn in Hell.

A new fear shoots through me as I start scanning the crowd. I'd been worried about a confrontation with my parents, but it suddenly occurs to me Sophia might consider Holland a friend. That's just what I need, an altercation with Holland Drake's plus one in my parents' house. At least it would give my dad more reason to hate *The Road*.

"Hey. I was wondering if you'd show."

My lips react in an automatic twist.

"Hannah Drake. Did you copy my social calendar or something?"

"It's not hard when it's bar, bar, bar, one-event-I-actually-have-to-attend."

"Ha."

My eyes brush over her smirk before continuing down the rest of her. Damn. I can count on one hand the number of times I've seen Hannah Drake in a dress. And now, on one finger the number of times it's shot straight to my groin. I wonder if she knows her tattoo is peeking through the cutouts on the side of her little black slip.

"So I guess you've stayed in touch with Sophia," I say.

"You've guessed correctly. She's the only one of you Altons who doesn't suck. Based on your expression, I'm guessing your parents still hate you?"

I cast a look toward the expertly composed couple chuckling with a set of clones. Must be over something hilarious like vacation home linens or restaurant reservations.

"You've guessed correctly."

She grabs my arm. "Come on."

"Where are we going?"

"I don't know. Somewhere we can't hear this elevator music."

"What about *Geoffrey*?"

"Working."

"Basement?"

I love the way her eyes ignite. "Definitely. Is the game room still set up?"

"You'd probably know better than I would. You and Sophia still hang out, right?"

"Yeah, but that was never her spot."

That spot belonged to Holland and Wes, we hear in the silence. But it's a damn awesome spot even with the ghosts.

"I used to love when Holland brought me along to hang with you down there."

"I know."

Her gaze shoots to mine, and I let my smile reveal old secrets.

"It's not because I had a crush on you so don't even look at me like that," she mutters.

"I didn't say a word."

"It's all over your face."

"My face is just on the hunt for my dad's good liquor."

Her glare doesn't believe me, and my smile widens.

"You were tall and scrawny back then, you know," she says.

"Yeah? So are most teenagers. The editor of *Alt Canada* didn't seem concerned during the shoot for Canada's hot 30 under 30 last year."

"Ugh. Don't remind me. You made my life miserable that month."

"Why? I was on tour around that time. I had to fly home for the shoot."

"Yeah, but everyone who knew we were friends was still around."

I laugh and wave her through the door to the finished basement.

"Don't worry. I'll be thirty in a few months so I won't be eligible anymore."

She rolls her eyes, but the slight pink in her cheeks as she slides past me sends my blood streaming again. Brain cells are ridiculously ineffective against wit like hers in a dress like that. I have no idea what's happening with my dick right now, but this is the one challenge I absolutely cannot accept.

"You understand that having a great body isn't an actual skill, right?" she says.

"Sure it is. You should see my workout regimen."

"I can't think of a worse way to spend five minutes. Oh! They still have the chairs!"

She skips the last step and launches onto an overstuffed recliner facing a giant screen. Spiky heels find their awkward grave on the floor.

"The command center is gone, though," she observes, and I feel a twinge at the loss as well.

"Appears so. Guess my parents decided gaming systems are just unnecessary clutter."

"Still, these chairs, though?" She pats the one to her right, and I sink into the soft leather. "Pass the remote."

I hand it over and try not to focus on her adorable anticipation. It becomes easier as my memories settle into the cushions with me. Holland cuddled against my chest as we annihilated bad guys and dreamt about changing the world with our music.

I assume my reflections are private until I sense Hannah's attention. One look, and I know she's sharing them.

"You two weren't right for each other."

"I know."

"Do you?"

"Hannah, I love you, but I'm not doing this with you."

"Oh, so who are you doing it with then?"

It's probably a glare I fire at her, but it's hard to tell from her reaction.

"I don't need to do it with anyone."

"No? I guess you could always just punch the guys she dates for the rest of your lives."

"Seriously?"

She cocks her head and dares me to finish.

"Or fill the void she left by sleeping with every chick who crosses your path. That's an option too," she says.

I force myself up with a lazy stretch.

"Where are you going?"

"Taking off. I'm not interested in this discussion. Remember to change the input on the TV if you want the satellite."

"Thanks. Have fun wallowing in your misery."

"I will. Have fun living a life you hate."

"You're still a dick, Wes."

She's told me that since she was ten. I only believe it half the time. Like now.

"Probably. It was good to see you, Han. Tell your family I said hi."

I pull a crumpled phone number from my wallet on my way up the stairs.

MIRANDA   BUSINESSWOMAN   LOVES   MY
APARTMENT. She loves the wine I offer her and the music
blasting from the surround sound. She loves my bedroom
décor, the feel of my sheets, and the way I pull my t-shirt over
my head. She especially loves every line and angle of my body
and proves it over and over again that night.

"You're amazing," she tells me as she gasps in recovery from
her latest rush. "I had no idea."

She must have had some idea or we wouldn't be here.

"Thanks" is my response because she's not listening and
I'm ready for another drink.

I avoid her gaze as I move toward the door. She'll just have
to enjoy my ass while it disappears down the hall. It's been
enjoyed at a national level thanks to *Alt Canada*.

My phone is buzzing where I left it on the island, and I
curse at the screen. Four missed calls. Three frantic SOS texts.
Someone better be dead, dude.

"Jacob."

"Wes!"

"Present."

"Funny. Look, Holland needs an answer."

"It's not a good time." I throw a look into the darkness
behind me.

"It's never a good time for you anymore. Just give me an
answer and we can get things moving."

"I can't."

"You have to."

"It's an impossible question."

"No, the question is simple. Yes, you agree to the new
terms, or no you don't."

"Fine, then, no."

"No?"

"No."

"Come on. I know you're upset but—"

I shift the phone to my weaker hand before my grip crushes the damn thing. "The answer is simple too. No, I do not agree. Holland has been the most important person in my life since I was a kid. Tracing Holland is our friendship. Everything about our music is from our history. We wrote those songs as soul-mates. The band exists from that bond, not as a collaboration of professionals."

"Fuck, Wes. We're scheduled to drop the new album in a month. The release tour is already booked. Get over yourself and fix this!"

It takes a deep breath to rein in my blood pressure. He's lucky my fist can't reach him through the phone. "I understand what's at stake," I manage through clenched teeth. "But some things are bigger than money. I can't work with Holland as a coworker and not as a friend. So if those are the terms then she needs to find a co-writer and lead-guitar player who can."

"Really? That's it? You're *this* close to cementing your legacy! One more platinum album and you're there. The tour is nearly sold out. You love Holland? You want to protect her? Then suck it up and don't fuck her over two steps from the finish line!"

It's his side of the line going dead this time.

"Tracing Holland is breaking up?"

Shit.

MIRANDA LEANS AGAINST THE ISLAND, gaze locked on me when I turn around.

Okay, so what did she hear? "We're just working through some contract issues."

"Really? Because it sounds like you're *refusing* to work out contract issues. It sounds like you quit the band."

I turn and level every bit of warning I've mastered into my gaze. "It's..." *It's what, Wes? Fucking* what?

Her expression changes as her eyes devour my body. "Hey, I understand. More than you know." She slides her palms down my chest, around my back. "I can help you."

"What?"

"God, your ass is edible," she breathes. Grinding against me, she grips hard with each distracting push.

I ignore her tangent. "How can you help me?"

She leans her head back to search my face. "Didn't I tell you? I'm the Executive Vice President of Ballister Data."

Shit! I step back. Alton Media's biggest rival? The cornerstone of Canadian media? What am I supposed to do with that?

The Label is going to slaughter me if they find out. Jacob, Holland. Dead man walking right here.

Miranda's eyes aren't flirting anymore either. Dark, menacing, even, they scream a warning I should've spotted that first night in the bar.

Dammit, I'm just paranoid. I run a hand over my face.

"I did my homework after we met. You have an album in the can, right? I know plenty of people who can fix this. Even if you can't work things out with Holland, all you have to do is keep the rift under wraps until the album drops and her people can spin the shakeup for the tour."

She's absolutely right which is absolutely wrong coming from a media queen who shouldn't know any of this. My pulse seems audible, my limbs twitching when her fingers trace my cheek. She holds my world in her hands and she knows it.

"Hey, relax, babe. We'll handle this."

"There's nothing to handle if nothing gets out."

"Of course nothing will get out." Those eyes though. Her hidden message lodges in my stomach.

"A lot of people could get hurt." Holland especially.

"This is what I do, babe. Trust me," she purrs against my lips. She pulls me in for a firm kiss, and I'm not sure what choice I have right now. "Let's go work through this in the bedroom."

My dick reacts on reflex, even as my fist clenches at my side. She kneads my hard flesh, drawing a groan that sends my reason to the wasteland of future regrets.

"What will it take?" I say, fighting for control over my charged body.

"What are you talking about?"

"You know what I'm saying. What is it that you want in exchange for keeping this quiet?"

"I can't believe you're asking me that."

Her coy hum grinds on my nerves.

"You know how I feel about you. What can I do to convince you that you can trust me? That I just want to help?" Her tone triggers every warning flare in my head. The way her gaze pierces deep.

"I do trust you," I lie because right now—crisis mode.

"Hmm... Good." Her mouth plays with the skin stretching over my abs. Down, down, until she's on her knees. "I'll make this better. Promise," she says, grinning up at me.

My response is totally forgotten.

"I'LL NEVER GET tired of looking at you," Miranda says, running her fingers over the lines of my chest, my stomach. Usually I welcome a woman's appreciation of my body. I've worked damn hard on it, but this woman has presented me with a lot of firsts in the last hour. She moves lower, and I catch her wrist. *Enough.*

"So you're not going to say anything?" Shit, I sound desperate.

"Of course not. Not until you want me to." She pushes up and straddles me on the bed. It's funny that I found her aggression hot a day ago. Now, I have to keep myself from shoving her off.

"How about this?" she continues, rocking against me. "I'll take a look at my contacts and put together an action plan for us."

Us? "I'm not a client."

"No, you're more than that."

Shit. "Miranda, really. You don't have to do anything. The best course is to pretend you don't know and let my people deal with it."

"But I *do* know." It's said with a leveled tone that drains the blood from my face.

"Okay, but—"

She stills. "I *do* know, Wes," she repeats. Her kiss is gentle at first, then hard enough to slam her point home.

PEOPLE USE the excuse of being drunk too often. I've never been much for excuses and have no intention of starting now. You fuck up, and you own it. Although this one is hard to swallow.

I watch the reflection of kitchen lights dance in my coffee after Miranda leaves. You'd think they'd move in a steady pattern, but they seem to follow their own course against the current of the dark liquid.

Miranda owns me. Fucking owns me.

I don't know what to do with that sentence. I messed up on so many levels with this one I can't even speculate on the repercussions. I don't know her well enough to recognize what she wants, but I'm a freaking goldmine for someone with no limits. I've been exploited and hurt enough to know you don't get close to people. You don't show weakness. And you never, ever, give them power over you.

I'm not a detail person, not a planner. I've never worried about the weather, the cost of toothpaste, or traffic patterns. So it's strange that my first thought when I see white flakes falling outside my window is that I should have known it was going to snow. I should have known the barometric pressure would drop and moisture would descend from the sky in a blanket of frozen mist.

I should have known if I gave up everything for Holland Drake, one day I'd have nothing. I especially should have known that no matter how much we hurt each other I would sell my soul to protect her.

4

NAME DROP

A week later, I'm still not sure what Miranda wants. Sure, there's the obvious, but it's not like I mind the sex anyway. Our time together is only a fraction more intimate than what I would have given her without the threat of implosion hanging over my head. There's no talk of commitment, no probing for Alton Media trade secrets, no demands for celebrity perks, just a few phone calls, texts, and the occasional uninvited buzz at my door. One of those times was only lunch she brought from the deli by her office.

It's not until she insists I escort her to her company holiday party that the darkness begins to settle in me again.

"You know this is a terrible idea." I'm hoping the hundredth time I mutter it will cement it in.

"It's fine. Everyone knows you're not associated with your father's firm. They're dying to meet you." So many things wrong with those thoughts, and my fist tightens on the door-frame of my closet. She pauses behind my rigid stance at the entrance. "You can wear jeans, but at least do a button-down."

She misses my glare when she returns to dabbing color on her eyes.

"You really don't have another date to this thing?"

"Why would I want to go with anyone else?"

I swear I've singed the back of the closet with my stare. "We're not together, Miranda."

"I know."

I turn my irritation on her again, but she's too busy applying shiny crap to her lips.

"I just don't want any hard feelings."

"Of course not. What do you think?"

She presents the final masterpiece, and I do a polite scan.

"Looks good."

"That's it? These shoes are exclusive Garnette's."

"They're black heels, I don't know."

I turn back to my shirts and regret the hesitation when greedy hands slip around my waist from behind.

"You could go like this," she murmurs, running cold fingers over my skin. They sink into the now-tense muscles of my chest as sequin shit scrapes against my back.

"Doesn't fit your button mandate."

I step away to grab the first shirt I see and shrug it on, those mission-critical buttons a helpful distraction from her lust. I try to ignore the gaze lingering on my tattoos as I roll the sleeves to my elbows and curse myself yet again for triggering this scenario.

"Wow. There will be a lot of jealousy at tonight's party."

Uh... "I still need a sec."

"Okay, but we should hurry. The car is probably here."

I nod and retreat to the bathroom for a long stare at the hypocrite in the mirror.

"THIS IS WES ALTON."

I swear, if I have to hear that one more time tonight I'm going to fling my fancy cocktail glass at a wall. Funny how your last name is so important when it draws shocked awe. I half-expect "of Tracing Holland" to follow. It's nothing I'm not used to. I've been "the namedrop" for a few years now. It's the excitement in her eyes when she says it I don't like. The situation spirals into sharp focus throughout the night, leaving me on edge as I count the seconds until we're alone, and I can fix this.

And I was right. It *was* a bad idea—crossing enemy lines to party with the rival king and his court. Duchess Miranda seems to revel in the raised eyebrows and awkward affirmation that I am, indeed, related to *the* Frederick Alton of Alton Media. Just as I thought, this is the celebrity status these people find most intriguing.

"What does your father think of you dating his competition?" Small talk with the C.F.O.

My real answer stalls on my tongue at Miranda's deceptively calm smile. "He hasn't weighed in yet," I say instead. He hasn't. He will.

"Really? Well, I'll be careful where I leave the books tonight." CFO humor. Thankfully, Miranda laughs enough for the both of us.

"I'm more into music than marketing," I say because I'm also hilarious. Extremely hilarious by the eruption of mirth around me. "Pardon me for a moment."

I beeline for the exit of the Grande Ballroom and turn left instead of right. There's too much risk of an encounter in the washrooms, so I find a service exit to the closed patio instead. No one in their right mind would spend a Toronto winter party outside. Then again, I have faith the fire raging through my blood will keep me thawed. Fucking...

I slam my boot into a wrought iron chair. The sting of

contact shoots up my shin then sinks back to a dull throb. Finally, a sensation besides hatred. Disgust. Fury. I kick it again to make sure the pain lingers.

I lock my fingers on my head and release a billow of air over the decorative barrier separating the patio from the pool. This place isn't just a current trial, it's a haunted relic from the catalogue of memories that's been consuming me lately. Memories of her. The good times which make everything now so much worse.

It was warmer then, the night Holland and I played a wedding reception on this patio. Hot, even. I remember the beads of sweat slipping down her neck. It was hard enough gripping the guitar pick with my own slick fingers, let alone when my bandmate was the picture of temptation in tight ripped jeans and an oversized tee because we *sure as hell* weren't going to be a wedding band. She made me wear jeans and a t-shirt also, not that I minded. If not for my mother's interference, I wouldn't have owned anything else.

We played an eight-song set. I remember because it was our first *real* gig as Tracing Holland. At least, real in the sense that we earned enough to cover our costs for once. Even a little extra to put toward the in-ear system we wanted. The extra details are also seared in my brain by the fact that Holland and I found a vacant conference room to release some of that restrained lust after we wrapped. Damn, now *that* is the memory I want lodged in my head when I think of this hotel. Not fucking accountant humor.

"Wes?"

My hands drop from their perch on my head at the interruption. Miranda, of course. "You ready to go?"

"Yeah."

"Okay. My place tonight?" Her hands feel warm for once as they grip my frozen fingers.

"We need to talk."

"Perfect. I just got a Cabernet Sauvignon you're going to love."

"Miranda—"

"I'll meet you at the car. I have to say goodbye to a few people." A way too intimate peck on the cheek and she's gone.

"MIRANDA, THIS HAS TO STOP."

We're inching through the Saturday night downtown traffic. Despite the spacious interior of the car, I'm suffocating from my latest mess.

I wish she were an idiot, that I could blink this away with some fangirl satiation, but Miranda is an executive for a reason. I'm a musician, an unemployed one at that, and way out of my league in this negotiation. Especially since her game seems to involve pretending there isn't one.

"What, babe?" So casual as she reapplies lip gloss.

"That! The 'babe' and the dinner-party 'plus one.' We aren't together."

"Of course not. We're just having fun."

"Yeah? Some casual fun?"

"It was one party, hon. Relax."

I search her eyes, but she's impossible to read. And clearly more interested in her makeup than locking me in the basement as a captive boyfriend. I sound insane. This thing with Holland has shot me completely off-axis.

"Okay, yeah. Just making sure we're on the same page," I mutter, focusing on a bus stop outside the window. A trash receptacle. A tree. Anything besides this woman.

"Oh! This one is so cute! Look what Jo posted from the

party." She shoves her phone at me. Three hundred likes and fifty shares? *Shit.*

APPARENTLY, Miranda now feels entitled to inform me of her business travel plans. I clamp the phone against my shoulder as I slide on a pair of jeans.

"Uh-huh."

"Ah I wish you were coming with me!"

I freeze and readjust the phone. "Um..."

"I mean, these trips can be tedious, that's all."

Sure.

"It's just two weeks, right?" I didn't mean for my voice to contain my eye roll.

"Well, yeah. I'll be in three different locations, though."

She's defensive now, but come on. *Try living on a bus for three* months. Thankfully, I manage to translate that to, "It'll go quick."

"I'll call you."

"Okay."

That was the wrong answer because she sighs into the phone. I know my "well, good luck" won't win any points either, but I never asked to be on her notification list.

My life gets no better when she hangs up. The truth is I didn't totally hate her call. It distracted me for a full six minutes from my upcoming trial at Reisler's Grille. A few hundred seconds of head-scratching bliss.

I button my jeans and find myself staring into the closet for the second time this week. What is it about your life turning to shit that makes you care about things like shirts? Holland always liked green on me. *It makes your eyes tropical,* she'd say or some other random slice of Holland poetry. Would she be pissed if I wore green tonight? Take it as an up yours to trying for a future that doesn't include the past? I hope so as I yank a green vintage tee from a shelf.

Luke will be there. Of course he will. I wouldn't leave my girlfriend alone with a guy who punched me in the face. Twice. Everyone keeps telling me he didn't deserve it. I was out of line. Even our peacekeeping drummer, Spence, told me I screwed up.

Our drummer. Dammit, *her* drummer now. A decade together leaves quite the stain on your vocabulary.

We're here.

That's a message from Holland.

We. I'm not *we* anymore. I type out a response letting her know I'm on my way. A couple quick shots from my minibar, and I am.

REISLER'S GRILLE. Of course she'd pick the most non-descript spot in the six blocks surrounding my downtown condo building. It's fitting for the meeting that has a high probability of ending in bloodshed.

I don't see them when I enter, maybe because the awe-struck hostess has her stars tucked into a secluded booth at the back of the restaurant. Heads turn as I weave through the maze that seems more fast-food than celebrity-ready. The patrons appear just as surprised to witness rockstars maneuvering through the red and white labyrinth.

Holland and Luke quiet at my approach; backs straighten. We push the limits of civility with a recitation of each other's names as a greeting. Hey, it's politer than I anticipated. No venomous diatribes, no fists to cheek or jaw bones. We're the picture of awkward reunion as I slide onto the bench across from them. The server comes over, and I order a drink even though they're on seltzer and lime thanks to Luke's struggle with addiction.

I'm not "we" anymore, though. Did I mention I can be a dick?

"Thanks for meeting us," she says.

"Sure. No problem."

"I'm serious, Wes. We need to solve this."

"Solve what, Holland?" I shoot my stare into hers. "Look, I get it. But I'm never going to apologize for protecting you."

"She didn't need protection. She needed you to act like a human being," Luke says, and I return his cold stare.

"Guys, come on. Not now?" Holland focuses back on me. "What happened on the tour is done. We're here to talk about what's next."

"I'm not going to be your guitarist for hire. It's *our* band. *Our* songs. It's all or nothing." My back creaks against torn vinyl as I cross my arms.

"I never said I was going to cut you out of royalties."

Fuse. Ignited. "Fuck, Holland! You think my issue is the money?"

"Watch it," Luke hisses, leaning forward.

I cut him a giant portion of my glare before returning the rest to his girlfriend.

"After all we've been through, I can't believe you'd sit here and think it's about money for me. That band was my life, Hol. I gave up everything. You know the hell I went through. What I had to do for this. For you!"

Her face wilts, and that eternal protectiveness knots in my chest. God, why can't she see she's my world?

"I know. It's just—"

"It's just she can't trust you not to be an asshole. She can't trust you, dude."

Luke again. Always helpful translating for the woman I've known since I was seven. She gives him a look, and he shrugs.

"You crossed lines," Holland says. "I have to protect myself and Luke and make sure you won't cross them again. Just read the contract. You'll see that—"

"I read it. It's not about the damn contract. I didn't come here to haggle over 4b and 3c. It's what it represents, the dissolution of our relationship."

"It's not dissolved..."

"You want it in writing that we will never be on the same hotel floor or share a dressing room."

"That's just standard."

"No it's not. And especially not for us."

"Well, it needs to be now."

"Fine. And the new bus? You're touring with your own bus now? Was that your idea?"

I fire that one at Luke, who sends simmering coals right back.

"You're at that level and you know it," Luke argues.

"Yeah? Night Shifts Black is two rungs up from where we'll ever be. Do you have your own bus?"

Again, dick move, because I just spent three months touring with their one shared band bus.

"We have a separate crew bus."

"Oh, so Holland is going to be riding with the Tracing Holland crew?"

"Wes..."

"No, I'm done with this." I slide out of the booth. "I fucked up. I get it. I will face the consequences, but they'll be the ones *I* choose. Not Luke. Not some Label lawyer. And not even you, Holland. Merry Christmas."

I HATE that I leave Holland with her face twisted in pain. It's *my* pain because she still loves me even when she doesn't. She has to because her heart is pure angel's breath and kitten purrs. She loves, it's who she is. She's forgiveness. Compassion. Freaking trust, which is why I refused to just sit back and watch the tornado of Luke Craven plow her down on their Greetings Tour. Yeah, irony's a bitch.

I crossed *lines*. Fine. I did. Fuck it, what lines don't you cross when someone you love is about to get torn to shreds? It doesn't help my case that she supposedly ended up happy instead. That Luke apparently has shed his magnet for trouble or whatever.

I don't even know what drink number I'm on when my phone buzzes.

> Can I come up?

My heart slams against my chest at the "H" and the "Drake." Oh, wait. Hannah?

> Sure.

I stumble toward the door and release the button so she can enter the building. It seems like I just pushed it when my door is being assaulted. I pull it open to be bulldozed by a petite fireball.

"Shit!" she says, running black nails through her light brown hair. It's been freed from its clip and washes over her shoulders. Wow, it's been so long since I've seen her hair like this. I have to suppress the urge to sample its texture. I'm just wasted, hurting, and yeah, the glare on her face would not approve of my investigation.

"Um, hi," I reply with a crooked grin. She pauses long enough in her stomping to return it.

"Sorry. I know. I must seem crazy right now."

"Well..."

"Ugh, I just didn't know where else to go!"

Alarms flare. "What is it? What's going on? Are you in trouble?"

Her bitter laugh isn't encouraging. "Not the kind you mean." She drops to my couch and rubs her hands over her face. That gorgeous hair. "I don't know, Wes. I'm sorry. I shouldn't have come. It's just..."

"What's going on? Why are you in my condo?"

She grunts and tilts her head toward me. "I quit."

"Huh?"

"I *quit*."

"Okay... Quit what?"

"Everything."

"Like your gym membership? Euchre club? Zoo volunteering?"

"Everything. Look I don't want to talk about it. That's why I came here. I just want to chill and figure shit out. Can we just watch TV? Where's your bar?"

I point to both, and it's then that I notice her suitcase.

"Oh."

She twists her head back at my utterance and stalls a generous pour. "Oh, right. Also, can you not tell anyone I'm here and let me crash on your couch for a while?"

Holland. Would kill me. The entire Drake family. Miranda. My family. The media. This is such a bad idea. Getting involved in the personal drama of my best friend and bandmate's sister during a bitter contract dispute? Movies are crafted about this shit.

"Sure."

Because, fuck it.

"SO ARE you ever going to tell me what's going on?" I ask after the second movie and her—I don't even know—drink.

Hannah blasts me with the dragon look that's made me smile since we were kids. Yep, even I'm intimidated by that laser.

"Sorry, I just thought your new landlord deserved a little information."

Her shoulders relax ever so slightly. "I'm sorry. No, you're right. Thanks for letting me crash. And I will talk about it. It's just..." Her words fade as her eyes graze the wall.

"It's fine, Han. You don't have to talk. But how long do you think you can hide here?"

"Ha. Where's the last place my family would look for me?" I smirk. "Here."

"Exactly." We exchange a smile, but it doesn't bring any peace.

"Your family is amazing, Hannah. Whatever's going on, I'm sure they're much better for you right now than I am."

Her eyes change as she studies me, or maybe it's the booze, but I swear she's surprised by my comment.

"I'm not so sure about that. At least not right now. Just... tomorrow? Over breakfast?"

"Sure."

"You won't even know I'm here." She pulls the throw blanket off the back of the couch, and I bristle.

"Not a chance. Get your cute butt into the guest room."

Her smile is all shy resolve. "Seriously, this is fine. You're already epically amazing for letting me stay here."

"I'm not kidding. Get in that guest room. Don't make me carry you."

"Ugh, chill, *Dad*. I'm fine! I've slept on much worse. Your couch is perfection."

"Hannah!"

"Nope."

"You're starting to piss me off."

"What else is new?"

"Little turd."

"Spoiled rich boy."

"That's it."

"Wes!" she shrieks, laughing as I scoop her off the couch. She half kicks, half clings, on our journey to the guest room where I deposit her on the queen bed.

She grabs my hand as I turn toward the door. "Seriously." I meet her eyes and cringe at the sudden sheen. "Thank you. I just..."

I squeeze her fingers. "As long as you need, okay?"

She bites her lip and a few tears escape before she tries to hide them from me.

5

TENANT

It's funny. Making breakfast for a girl is usually an angst-ridden formulation. Do I want to see her again? Does she want to see me? Do I play the gentleman or the asshole?

And yet, here I am, eggs on the plate, French toast stack growing, coffeemaker beeping before the thought even enters my head that I'm preparing breakfast for a woman who slept over. That's Hannah, though. Not a "woman" but my sister for every reason except blood. I watched the girl learn to ride a bike, find her first boyfriend, get her heart broken by her first boyfriend, then break a long streak of hearts herself. I saw her in a prom dress and almost a bridesmaid's dress if Holland and I hadn't broken off our engagement after two months.

No one ever understood my complicated relationship with Holland like Hannah did. How you can desperately love a woman and not be in love with her. How you can imagine her as your wife but realize neither of you would be happy. Hannah got it. Hannah was also the only one in our lives with the guts to tell us our engagement was bullshit. That great friends don't automatically translate to great spouses.

At the time I thought she was jealous, but it turned out Hannah Drake was just developing into a woman who didn't give a crap about the consequences of the truth. I didn't think she gave a crap about any expectations or social pressure until she did a complete 180 halfway through university and pursued politics and law instead of vocal performance or whatever degree she was working on that made her happy. I remember being sad the day her family praised her for coming to her senses. Self-projection? Totally.

Hannah makes a great lawyer. The girl is razor sharp and brutally honest. She would have made a great anything. Well, okay, maybe not a politician. Or a preschool teacher. I snicker at the thought of terrified four-year-olds absorbing Ms. Drake's critique of their crappy drawings. But aside from that, she was always one of those people bursting with unrealized potential. Sure, on the surface earning her law license was a huge accomplishment, and for many, would represent the pinnacle of achievement. But my Hannah has a breathtaking tattoo climbing her torso, notebooks of poetry, and a hypnotic singing voice even her rockstar sister envied before she stopped using it, for some reason. Oh, right. Lawyer stuff. Scotch tastings, client dinners. All the shit I ran from the first chance I got, and there was Hannah, embracing it with open arms. Everyone else applauded her for it.

Outwardly, I did too because it wasn't my business. Still isn't really. No, my job now is to provide room and board for my ex-best-friend's sister while she sorts through whatever bombshell just exploded her life.

Wes Alton: failed rockstar, innkeeper.

IT MAKES no sense that Hannah Drake is shuffling down the hall toward my kitchen and open living space. Messy hair, yoga pants, and sleep weighing down her eyelids. I can't help but grin at the sight, certain I'm in some alternate reality that's going to screw the shit out of me. God, I love playing with fire.

"Morning, sunshine."

"Shut up," she replies. "Oh my gosh, that smells amazing." She skirts around me to search my cabinets for plates.

"Above the coffeemaker."

My instructions earn me a look. "You don't keep your mugs above the coffeemaker?"

I shrug.

"Men," she mutters, yanking two plates from the shelf. She studies them and snorts. "Dragonflies? Wesley Alton."

"Karine's one contribution to our relationship."

"Ah."

"Oh, and the towels. Wait until you see those."

"Can I not? She was the ballet dancer, right?"

"Physical therapist."

"Oh, right. Barbie."

"She did not look like Barbie. You never even met her."

"Uh, yeah I did. You brought her to that release party for Unending Circus, remember?"

"I did? Wait..." I did. "Shit, okay."

"That girl needed to eat a burger like nobody's business."

"Wow. Someone's bitter."

She snickers as she starts scooping food onto the plates. "Forks? Let me guess, the linen closet?"

"Hilarious. Drawer next to the dishwasher." I grin at her expression. "Impressed?"

"A little. Although not so much with your threads. What is this?"

She tugs my gym shorts, and I smack her away. "You should be thanking me. I usually walk around naked."

"Then why would I thank you?"

Damn. By her look she knows I felt that low and hard.

"You shouldn't be hitting on your landlord. That's gross," I say. "Maple syrup?"

"Duh. Coffee?"

"Yes."

She pauses mid-stride. "Okay, so where are the mugs then?"

HANNAH DRAKE HAS OPINIONS. She has a lot to say about my wall color, living room layout, and the travesty of my dragonfly cookware. The prime minister, Toronto sports teams, and whacky weather. Oh and Christmas. It's in three days. Plenty of feedback on that topic. What I don't get is anything remotely close to an explanation about why she's moved in. Every time I broach the subject I get the death stare, so Christmas it is.

"You spending it with your family?" she asks, shoveling more food into her mouth. The girl can eat and doesn't care who knows it. Is it crazy that I find it sexy? I clear my throat.

"Probably not. I got enough of an ass-kicking at Sophia's engagement party."

Her eyes narrow. "From your parents or me?"

I shake my head. "Please. You couldn't take me if you spent a lifetime trying."

"Wanna bet?"

"Not particularly, no."

Her pout is almost as charming as watching her suck French toast down her throat. When was the last time she ate?

"What about you?" I ask even though I know the answer. Drake family Christmases are not optional. I bet Holland is even flying home. My pulse picks up at the thought. Not that I have any hope of seeing her after burning her final olive branch.

"The usual."

I nod. I've been involved in enough of the Drake "usual" festivities to understand the definition.

"So what, you're just going to spend Christmas alone?" she asks.

"I'm sure there are bars around that will be open."

"Christmas in a bar? You're that guy now too?"

"Apparently, I am. What of it?"

And just like that, she's finished eating and jumps up from the table. "Play me something."

"What?"

"Where's your guitar? Play me 'Viper,' the one you wrote after I got my tattoo."

"Hannah..."

"What? It's been like ten years. I want to hear it."

"Ten years? You only got your tattoo eight years ago."

"Please! Don't make me beg."

"You're already begging."

"Don't make me punch you then."

I cock my head. "I dunno. That actually sounds kind of hot."

"Whatever. Just get your guitar, Casanova."

When I return, she's on the couch and points to the other end. I lower myself as well.

"I don't know if I even remember all of it," I say. "That was a long time ago."

"Just try?"

Her eyes are different now. Darker, the smile is gone. Red

vessels corrupt the white around her blue irises, and I know her tears are close again. Dammit, I *will* try.

"I haven't played much since the tour."

I expect some snide comment about needing help to tune but there's only silence as I do just that. I don't like Hannah's silence. It brings me back to a much darker time in our lives. A time when a viper tattoo snapped us into a bond that can still pull us back eight years later.

> "Let them stare, they won't dare to touch your
>   soul.
> Let them laugh, their wrath is where they
>   hide.
> They lie. They cry—too—because you, you're
>   the brave one, the safe one, the irreplace-
>   able one.
> Let them bleed while you release their ugly
>   truth.
>
> Let them bury their joy in baseless hope, face-
>   less, nameless, shameless they scream their
>   joke.
> Let them breathe the poison of their worthless
>   spite, their eyes,
> Descend, yours amend
> Fate.
> So lie in wait, hold tight, let them fight
> Until you strike
> Them dead."

Her cheeks are wet when I finish and dare a look across the couch. I'm not good at this. Consoling. Compassion. I'm usually last on the list of shoulders people want to soak with their tears. But Hannah is alone. Stuck with an asshole who cares deeply about her even if he has no clue how to say it.

So I don't. I rest my guitar against the couch and move beside her. A few buttons on the remote to find a movie, and I slip my arm around her shoulders. She settles into my hold, soft hair brushing my chin as she nestles close. Then we observe some crazy shit go down on a distant planet.

***

"SORRY ABOUT EARLIER."

"Earlier?"

"Yeah, my mini meltdown."

"Wait, that was a meltdown?"

Her sandwich remains mostly untouched as she studies the wood grains etched into my table.

"What's going on, Hannah?" I ask finally. Her gaze trickles up to brush mine before returning to its post.

"I don't know yet."

I believe her and wait.

"I was trapped." Her eyes search mine again. "I was living a great life, a perfect life, but it wasn't mine."

"It was the one you thought you were supposed to live."

Her expression softens as it rests on me. "You are the only one who got that. You never judged me."

"You were perfect the way you were."

Oh god. I don't know where that came from. It may be true but had no business coming from my lips.

"What I mean is, you should have felt comfortable pursuing your own goals instead of the ones you forced on yourself."

"Yeah, that's what you meant?" and the glint with her sudden smile makes me cringe.

"You know what I meant."

"It literally kills you to give compliments, doesn't it? Like rips out a piece of your badass soul."

"Shut up."

"It's fine. Go find a puppy to kick. I'll wait."

I laugh and throw a chip at her. "Whatever. You know I'm not good at this shit."

She giggles as she picks the chip off the table and pops it in her mouth. "Actually, you're great at this *shit* because you don't care about consequences or what people think." She cocks her head. "Well, maybe you could care a *little* more about what people think."

"You mean, not piss off your sister to the point where she wants to dissolve our friendship in writing?"

"Wait, that's what's in the contract?"

I sigh. "Sorry, I shouldn't have said that. I don't want to put anything between you and Holland. This is our issue."

Her brows knit, but I infuse enough indifference into the pursuit of my own sandwich that she has to let it drop.

"Okay, yeah, I guess that's a good example. Maybe don't pick fights with rockstars in the midst of highly publicized comeback tours either."

"Noted."

"Or recruit their ex-stalkers to try to ruin their relationships."

"Shit. You heard about that too?"

She shakes her head and pokes a finger at the bread pillow on her plate. "That was low even for you, Wes."

I grunt. "Yeah, well, it wasn't what it seemed."

"No? You didn't contact Luke's old groupie and convince her he wanted to hook up just to wreck his relationship with Holland?"

"Okay yes, but I was really drunk and desperate. I tried to

take it back the next day. I was just as shocked as anyone when she showed up."

"Why wouldn't she have? Geez, if someone told me my hottest crush ever wanted to see me, of course I'd show."

"Because I told her it was a lie."

Her eyes attach to mine. "Wait, what?"

I sigh and pull out my phone. Evidence, I guess, for no one but me. I never showed Holland. There was no point, and it didn't matter anyway. What use is intent when your actions blow apart any rational explanations? No, this text stream is for me, for my sleepless nights, and what's left of my conscience. Because sometimes I have to prove to myself that I'm a dick, not a monster.

I turn my phone to Hannah, and her eyes widen.

"I didn't know that the message telling Laurel not to come hadn't gone through until she showed up that night. I checked right after the confrontation and just about puked. That's when I knew I'd blown it. Holland would never forgive me at that point."

"Why didn't you tell Holland you tried to take it back?" she asks, still in disbelief.

I study the label on my beer. "What was the point? It happened, and she hated me. I wasn't going to whine and beg. I deserved what I got. But I'm not going to punish myself for the rest of our lives with this new contract because of one screw-up."

"Two."

"Whatever."

"Three, actually."

I roll my eyes, and she grins before growing serious. "You're hoping she forgives you and believes you've changed?"

I shrug. "Honestly, I don't know what I'm hoping for. I'm not sure I *have* changed. Just because I can admit when I screwed up doesn't mean I won't do it again. I'm never going to be the saint."

"Okay." She stares me down and rises from the table. "The thing is not everyone needs a saint, Wes Alton." She's on her way toward her room before I can respond.

I WAKE TO POUNDING BLOOD, excruciating pleasure. A wet dream? No, hot pressure controls my body. Dissolves me into my mattress. Oh god. My groan is cut off with a tongue, determined lips. Fingers push down my hips and clench.

"What are you doing?" I gasp. I'm her friend. I need to stop this. I... ah.

"Just this one time, I promise," she breathes. I feel her nakedness. She didn't invade my sleep to negotiate.

"Hannah, come on. You're upset, you—"

"Now's your chance to say no. Tell me to leave."

She's doing everything in her power to make sure I don't.

My body is trained for this. My brain, not so much. When her mouth attacks me again, reason loses the rest of its weak protests. Some distant siren screams through the background. Regret. Guilt. Pain. But not yet. Tomorrow's poison. Right now it's skin and heat and pulsating need as she slides over me.

"What about..."

"Here. Found this. Your place is stocked." I barely hear the tear of packaging. "Damn, Wes. Are you always ready?"

I know, worst time for irony, but there's a definite smirk before she consumes me again. Hard this time. Deeper, her own moans make me crazy.

"I want you to own me like the others," she gasps, and that siren screams, radiates through every cell corrupted in ecstasy.

"You're not the others, Han. You're..." There are no dirty

words. There are no words at all for this. Just. Her. Hannah Drake. The only woman in the world I should not be fucking.

SHE DROPS BESIDE ME, sucking in air while I'm still trying to process what just happened.

I almost choke at the gloss in her eyes when I dare a look. Oh shit. Oh shit. Oh shit!

"Hannah, I..."

"Don't," she hisses. "Don't you dare apologize. You didn't do anything wrong. I was the one using you. So, thank you."

Nope, does nothing for my guilt.

I throw an arm over my face and struggle to catch my breath.

"Why did you do that?" I hate that it comes out gravelly, but what the hell? I'm desperate for something to make sense for once in my fucked up life.

"I know. I just... had to feel something good."

I scrub my face, confused, horrified, and charged enough for another round. "You quit your life, didn't you? You're dark again."

I know I'm right when her glare shoots at me.

"If I wanted a lecture about being a massive disappointment to the universe I would've gone home."

"I'm not judging you. I'm trying to figure out what the hell is going on. You show up at my place ready to move in and then throw yourself at me while I'm sleeping. Don't you think I have the right to a couple questions?"

She sighs and shoves small fists into her eyes. "I know. I'm sorry. You're right. It's just..." She turns away and the tears are audible now. "I'm sorry. I'm so sorry."

"Aw, Han..." She clings to the arm I wrap around her shoulder, and I gather her against me. "Hey, I get it. You know I do. You're my viper, remember?"

Her nod grazes my chest, and I hold tighter as she breaks down. I don't have any more ideas as she cries, and I let her sobs weaken into the barest of breaths. Just when I think she's finally asleep, she grips my hand with a new intensity.

"I need you to kick the world's ass for me while I hide. That's why I came to you. I need you to be *my* viper."

6

QUITTING

I know the script.

Things should be awkward the next day. I should find mascara-stained eyes blinking with hope inches from my face as I wake. Or in the bathroom trying to clear any evidence of sleep. Maybe struggling with the zipper of a dress or searching for missing accessories. But no. None of that. In fact, I don't find Hannah at all until I move toward the kitchen and pass her mop of hair secured above the neckline of my t-shirt.

"Morning," Hannah tosses over her shoulder from the couch, then raises a bowl to invite me to my own cereal for breakfast.

"Morning. You sleep okay?" I help myself to coffee she's already made and study her from the kitchen as she watches some sports recap. That shirt doesn't look nearly as good on me.

"I guess. Well, no, but whatever." She turns back to her show, and I listen to the crunch of whatever treasure she found in my cabinets. I didn't even know I had cereal. Maybe I don't. It's Hannah Drake so normal rules don't apply.

"Hey, Han. About what happened—"

"Geoffrey kicked me out."

"Damn. I'm sorry."

She shrugs, and I join her on the couch. Her gaze still rests on the TV screen, but her eyes aren't watching. "Whatever. Boyfriends suck."

"What happened?"

"He 'doesn't know who I am anymore.' How classic is that? Three years together, and I get tossed aside with a line from a soap opera. At least pick a better cliché. Do you think he could be a long-lost brother who's just returned from some exploration of the Amazon? Ew, I've slept with him. Gross."

Yeah, I kind of smile at that. Such a smartass. "Do you actually think Geoffrey would survive a day in the Amazon? The guy carries a messenger bag to get coffee."

"Hmm. Good point. Can't believe I actually thought he was the one."

"Really? Wow."

Tears accompany this shrug, and I know she's more wounded than she's letting on.

"Hannah, come on. It's me. I'm the last person anyone you care about wants to gossip with."

She swats at her eyes. "Another good point. Who's the lawyer here? Oh wait, there are none in this room."

I pull her hand from her face. "Were you fired?"

"I quit."

"Quit? Why?"

"I don't want to be a lawyer anymore. I never wanted to be a lawyer. I knew I could be and it would make everyone proud and make my life important..."

She stops. I wonder if that's the first time she's heard that out loud.

"So don't be a lawyer."

Her gaze crashes into mine. "Right," she scoffs. "It's that easy."

"It is."

"For you."

I let her accusation settle between us before she huffs an apology. "Sorry, that wasn't fair. You gave up everything to follow your dreams."

"It sounds so poetic when you say it like that. I just remember years of fucking pain."

She absorbs something from my confession with closed eyes. "I just want to disappear, Wes. I don't want to do it anymore. I can't."

"Do what?"

"Never mind. Can we just chill for a while?"

My phone goes off before I can weigh in on her request. Shit.

"Are you going to answer that?"

"No. I'll call her back."

"Seriously, Wes. I came here to escape my life, not invade yours. Go take care of your business. I want to see how the Leafs did last night."

It still feels wrong as I push myself up from the couch and brace for the call, but Hannah's clearly done with me for now. Besides, I've ignored the last two already.

"Wes! Where have you been? You haven't responded to any of my texts either."

"Sorry, I've been busy." I haven't thought about Miranda since Hannah showed up at my door. "How's..." I have no idea where she is.

"New York is great."

"Great."

"Wish you were here though. There's this amazing restaurant we found last night that you would love. I know how you like a good burger."

"Yeah?"

"We should go when I get back. A weekend trip?"

"Miranda..." We are not together.

"It's the strangest thing. I've heard probably three Tracing Holland songs since I left. I so wish I'd had the chance to see you play. Maybe one day, eh? How's all of that going?"

Bitch. I swallow my anger. "Fine. We had dinner the other night." It's a fact no one can argue.

"Oh yeah?"

Is she actually disappointed?

"Yes. Look, I'm kind of in the middle of something." My dining room. "Talk later?"

"Of course, babe. I have to prepare for a meeting anyway. I'm sorry I won't be there for our first Christmas together. I would have loved to meet your family."

I don't even know how to respond to that. "Don't worry about it. I probably won't be seeing them." My stomach hurts just thinking about that disaster.

"Really?"

"Miranda, I've told you. I'm not on good terms with them. I have nothing to do with my father's company, and I never will. They've practically disowned me."

"I know, babe. Don't get upset."

I don't do much to block my irritated sigh.

"Have a great day. Miss you."

"Enjoy New York."

I mutter a curse as I glare at my phone.

"Wes, I'm so sorry. I didn't even ask if you were seeing anyone."

I CAN'T STAND the genuine remorse on Hannah's face. I also have no clue how to explain Miranda.

"I'm not really. It's complicated."

She nods and looks as tortured as I feel. "Are you going to tell her about last night?"

I'd laugh but that reaction would be even harder to explain. "No. Of course not."

"I'm sorry for making you cheat on your girlfriend."

"She's not my girlfriend."

"The woman you're dating then."

"I'm not dating her."

"The woman you're sleeping with?"

Well... "It's complicated."

She sighs, and I don't miss the darkness that washes over her face. It's not for me. I'm afraid it's not even for Miranda. "I'm going to go take a nap."

That makes perfect sense to her at ten in the morning.

"Han, you okay?"

"Fine. Just tired. I didn't sleep last night." It would be a funny joke if the humor was in her eyes too.

"Han..." I get nothing else as she disappears into the guest room.

I TRY to think of a time in my life when I've had more people pissed at me at once.

There was the night I skipped Dad's annual show-off-his-perfect-family-to-the-board party to play a show with Holland when I was eighteen. I was homeless for four days because of that. Three furious faces that I remember, but only because I'm counting the entire Alton Media board of directors as one.

There was the time I took Hannah to get her tattoo when

she turned eighteen and my guy was willing to work on her. Six, I think? That's up there.

When Holland and I got engaged: four. When we broke up: two. My parents were insulted. Pretty sure hers threw a non-engagement party.

Now? "Now" wins. My list is "one" of people who aren't pissed at me. Although Hannah's been in her room since Miranda's phone call, so I'm not entirely positive about that. Wait, she seduced me while I was asleep. I'm standing by one.

"Hannah?" I knock for the fifth time since she ran off. Still no response, and I finish the journey to my room for the night.

I've seen Hannah Drake dark before. She always had an edge, a melancholy cloud to her existence that used to express itself in some incredible art she believed in. She designed her own ink, and even Matt, my artist who brought it to life, was impressed. The viper slithers from her hip to her shoulder, dormant in its aggression, but eyes wild and ready for violence.

"Vipers are badass," Hannah explained to Holland and me. *"They seem lazy and slow, and then bam! Surprise strike out of nowhere. And they can measure their venom too. Did you know that? Yep, they control how much they want to release into their prey."*

For a long time Hannah was just Holland's quiet, sarcastic, artsy sister. Then she stopped being sarcastic. Then she stopped being artsy. Then she just stopped *being* during her second year of university. I'll never forget Holland's long, frantic calls with her family during that time. We were on tour and it killed her that she couldn't not-help at home instead of not-help on our bus. That part I didn't get.

Thanks to the push of the love surrounding her, Hannah found pros who could help. Their collective efforts helped her piece her life back together in time to graduate with an impressive transcript and solid plan that made her family and therapist happy. She was happy too, I'm sure. And I was happy she was happy, but even happier Holland could breathe again. The plan didn't make sense to me, but it was none of my business.

But the thing with depression is it seems lazy and slow, and then bam! Surprise strike out of nowhere.

7

BROTHERS

My tenant has emerged from hiding the following morning. Her hair is even wet enough to suggest a shower.

"Morning," I say.

"Morning."

"I'm heading to the gym. You want to come?"

"To watch you work out? No thanks."

"They have more than one machine at the gym. It's one of those fancy ones with several."

I finally get a lip quirk. "Does it have a water cooler?"

"Hot and cold spouts."

"Who wants hot water at the gym?"

"Fancy people."

Another twist, and I return it. "I'll bring food back."

MIRANDA CALLS AGAIN while I'm on the treadmill. I guess this is going to be a daily thing. At least Hannah is spared from this one.

"You sound out of breath."

"I'm at the gym."

"Oh, I see. Pinot Noir or Pinot Grigio?"

"I'm not a big wine drinker."

"Oh, right. I want to grab something for us at Duty Free on my way back. Whisky, eh?"

I have to keep the panic in my blood out of my voice as I respond with, "I thought you were going to be gone for a couple of weeks."

"I am. I just like to plan. You know that. It's sweet that you miss me though."

I can't tell if she's joking. What if she's not? "Hey, I don't want to let my heart rate drop. Call you later?" I hope no one else heard that. I'm cool with Miranda's disgust, but I like this gym because it's not stocked with asshats who say shit like that.

"Oh, sure. If I don't answer it's because I'm with clients. Just leave me a message."

"Sounds good."

So I just have to make sure I call when she's with clients.

I'M STILL NOT USED to finding Hannah Drake on my couch when I walk in the door. She offers a casual "hey" that I answer with a nod.

"So this is your life now? Cereal and daytime TV?" I ask.

"You said you'd bring food back."

I hold up the bag. "But you have to move your ass from the couch to the table to get it."

She must expend most of her energy on the eye roll, because her walk across the living room appears to be excruciating.

"I don't remember you being so bossy."

"Really? I don't remember you loving judge shows."

There's the grin as she takes the chair across from me. I arrange the food containers between us.

"Hope you like Indian."

"Love it."

I'm skeptical when she frowns.

"I have to go get my stuff from Geoff today." Her announcement comes with a stab at her food that almost makes me fear for the guy.

"Okay. I can go with you."

"No. I don't want anyone to know I'm here."

Right.

"Have you told your family at least? They have to know you broke up with him by now."

"I told them I need some time to sort things out and I'm staying with a friend."

"A friend," I snicker.

"You're not exactly their favorite person."

"Yeah, well, I'm no one's favorite person." It comes out on its own. I add a laugh to correct the error, but her eyes still shoot to mine.

"Is that what you think?"

"I didn't mean it like that. Hey, pass the naan?"

She holds the foil package out of reach, searching my face for the angst she won't find. Not if I can help it.

"It's all an act, isn't it?" she says.

"Hannah, come on. Seriously?"

"This alpha-bad-boy-I-don't-give-a-shit thing. It's an act."

"I was making a joke." I was, and I'm so not interested in this conversation.

"I see. So are you ever going to actually be real with anyone?"

"You're one to talk."

"Pardon me?"

"You really want to take me on in the who-needs-psycho-therapy-more debate?" God, I'm such an ass.

Her frown lets me know she agrees.

"Nice. That's great, Wes. Sorry for fucking caring about you." She slings the bread at me and stalks off to her room.

MY SHOWER IS LONG. I can tell by the cloud of steam obscuring the room that I'm escaping. Reality? Her? I don't know but there's a reason I don't do relationships anymore. Hannah thinks she uncovered some deep, dark, pain of isolation when all she touched was the very reason I avoid this shit. We were happy with a few containers of Indian food and cheesy movies. Throw in expectations, though, and lunch take-out becomes daytime drama.

My palms tingle from the heat. I lower the temperature and turn my face into the stream. Water pounds at my eyes and slips down my cheeks to my chest. I watch the rivers crisscross over black ink and contoured muscle. Down it flows, caressing me like the many hands that have traced that same pattern. How many have there been? How many that I can't remember or wish I didn't? And yet, none have ever left me hiding in a damn shower. None make me consider bullshit like the "caress of water."

I curse and brace against the wall. It's official. I'm trapped. Hannah Drake is a problem. A fucking disaster in my life that I don't want to go away.

THE APARTMENT IS empty when I emerge from my suite. I see Hannah's suitcase through the open door of the guestroom as I pass, and shudder at the relief that spreads through me. Then, I remember her appointment with Geoffrey. I never liked the guy, and it's good I didn't go along. Geoffrey would not have enjoyed a confrontation with me. I pick up my acoustic in an attempt to tame my hot blood.

Guitars are rigid, constructed from firm wood, so I always found it strange that this one feels soft in my hands. Some are rods of steel I have to wrestle into submission. Others beg to be handled but never satisfy. It's only my old Martin that reads my soul, soothes my turbulence. She sings every time, the ancient frets molded to my fingers after years of forgiving my sins.

I'd always loved her but our bond became permanent after my father sabotaged my first record deal "for my own benefit." She saved me from murder that night, transforming the rage into the song that finally hooked Holland Drake and launched our career together. My Martin also saved me from implosion when Holland decided we were better friends than lovers. The weathered curves even forgave me the day my feud with Luke Craven exploded into regret, and now here she is again. Infusing life into voids.

Hannah was wrong. I'm not alone. I'll never be alone no matter how much life has forced failure down my throat.

> "Fire of mine, ashes of regret
> Redeem the manic truth.
> Proving scars in vain effect
> With no doubts left to lose.
>
> Seven scars from timid youth—six I've left
>   undone.
> Since here I am unraveling

And it only took the one."

I don't know how long I write. It's a haunting melody, so lonely without the intricate harmony of a female voice to twist around my lead. I stare at the vacuum on the other end of the couch where Holland should be, notebook in hand. Saying things like, *"ashes of regret is too cliché. How about ashes of regard? Give the fire more power."*

She'd be right, of course. She'd also want to change the progression in the bridge. She hates when I do a 6-5-1 ending. *"We're building, not resolving."* But I was good for her music too. I brought an edge, kept her from falling into the pop princess abyss where she was headed with her perfect vibrato and sweet melodies. Her music is poetry. Mine bristles, and together we found perfection.

Now, I'm a repertoire of thorns.

My door clatters, then erupts into an anxious knock. Surprised, I set my guitar aside and move toward it.

"Wes, it's me. Some guy let me in the lobby."

I pull it open and find the most beautifully sad woman I've ever seen. Her eyes are wells of grief, too full to hold the tears that slip down her cheeks. I take the large box from her hands and set it inside the door. Then, I pull her against me.

Sobs escape from Hannah as her arms tighten around my back, and I send my fingers through her hair. It's as soft as I imagined, warm when I cup her head and hold her to my chest.

"It's not okay. I'm not okay," she whispers.

I close my eyes and mumble the truth I've known since that first day back. "I know."

"HAN, YOU AWAKE?" I graze her door with my knuckles. "Freddy wants to meet up for drinks. You want to come?"

"Junior or Senior?"

"Would that make a difference?"

Pause. "No thanks."

I poke my head in to find her curled up on the bed, down-comforter pulled up to her neck, eyes stabbing me through the dim light.

"You're really going to make me face my brother alone?"

"So... it's Freddy Junior?"

"Senior wouldn't ask to meet up for drinks."

"True. I'm too tired though."

"You've been in bed all day."

"I went to the washroom. Three times."

I grip the door jam. "Okay, well, I'll bring food back for you," I say, pushing away with a decisive tap on the wall.

"Not hungry."

"Don't give a shit. See you in a few."

FREDERICK ALTON, Jr. is the most intelligent and boring man I know. His sour face physically hurts to look at, probably a result of being the only person who buttons the top button even without a tie. He also never invites anyone out for leisure. Freddy Jr. doesn't believe in leisure. Or laughter. Or ponies.

Truth be told I invited Hannah more for my own benefit than hers. Anything to tame (shorten) the stoic diatribe I'm about to receive. Why am I going? Because Freddy Jr. has our father's trust and there's something I need them both to hear.

"Hello, Wesley. Good to see you."

My brother offers his hand because god forbid we risk a relationship beyond *cordial*. I give him my best Alton death-grip handshake and drop to the seat across from him. "Drinks" is something he does at a four-star restaurant over lobster and truffle butter.

"'Sup, Prince Charming?"

His sour face scrunches into a downright rotted face. Not his favorite nickname for sure, but when you spent your formative years in the shadow of another Freddy (Prinze) Jr., well, you know.

"Don't you think we've outgrown that?"

"How can I when it makes you light up the room with your smile?" I have to bury my face in the menu to hide my snicker. I'm already in trouble for something.

"So you're back from your tour. How was it?"

"Great. So great," I lie since his question was bullshit. "How's being Dad's manservant?"

Another Freddy bristle. "It's an honor to represent our family."

"Couldn't agree more."

The server approaches and takes my order for a double whisky and grilled cheese.

Grilled cheese, you cretin? Says Junior's face.

"I'm on a diet," I explain. I can almost see the brain shards launching from his ears. Plus, four-star grilled cheese has to be epic, right?

"Is everything a joke to you?"

"Most things."

"You're almost thirty years old, Wesley. Don't you think it's time you start taking life seriously?"

"Hmm... I guess I could start a platinum-selling rock band that tours the world. How many magazine covers did you do last year again?"

His eyebrows knit in classic Freddy Senior exasperation.

Do they practice their mannerisms together? God, I'd pay to see that.

"You know exactly what I mean."

"Right, well, tell you what, when Dad spends all of his vast resources on trying to break *you*, then we can have this conversation. Until then, why am I here, Freddy?"

"Is that really how you see things?"

"How else would I see them?"

"He was trying to protect you."

"Protect me? Are you fucking serious?"

"You were a dreamer."

"I was a prodigy! I could have been something amazing and instead the bastard threw my guitar from the balcony just because he could. Do you have any idea what it was like to watch the one thing I valued shatter on the pavement? To stand there and be called a piece of trash just like the tangled splinters of the only thing I cared about?"

"You're being melodramatic."

"I'm being a musician! God, why can't you all just accept that? I'm not a suit; I'm an artist. So what? I've walked away. I've done everything I can to remove the stain that I am from your lives, so why can't you just accept that and leave me the fuck alone?"

Eyebrows, again. *Language.* One doesn't use *language* in a four-star restaurant.

"What do you want, Freddy? Seriously, spill it or I'm gone. The only reason I'm here is to show you and Dad that you don't control me anymore, and I don't give a shit what you think. Feel free to quote me on that."

He sips his wine to buy a few seconds of processing time. "Okay, well, if that's your preference, I'll get right down to it. We're here because of Miranda Rivenier."

And that was totally in my script for this meeting. "What about her?"

"Do you really not know who she is?"

"She's a school teacher who trains service animals, right?"

He's never been able to read my dry humor.

"No, Wesley. She's lied to you. She's the—"

"Relax, I'm kidding. Of course I know who she is. So what?"

"So you don't think it's inappropriate for the son of Alton Media's CEO to date Ballister Data's executive vice president?"

"Totally inappropriate, but only because the woman's nuts. No one should date her."

He buries himself in the $200 merlot again. He'll be drunk soon if he doesn't find a new defense mechanism for dealing with me.

"So you're saying you're not dating her?"

"I'm not."

"Then how do you explain this?"

He scrolls through his phone to find the picture I've seen a hundred times in a hundred places. "Don't bother. I went with her to a holiday party. Again, so what?"

"You willingly attended a Ballister Data function?"

"I wouldn't say *willingly*."

Another sentence he doesn't know what to do with, and he has to refill his glass. Good thing he ordered the whole bottle. My whisky finally arrives, and I throw it back in three gulps to catch up to my wine-whore brother.

"I don't understand."

"I didn't expect that you would."

He waits for more. I shrug.

"Well, Dad is furious."

"Not surprised."

"He's hurt, Wes."

Okay, now I snort into my empty glass. Should have ordered two. "Hurt? Please."

"He is. He feels like—"

"Like what? Like how it feels to be locked out of your own house for four days? To shiver humiliated on the street in the sleet and freezing rain while your parents tell you to fuck off through an intercom? But wait, that's another thing you've never experienced. Christmas alone in someone else's house because you were barred by security from your own."

"You're still upset about that? You shouldn't have skipped the board dinner to play that stupid gig. You knew how important that dinner was to the family."

I'm sure the Alton sour face has now spread to me as well. Downright contagious, that sour face. "And what about what was important to me? How do you think we got the studio time to record the demo that launched our career? We had to play that... You know what, forget it. If that's all you've got, I'll leave you to your lobster tail."

I shove my chair back, and Freddy's vinegar face transforms into a painful-looking compassion face. Well, his version of compassion. Looks more like a snail giving birth to a watermelon.

"Seriously, Freddy. Don't hurt yourself trying to figure it out. All I want is freedom to do my own thing. Freedom from *Alton*."

It's then that I see he's consumed all of glass two. Glass three passes the line of a proper pour, and I know my efforts have gained nothing.

"Tell Dad I said hi and to mind his own fucking business."

I have the server box my grilled cheese for Hannah on the way out.

"OH MY GOSH. THIS—IS AMAZING."

I'd suffer another drink with my brother to watch Hannah Drake eat $30 grilled cheese. I reach across the table for the other half and steal a bite. Okay, so that meeting wasn't a total disaster.

"How was Junior?" she mumbles through a mouthful of imported cheeses we can't pronounce.

"How's any meeting with Freddy?"

She tilts her head. "He still give you crap about your dad?"

"'Crap' has such a broad range of meaning."

"Not when it comes to your family." I can't help the smile at her tone. She motions for the rest of the sandwich back, and I hand it over. "You okay?"

"Sure. Nothing I haven't heard before."

"I'm sorry."

"Whatever. It's not like I expected anything different."

I think she believes my indifference as she works on her grilled cheese pile. When she looks up again, I'm met with no-nonsense Hannah. Viper Hannah. "Except for Sophia, your family sucks. You know that, right?"

I almost laugh. "Believe me, I know that."

8

CHRISTMAS

Christmas comes every year. Which means every year I'm stuck with the bitter choice of confronting my parents' wrath at their house or absorb a compounded version for not going. The Drake household, though? A full-on holiday movie.

"What do you mean you're not spending Christmas with your family?" Maybe this makes me a hypocrite, but come on.

I'm talking to her cute butt because the rest is buried in the fridge. "I'm not up for it."

"Yeah well, that gets you out of a lot, but not this." She ducks out enough to throw me a glare. I leave no room for negotiation, though, so she returns to her furious search. "Han, I'm not letting you skip Christmas with your family. That's a regret you don't want and don't need."

She clearly disagrees as she shoves fridge contents around with way more force than required for creamer.

"I'll just use milk," she mutters, grabbing the pitcher.

"The creamer is in there. I picked some up yesterday."

"Yeah? Well, I don't fucking see it."

"It's probably hiding from you."

Her lips crack into the slightest of smiles as I grin and lean against the counter beside her.

"Sorry. I know I'm not the nicest person right now," she huffs.

"Well, you're in the right place. Prime Minister Asshole right here."

Her eyes change when they turn on me. Soft, heavy with some emotion I can't read. Petite arms slip around my waist, and I respond with an instinctive embrace. I can't tell if there are tears this time, but there's definitely a thunder of blood through my body at the contact. Hers too, I fear, when her hands slide up my back and grip my shoulders. She burrows into my chest and triggers every protective reflex in my DNA.

"You need to go home for Christmas," I tell her hair. There's no space between us now. No room to protect myself from how important this woman is to me. I draw in a deep breath. "Tell you what. I will if you do."

She tilts her head back. "Seriously? With everything going on? You hate Christmas with your family."

"Yeah, well, I hate the idea of you missing yours more."

Her eyes. Dammit. It's supposed to be a sweet moment, but my dick ruins that and forces me a step back. I clear my throat.

"All you have to do is send me a text and I'll call to help you escape."

She's silent as her gaze touches every inch of my body. I feel it, burning from my chest to my arms to... It rests on the one place I can't control, and my brain completely malfunctions.

"I'll go," she says. "If you promise to rescue me."

I GET Hannah's text while I'm preparing for my own trial. The Altons do evening celebrations—it's better form—so Hannah had first dibs on drama. With the phone on speaker, I finish running a towel over my body.

"Merry Christmas," I say.

"Shut up," is Hannah's greeting, and I grin.

"Not going well?"

"No. They're sweet and concerned and all that crap."

"Yeah, they're the worst."

"I hate you."

"I know. Hey, seriously though, I get that it's annoying right now, but just keep hearing 'I love you' every time they try. That's what they're really saying."

"Ew. What's wrong with you?"

"You, apparently," I laugh.

"Jerk. Are you on your way to the castle yet?"

I suck in a hiss with the slide into my jeans. "Getting dressed."

"Wait, are you naked right now?"

"Not anymore."

"Damn."

"Are you flirting with me, Hannah Drake?"

"Never."

"Okay, good. Hey, Han? You got this. We'll exchange war stories later."

"First we have to survive the gift exchange. Emma made us stuff this year..."

"That's adorable."

"Have I mentioned I hate you?"

MY PARENTS' foyer is Christmas-ready with a spectacularly red flower arrangement and single strand of garland laced up the grand staircase. Probably made from baby peacock feathers or something. I have plenty of time to examine the two decorations as I wait for Alfred to inform the hosts that the black sheep has arrived. Funny how the place I spent most of my life seems foreign to me. Maybe it's because my parents expect things like forcing their son to wait in the foyer.

"Wesley, we're so glad you've joined us." My mother glides —*glides*—across the marble floor. She's full-blown Alton Holiday Chic in a shimmery silver dress and obscene diamond jewelry. I match perfectly with my jeans and rolled-sleeve plaid shirt. At least it's *red* plaid.

"Merry Christmas, Mom." I kiss her cheek and hand her a ridiculously expensive bottle of wine for their collection.

"Oh, honey, you didn't have to," she gushes, but still scans the label to make sure I was successful since I did. Satisfied, she leads me into the less formal of the formal sitting rooms where my sister shrieks and throws herself into my arms.

"You came!"

"Of course." I kiss her cheek too, but this one comes with affection. "And here." Her face lights up at the large envelope. "Wait, is this..." She starts pulling out autographed swag and squeals at the personalized band photo of Limelight. I snicker remembering how frontman Jesse Everett and the gang were just as amazed my sister would go nuts for this crap. Limelight is only starting to gain traction, but Sophia always had a radar for up-and-coming talent. After touring with them for the last few months, I agree with her on this one. Plus, Jesse was a cool guy, talented, and one of the few bright spots on our last tour.

"Wesley."

"Dad."

His nod tells me that unlike Sophia, he's not thrilled I showed. That makes two of us.

"Where's Freddy?"

"Your brother had some things to finish up at the office. He'll be here for dinner."

My father has a special ability to turn any sentence into a criticism. This one: *I should be half as dedicated as Frederick Jr.* Got it.

"Sounds fantastic," I say, popping some seared scallop contraption in my mouth.

"Perhaps if you spent more time working you'd have less time to date the likes of Miranda Rivenier."

I force away a wince.

"Did you think we wouldn't find out? Another of your attempts to get back at me?"

My pulse picks up, but I manage a shrug to go along with an inspection of the assorted cheeses. Guess Junior didn't relay my message. "We're not dating."

"No? My PR team is lying to me?"

"I said we're not dating, not that I didn't know her."

"Dammit, Wes! One scandal at a time isn't enough for you?"

The cheese tray loses its power, and I tighten my fist. "I told you I wasn't dating her."

"Then why are there fucking pictures and headlines all over social media?"

"There are always *fucking* pictures and headlines all over social media about me."

"So you weren't at a Ballister Data party with her?"

"It's complicated."

"Ballister Data! You're an Alton. How do you think that looks?"

"Like I don't give a shit."

He grips my arm and yanks me around. Hot breath fires centimeters from my face. I remember those eyes. They used to accompany spit-laced tirades. They smashed a guitar against a driveway and convinced a record label they were about to sign a huge mistake. I don't know why I let his fingers cut into my biceps now. I could drop him with one punch, but that's the one thing I've never done—fought back. I'm ten years old every time I face this man.

"You know what? It's not complicated, Wes. It's very simple. You are a self-centered screw-up who doesn't give a damn about other people or the consequences of your actions. If you want to waste your life partying and sleeping with every piece of ass that throws itself at you, fine, but when your filth affects my life and the health of this family, we have a problem."

I try to pull away, but his grip intensifies. "Let go of me."

"Break it off with Miranda."

"It's none of your damn business who I date."

"It's my business when your shit affects me!"

"You have no idea what's actually going on!"

"Oh, I know you and—"

I yank again, triggering a shove that sends me into an end table. He steps back to avoid my crash to the floor along with an heirloom lamp.

"Fuck!" I gape at the blood streaming from a deep gash below my elbow, hardly even hearing the resulting commotion around me. Pain sears up my arm, but no way in hell does this man get to know that.

My mother reaches for me as I push myself up, and I duck away. "Merry Christmas," I mutter, stalking to the door.

"Wesley, wait." Mom's voice is strained like it is every time she tries to hide in her bubble. Tries to pretend her husband isn't a demon and I'm not their only regret. "Don't leave."

"Pretty sure dinner is a no-go. Enjoy the wine." Apparently that was the extent of her mothering instinct, and I'm relieved she doesn't follow.

"Wes!" Sophia is harder to brush off. I let her stop me in the foyer and I stare at the eerily beautiful trail my blood carved on the pristine marble. Matches the décor, and I hold my arm steady to complete the design with a dark red pool at my feet.

"Oh my god." Sophia must not be as impressed with my macabre artwork.

"Watch your shoes."

"Wes—"

"I'm not going back in there."

"I know."

Tears shadow her eyes, and I have to clench my jaw to block the heaviness in my own chest.

"Are you okay? That looks bad."

"Fine."

Her fingers brush my hand, but I can't look at her. I stare at the staircase instead, blinking, breathing, anything to keep my brain from allowing the previous scene to sink deeper. I will not give power to the pain. I will not give power to him.

"He's never been fair to you. Never."

"Yeah, well, it doesn't matter anymore."

"It matters to me. He's wrong. He—"

"Sophia, I can't. Not right now, okay? I have to go."

"But your arm!"

"I'll take care of it at home."

"At least let me give you a ride. Here."

I do accept the cloth napkin, but position her firmly in place when she tries to approach. "I'll be fine. Merry Christmas, sis."

Yep. Merry effing Christmas.

THE UNIVERSE IS NOT on my side when I enter my condo and discover it's already been accessed. Maybe I regret giving Hannah a key. Yeah, definitely when her gaze darts to me and lands on the bloody mess.

"Oh my god! What happened?"

I kick the door shut as she charges toward me. "It's nothing."

"Were you mugged?"

"Kind of. Dad is a beast with a table lamp."

"Your father did this?"

"How was the gift exchange?" I brush past her to reach the safety of my bar.

"Wes..."

"Merry Christmas, eh?"

I toss back a shot and pour another. She stops my hand. "Let me look at that."

She turns my arm and cringes at the dark streak framed by a torn sleeve. "Crap. You need to get that fixed."

"It's just a cut."

"You probably need stitches."

"You learn that in law school?"

She swats my other arm before dragging me to the couch. "Be nice. Where are your supplies?"

"Hall closet."

She returns with the first aid kit and examines my arm again. "Time to strip."

"Really? Not even a glass of wine first?"

"Knock it off, hot shot."

"I'm wrong?" All I can think about is her body pressed against mine in the kitchen. Her eyes as she soaked up what she did to me.

"No..." She releases the first button of my shirt. Deliberate, rebellious. Mission abandoned as I'm consumed by a different kind of fire. Sparks dance on my chest when her gaze scans my exposed tattoos. Another button. And another. Her hand slips in the gap, and I close my eyes.

"Hannah..."

"What?" Her mouth is right there, so close I can almost feel the brush of her lips on mine. Her pursuit moves down my abs, exploring, demanding.

The kiss isn't optional. I suck her lip, my fingers tangling in her hair. She climbs forward and rips at the rest of the buttons. The shirt is garbage anyway, stained with a past that shouldn't allow a moment like this. She goes for my jeans next, a button, a zipper, and...

"Are you sure?" It comes out as a groan because she's way ahead of me.

"So sure," she breathes, and I free a clasp under her shirt. My fingers trail smooth skin, small curves that harden with my touch. Her breaths come harder with the pressure of my movements. Her hand clasps over mine, guiding, insisting.

Water caresses...

I can make her scream. I will too.

"Dammit!" I hiss, straightening. "Fuck!"

I stare at her in horror and grab my shirt to wrap my arm.

"What? What's wrong?"

She follows my gaze and sighs at her bloody torso.

"Han, I'm so sorry. I'm such an idiot. Go clean up. I got this."

"Come with me?"

My eyes can't stop scanning her gift, absorbing the beautiful flow of hair over pale skin. Then, blood. Streaks of violence where there should be beauty.

I'm not the kind of viper she needs.

"I want to, but I should really take care of this," I say.

"Bullshit. You're backing out."

I shake my head, unable to face her disappointment. I pretend to sift through the first aid kit. It *is* a bad cut.

"Since when did Wes Alton have a conscience when it comes to having sex? Oh wait. It's just me, I guess," she snaps, moving toward the guest room.

I let her anger settle over me. I deserve it, but Hannah Drake is not a "fuck." She's right; I know women, and I know when they understand their hearts. Hers wants more than I can accept right now. Probably ever, because I'm not safe. I'm not the knight she thinks I am. I have blood on my hands and thorns in my soul. She came here for protection, and it kills me that I'm her biggest threat.

I'm still Christmas Day Night eleven years ago.

"Please, Mom. Please!"

Of course the soft snow had turned into painful stabs of sleet as I stood shivering at the security gate of my own house.

"You know I can't, sweetheart." Maybe she sounded sad. It was hard to read inflection over an intercom.

I'd already been locked out for two days and had nowhere to go. I'd been staying with Holland but they'd just left for Ottawa. None of that mattered to Frederick Alton who quickly took over the conversation and told me to "get the fuck off his property."

And like a little dog I begged. Yeah, I did, fucking *pleaded*, but it made no difference. Probably just pissed him off more. The rest of the conversation was instructions for the security guard to get rid of me. I was eighteen and no longer his problem. If I gave Keith a hard time he had permission to involve the cops.

Maybe that's my most vivid memory of the night. Security guard Keith's look of genuine distress when the line clicked dead. He reached through the window of the guard shelter to show me his hands were tied. Even offered to "get me into the garage" which wasn't as cold and would protect me from the sleet. And I considered it. I did because ice was pounding my face, the wind was beating my body while I absorbed how little I mattered.

I didn't stay though. Somehow even that small mercy felt like a win for my father. I preferred to freeze to death.

BY THE TIME I finish my own cleanup, Hannah is stationed on the couch again. I almost laugh at her appearance, the picture of regret in a loose tee and baggy sweatpants. We make quite the pair of repentant lovers.

"Nice outfit," she says when I emerge from hiding.

"Thanks." I grab a beer from the fridge and smile to myself as her eyes travel over my bare chest, down, down to the elastic of my own sweats resting precariously low on my hips. Her gaze lingers on the V there I know she likes.

"You have bruising on your ribs too."

"Yeah, I noticed that in the shower."

"Also from your dad?"

"Same fall. Same table." I don't need her thinking about that right now. "You still pissed?"

"Depends. Are you still pretending to be some self-righteous badass?"

"Self-righteous? That's a first." I drop to the other end of the couch.

"Not the badass?"

I smirk. "What are we watching?"

"Okay, so that dude with the bandana insists the other dude owes him four hundred dollars for an unpaid debt."

"Oh yeah? What does the scary-ass judge say?"

"Don't know yet. But the smaller dude kind of looks like Rice Harrison, don't you think?"

"Wait, the scrawny kid who lived next to you in high school?"

Her expression lifts at the memory. "Remember when he tried to start the landscaping business and re-did my parents' entire backyard without asking?"

"Oh my god. The pond?"

"So many dead fish."

"A dead squirrel too, right?"

"I thought my dad was going to call the police," she laughs.

"He should have. That design was criminal."

"A clear felony."

The scary-ass judge decides the debt is valid. Bandana dude is ecstatic.

"Aw, Rice Harrison lost," I say.

"Good. That haircut alone deserves a lawsuit."

I laugh, and Hannah shifts closer to present a fist. "Friends?"

I tap it with mine. "Always."

9

WRITING

"So tell me about this year's Drake Family Christmas." I say over breakfast eggs the next day. "You heard all about mine."

"Um, no I didn't. You told me nothing, but I'll go first because oh my gosh. Sylvie has a boyfriend."

"Wait, what? And it's not Casey Barrett?"

"Hilarious. Hold on, it gets better. He's some road crew guy for The Thalias she met at that charity thing in the Bahamas. She went with Holland."

"Wow. Sorry I missed that." I chuckle at her reaction more than the story. Instalove is definitely a thing in our chaotic world that moves with zero patience—even if it's not my thing. Then again, maybe it's *love* that isn't my thing.

"Oh, and his name is Shandor!"

"Shandor?" Now I know she's lying.

"Yep," she assures me.

"Huh. And your family is cool with this match?"

"Honestly, yes. Even Holland approves of the guy. I dunno. He seems cool. He's obviously into Sylvie as much as she's into him, so I'm a fan."

"Musicians are trouble."

"Tell me about it."

We exchange a smile.

"What about your situation?"

A shadow drifts over her features. "Yeah. That came up too."

"And?"

"I didn't tell them anything they didn't already know."

"Hannah..."

"What? I will. I'm just not ready yet. It'll destroy them to know I've quit."

"They'll be more supportive than you think. They love you. They just want you to be healthy."

"You of all people know it doesn't work that way."

I clench my jaw.

"Okay, your turn," she continues, striking while I'm down. "Tell me what happened."

"What do you want me to say? My dad picked a fight thirty seconds after I got there and shoved me into a table. I left. That was my Christmas."

Shit, forgot the hot sauce.

"Wes, I'm sorry."

"It's not like I expected anything different."

"Yeah, but it's my fault."

I lower my fork. "Huh? In what universe?"

"If not for me you wouldn't have gone."

"Oh please. Don't start with that."

"I'm serious! It's because of my—"

"Hannah, stop. It was my idea. My drama. My father's anger issues. You're not even in the equation."

"But—"

"I'm not letting your self-hatred speak for you." I stare her down across the table and hold up my bandaged arm. "This. Is. Not. Your. Fault."

"How is it anyway?"

"Fine."

"You're lying."

"So?"

"Trying for badass points?"

"Is it working?"

"Maybe."

"Hey, what are you doing today?" I ask, studying her until the self-conscious smile spreads across her lips.

"What?"

"You want to write with me?" I sound almost playful.

"Write what? Music?"

"I was thinking articles of incorporation, but whatever."

"Shut up," she laughs, then grows serious. "You want to write with me?"

"We used to do it all the time."

"Yeah, *with* Holland! And before you two were a super-famous rock band!"

I shrug. "Okay. Well, Holland may not be here, but I'm also not in a rock band anymore, so I guess that's balance in the universe, right?"

"Stop it. You and Holland will work things out."

"You're changing the subject."

Her eyes are still orbs of skepticism, but eventually squint into acceptance. "If you're serious..."

"I am."

"Get your guitar."

I FORGOT how much I love Hannah's voice. The slight rasp, the way she phrases lines in a way you never see coming—captivating. Perfect for my edgy song structures. I get that it's hard to waste time on music when you grow up in the shadow of Holland Drake, but the creative universe has been robbed.

"Damn," I say, biting down on my pick so I can scribble some notes.

"Was it bad?"

"Not even close," I mumble through the plastic in my teeth. Pick back in hand, I turn to her. "That was sick. The run you did on 'replay?'"

She's clearly self-conscious so I'm not surprised when she deflects the attention back to me. "You're not so bad yourself. I know Holland gets all the credit, but you could front your own band if you wanted to."

"Nah, I'm not much for the spotlight."

She legit snorts. "Right."

"Seriously, though. It's always been Holland's band. I was fine with it. She deserved the attention and never abused it like I probably would have. It's a miracle I didn't fuck things up sooner."

Her silence isn't a good sign. "That sounds like your father talking."

I manage a shrug as I lean my guitar against the couch and stretch. "Just because he's an asshole doesn't mean he's always wrong." I distract myself with a hunt for beer in the kitchen.

"You only say that because you've been hearing it all your life."

Bottle opener. Shit, what did I do with the thing? I give up on the drawer and start searching the counters.

"I know you can hear me."

"Trying to find the bottle opener. Did I leave it over there?"

"Oh, okay, so you're just going to avoid my analysis."

"What analysis?" I tease, and earn an eye roll. She grabs something off the coffee table and approaches the kitchen.

"My badass alpha feels no pain. I get it."

But she doesn't seem to be too against the description when she closes the gap and deposits the bottle opener in my hand. There goes her gaze again, wandering over my body. Locking on hard lines and harder... damn. This girl has no mercy on a guy trying to be a decent human being for once.

It's way too easy for her palm to slide past flimsy elastic.

"Shit," I groan.

"I knew it," she whispers, hot breath sending sparks over my skin as she discovers my neck, the line of my jaw. Dark nails sink into my chest.

"You're making things damn near impossible for me, you know that?"

Her mouth curves into a smile I want to suck off her face. "What girl wouldn't want to play with one of Canada's Hot Thirty Under Thirty every chance she gets?"

I devour that smile. Her lips, her tongue. It's not enough, and she gasps at the violence of my hips shoving her into the island. Her fingers dig into my back to pull me into an intoxicating rhythm that sends my thoughts down the hall to the bedroom.

I guide us toward the opposite counter where my right hand searches a drawer while my left works on coaxing moans from the woman who's uprooted my world. I strike gold with both and rely on my teeth to conquer stubborn packaging. She's so light as I lift her onto the counter and scale her thighs, already open and inviting me in. Head back, eyes closed, chest rising and falling in an unnatural race for oxygen, she's every woman in my songs.

"You're sure?" I say. A hand that was gripping the edge of the granite, grasps me instead, low enough to send my blood pounding in desperation.

"Yes. Now!"

But I don't. I can do better than this. She deserves better than this.

Her legs tighten around my waist as I lift her from the counter and carry her to the couch. She's already mine, so impatient.

> "Hell's fire and Hades' desire, have nothing on
>   you, babe.
> Nothing on you.
> Reigning kings tossed worthless rings with less
>   hunger than my desperate plunder for your
>   treasure.
> Better, you tell me no, and save my soul,
>   before..."

I've surrendered too. I know it. We both do. I groan into her *"Before..."*

"Before your charm, disarms all that I am. Breathe my last, through your lungs. The sweetest death."

And I do.

"I HAVE AN IDEA." Hannah tilts her head up from my chest.

"What's that?"

"How about we do this every day? Maybe a few times?"

I laugh and run my finger down her cheek. After my gentle kiss, she settles against me again, fingers tracing the art etched into my skin.

"I mean, we can be flexible," she continues. "Location, position, things like that. I'm open."

It's a tempting offer. More than that. An irresistible one. Too bad she doesn't understand what she's offering.

"I've always loved this one. Even more so now," she says. By the location of the chills rushing along my nerves, I can tell she's outlining the detailed likeness of a burning Hades.

"Ah. That's one of my favorites too."

"Did you get it before or after 'The Death of Hades.'"

"Before."

"Is the song about Holland?"

"Basically."

"And the tattoo?"

I follow her fingers over the lifelike shading. "Actually, the tattoo that inspired the song is the opposite. It's about the moment I committed to this journey and accepted the Hell that comes with it. 'The Death of Hades' is about Holland's power to make it worth it. She transformed the pain into beauty."

"My god," she whispers, now tracking my jaw. "You really loved her."

"It was more than love, Han."

"I know you two are long over, but she'd freak if she knew I was here."

"Sister code?" I say with a laugh. "Holland's not petty like that."

"No, but she's protective." Her grin says it all.

"Yeah, she'd kick my ass for corrupting you," I say.

My phone erupts, and we both stiffen at the name.

"Miranda," Hannah mutters. My blood freezes as she pushes herself up and waves me toward my chariot with a bitter hand.

"I'm not going to take it."

"She calls you a lot for not being your girlfriend."

I stare at the display, the bright red decline button. "It's complicated." I really need a better response for this.

"Do you even like her?"

I sigh and rub my face. "Not really." I regret sharing the truth which is so much worse.

"So, what? You're just screwing her because she's that good?" I search for amusement, but only get resentment.

"No, it's not about that."

"Then what?"

This should be easy to explain. To this person who would also keep my secret to protect her sister. Then again, explaining how badly you screwed up is never an ideal topic. "She knows things."

"Knows things?"

"Yeah."

"Your bank account? Social security number? What?"

"She knows about the breakup of Tracing Holland. If she leaks it... God, I can't even think about what would happen."

Hannah pales. "Wait. Is she extorting you?"

I curse and rest my head on my fists. "No. I mean, I don't know. Maybe."

"Dammit, Wes! Why didn't you tell me? I'm a lawyer. We can—"

"We can, what?" I snap. "File a lawsuit? Go to the cops?"

"Okay, no, I get it, but—"

"She hasn't even admitted that's what she's doing. I can't explain it. She's never threatened me openly. It's just been understood that I play along, and in exchange, she doesn't ruin us. You know what would happen to your sister and her career if our feud got out right now. To all of us."

"Worst case? The album would flop."

"And the tour. Everything—over."

Hannah quiets, eyes softening, and I have to look away. "Does Holland even know?"

"About Miranda? Of course not. And she won't, okay?" My gaze bores into her. "Promise me, Hannah. I'm keeping your secret. No one can know about this."

"Okay, okay, I promise. But Holland despises you right now."

"I know."

"And you're still protecting her?"

"Of course."

"But maybe if she knew about this—"

"She won't. I'm serious. She deserves to have the life and career she's earned. I'm not going to take that away from her because I messed up with Miranda."

"I get that, but what about you?"

"It's my own fault."

Hannah crosses her arms. "So that's it? You're just going to be some woman's sex slave until she's done with you? What if she never gets bored?"

I roll my eyes. "It's not like that."

"No? What is it she wants from you, then?"

"A fantasy, I guess."

"What, like princess dresses and tiaras? No sex?"

I don't have an answer for that.

"Fuck! And what about me? About this?" she cries, bursting up from the couch.

"This is amazing, Hannah. I'd do anything to make it work with you, but you knew that was never going to happen. I'm not wired for happily ever after."

"Wait, so you were just going to screw me when your fake girlfriend wasn't around?"

"Come on. You know that's not what this is."

"Do I?"

"I tried to warn you. I—" Not my best speech as she grabs her bra and stomps to her room. "Stop! Will you just—"

"Screw you!" And the door slams shut.

I CAN'T STAND the sound of tears. Especially from those I care about. Especially when I'm the cause. Damn the thin walls of my condo. Didn't the contractor believe in privacy?

I want to intrude, my hero complex raging at full blast, but this one is beyond my expertise. Apologies do nothing without promise of change, and to be perfectly honest, she's much better off hating me than pursuing me. I'm a dead end. Still, it's pain, and I deal a lot better with my own than someone's I care about.

I don't expect an answer when I tap on her door so I'm encouraged by the, "Not gonna happen, Wes!" that blasts through.

"Hannah, please? Hear me out."

"I did."

That lie is an invitation if I ever heard one. I push through and suppress my smile at her exasperated curse.

"You're trespassing," she mutters.

"You'll have trouble proving that in a court of law."

"Asshole."

"Drama queen. Move over."

She shifts just enough to give me the edge of the bed.

We're both silent as the space between us shrinks, and I finally brave her pain. "Hannah, I'm sorry for my role in this."

"But?"

"No buts for that part. I'm sorry. I did a terrible job

explaining the situation with Miranda. With you, it's just, I don't know." I scrub at my eyes and focus back on the floor. "I don't even have a handle on what's going on with all of that, so I have no idea how to explain it. The thing is, and don't bite my head off, you and I both know I'm not the only reason you're in here right now." Her eyes narrow, and I shrug. "You're an intelligent, rational woman, Han. You know this isn't just about me."

"Oh, so now you're going to give me the mental illness speech on top of it?"

"No. You don't need it. You could give that speech in your sleep, which is why you are not going to be surprised that I'm setting a condition for you to stay here."

"What?"

"You heard me. Rent, babe. You're paying rent."

Her nose scrunches at my smile.

"Rent?"

"Yep. I'm going to guess that quitting life also means you quit therapy, so if you want to hide here, you're going to have to keep seeing a therapist."

"Bullshit."

"You want to test me?"

"I want to slap you, but it's too much effort."

I smirk. "Exactly, because deep down rational, intelligent Hannah knows I'm right."

"Damn you."

"Sure, as long as you go to your appointments. Hey, I don't even care if you spend the rest of the day brooding and watching judge shows, but you're going to talk to someone about what's going on. Non-negotiable."

She throws an arm over her face. "You suck."

"Maybe. I also care about you. A lot."

She peeks out from under her arm, and I plant a quick kiss on her forehead.

"Non-negotiable," I repeat moving to the door. "Also, no more sex because seriously? How fucked up is this?"

She turns toward the wall. "I bet that one is still negotiable."

10

PROVE IT

A week ago I longed to see Holland's name light up my phone, and now? I check the guest room door to make sure it's still closed before accepting the call.

"Hey, Holland."

"Wes! Thank god."

"Good to hear your voice too." Except based on the quaver, I'm not.

"Wes, I know you hate me right now—"

"I don't hate you. I will never hate you."

She quiets for a moment. "Okay, well, I know we're at odds, but I need your help. Do you remember that girl Hannah brought to the Acrobat release party?"

"Uh, what?"

"From her law school. Tall, disgustingly gorgeous. Come on, think. She was all over you. You probably slept with her."

"Wow, thanks."

"Don't pretend to be offended. Just think."

I sigh. "You mean Charlotte?"

"Yes. That was her name. Do you still have her number?"

"I don't think I ever had her number."

"You're sure? Do you know where she lives? Her e-mail? Last name? Anything?" I feel her disappointment through the phone.

"I haven't spoken to Charlotte since she left my room the following morning. What's going on?"

"It's Hannah. Something's wrong, and I'm scared."

I clench my jaw and force air into my lungs. "Yeah?"

"Please, if you know anything... You always saw her as a little sister. Help me find her."

Yep, this is *totally* messed up.

"Why do you think something's wrong?"

"Because she just dropped off the grid."

"You didn't see her at Christmas?"

"She was present but completely evasive. She broke up with her boyfriend and said she was living with a friend."

"Okay? And that concerns you?"

"It's not just that. Trust me, she wasn't right. She wasn't healthy. I'm afraid she's headed in the wrong direction again and if she's alone..." Her pain twists through me as her voice trails off.

"Holland, I'm sure she's okay. Have you tried calling her and seeing what's up?"

"Of course I have. She answered the first time and said she was fine and we shouldn't worry. She's been ignoring everything since."

"Okay, well, there you go. She's fine." I roll my eyes on her behalf for that one.

"Seriously? If Sophia suddenly got all secretive and started ignoring your calls, would you accept she was fine just because she said so?"

Shit. I let out a breath.

"Exactly. We've contacted her friends, and now we're

trying to track down anyone else who might have a clue where she is."

"I wish I could help, Holland."

God, I hate this.

"No, I know. It was a long shot. If you hear anything, though..."

"Okay."

If I hear anything, I'll still be a liar.

I pause at Hannah's door on the way back to my room. This has to stop. All of it, and my fist finds the wood. I push through when she ignores me. She must have expected as much because my spot is open on the edge of the bed.

"That was Holland?" she mutters toward the ceiling.

"You heard the call?"

"Your walls suck."

"They do." I study her as she shifts to face me. "Also, your sister loves you. It killed me to lie to her."

"It would kill her to know the truth."

"No it wouldn't. You're not giving her enough credit."

"What do you know about it?"

"Nothing. I just know Holland. She takes the hard fight for those she loves."

"Oh, so I'm a fight now?"

"When have you ever not been one?"

I get a scowl for that.

"Thanks for not betraying me," she says after another pause. "It must have been hard."

"Fucking brutal. And you're welcome." I force her to look at me. "Please don't do this anymore. You have to tell your family what's going on."

There's no evidence I got through. Her poker face is damn impossible when she wants it to be. Not sure if it's a lawyer thing or a Hannah thing. After a long silence, I rise to leave.

"Hey, Wes?"

"Yeah?"

"You should know that I decided I don't hate you after all."

I grin. "I already knew that."

"Asshole."

"Yep."

She smiles and absently runs her fingers along the edge of the mattress. "You're also a really good friend." Her eyes turn serious as they journey to mine, and I swallow the twinge in my gut.

"Yeah well, I like the hard fight even more than Holland."

SURPRISES SUCK. Anyone who knows me understands I never want to walk into a room on my birthday and be audibly assaulted by hiding acquaintances. I don't need random gifts or unannounced reunions with old friends. I certainly don't want Miranda Rivenier asking to be buzzed up to my condo four days earlier than expected.

"Shit," I mutter, after instinctively pushing the button.

Hannah emerges from her room, working a towel over wet hair. "Did I hear the bell? Is someone coming up?"

"Miranda's back early."

"Oh, crap! Your girlfriend?"

"She's not my girlfriend."

"Fine. Your twisted *whatever*. Do you want me to hide?"

Not sure I trust her offer with that expression. I huff a laugh. "Yeah. Go hang out in your closet for a few days. I'll slip food under the door."

She rolls her eyes. "I'm just trying to help."

"I know what you meant. Thanks, but it's cool. Just don't tell her we slept together, okay?"

"No problem, genius."

She gathers her hair in a ponytail and ducks back into her room. I get the knock a second later.

"Hey, gorgeous," Miranda purrs. "Surprise."

Her greeting tells me her expectations don't include a roommate.

"Miranda. Hi."

"You gonna let me in?"

"Yeah. Um, come in." I step back so she can enter and cringe when cold hands slide into my jeans and grip my ass. Hard. Yep, definite expectations.

"I felt so bad for missing our first Christmas together. I wanted to surprise you for New Year's."

"Uh, huh. Well, you did." I clear my throat and pull her hands away. "Here's the thing, though. I have a friend staying with me at the moment."

"Oh." She scans the space. "Is he here now?"

"Well, her name is Hannah and yes. She's in the guest room."

Virtual eye-bullets say she remembers more than I hoped. "Hannah, the lawyer?"

"Hannah, my friend from childhood who needed a place to crash for a while."

"I don't think—"

"Oh hi. Miranda, right?" Hannah enters the room, wet hair twisted up in a sexy pile on her head. Dammit, she looks amazing in a ripped band tee and tight jeans. Hannah looks like Hannah for the first time in years. And she knows it, the way her eyes travel over me for a response. I try to keep my reaction private while this nightmare plays out. Worst nightmare? I don't know. Atomic bombs go off. Some people are actual cannibals. You never know when you'll fall into a sinkhole and get buried alive. But yeah, this moment is definitely on the list.

Miranda shakes her hand. "Right. Hannah. From Regis, Whitlock & Sons."

"Not anymore."

"Oh? They let you go?"

"I left."

"Really. Are you with a new firm?"

"Nope. Just crashing at Wes's and watching judge shows."

"I see." Distaste parades across her face, and I have to suck in a snort at Hannah's joy over it. "Well, if you'd like a few leads, I can poke around at the firm we use."

"Aw, thanks, but I don't need you poking anything."

I bite my cheek because *ha*. Miranda's lips tighten into a thin line.

"Well, good luck to you with your new... career."

"Thanks!" Hannah adds her brightest fake smile. "Okay, I'm gonna go back to the room and brood. Enjoy your night. Hope you had a good business trip."

"It was great, thanks."

And I'm alone with Miranda's wrath.

"Are you dating her?" Her cool tone is worse than violence. I'd love a furious slap right now.

"No. I told you. She needed a place to stay and I had an empty room."

"I see. And the fact that she's young, beautiful, and obviously into you had nothing to do with it?"

"Just an added bonus." Damn my sarcasm. I might get that slap after all.

"Well, clearly you have your hands full so here's the whisky I bought for us. I guess you can share it with your *guest* instead."

Uh-oh. "I told you it wasn't like that."

"No, I suppose not. Nothing is *like that* with you, is it?

We're all just games in your little toy chest. Pull us out and play with us when you feel like it."

Solid fighting words right there. Cue the panic. "What? No. Miranda, come on. You're not being fair. I told you from the beginning we're not together."

"Oh, so you *are* sleeping with her?"

"Huh? I mean..."

"Wow, Wes. This is just... I thought we had this all worked out. Apparently not. Good luck with your band split."

Shit! "Miranda, wait!" I grab her arm, and she turns on me.

"You know, I get it now. Why your ex kicked you out of the band? You're a lying piece of shit. The world deserves to know what you are."

I flinch, and let her go. I knew what she was, what I am. Fucking saw this moment coming from the second we met. Doesn't mean I have a clue what to do with it now. As if I'm not close enough to the edge of watching my world blow up even more, we're startled by a clattering sound.

We turn just as Hannah slams a pill bottle on the island. "Depression and anxiety."

She deposits another next to it. "Sleep aids."

Two more. "And these are for migraines. Preventative and acute." Her eyes lock on Miranda. "I'm not well right now. I have a lot of issues I need to work through and have been fighting for years. No one has ever accepted me the way I am like Wes has. I came to him to help me pick up the pieces. You're upset at the wrong person. I'm the problem here."

Stunned, I barely react to Miranda's hard stare. All I can do is wait for her to process the surprise performance. Her eyes narrow; Hannah crosses her arms.

"Prove it," Miranda says finally, gaze cold and locked on me again.

I swallow and cast a look to Hannah, who visibly pales.

"What?" I hide my clenched fists in my pockets.

"You want me to believe there's nothing going on between the two of you? Then prove it."

My pulse is audible now, brain firing signals in all directions at once.

"Prove it how?" We all know the answer. The stench of it pulsates around us.

"Wes?" Hannah's voice breaks, and I can't even look at her.

The album.

The tour.

Holland.

Fucking Hannah who deserves so much better than this.

"What's wrong, babe?" Miranda buries her fist in my shirt, forcing my attention. Her other palm slides into my jeans, and I flinch at her sudden grip. "Certainly, your *friend* would have no issue with us heading back to your room for a while. She'd understand how much I've missed you." This speech is for Hannah as much as me. I see it in every slithering movement of her eyes toward her prey. Hannah hasn't moved. Neither have I. No, this is Miranda's show and she returns her focus to me. She traces a manicured finger over my lips. "But I mean, if it's a problem, I guess I can go implement that action plan we've been working on."

With a slight shove, she lets go and starts moving down the hall. Her dark gaze reaches over her shoulder and locks on me as her coat slides down her back. Next, it's a sultry grin, thick with warning, a turn to show me the release of buttons on her blazer. Soon it's expensive black lace drawing my eyes down the hall, bare skin explaining in no uncertain terms what "proof" means to this woman.

My instinct knows what to do. I'm moving. God, I'm actually going to do this. Another wrong choice? I don't even know anymore.

"I'm sorry," I whisper to Hannah. Our eyes only connect for a second. Just enough for her silent plea to rip my heart out. "I have to. I—" A trail of clothing directs my path, lures me to the consequences of my sin. *I have to, Hannah.*

Tears glisten on her cheeks when my gaze ventures back. Her teeth sink into her lower lip as she crushes me with a slight nod.

"Are you coming, babe?"

"Coming."

———

"I NEED to check in with the office. I stopped here first." Miranda adjusts her bra as she examines herself in the mirror. "That was amazing, hon," she adds, turning to me. She leans in for a lingering kiss that deepens beyond what's necessary for after-sex debriefing. "Ah, I missed you so much."

All I can muster is a twist of the lips. I despise her for not letting my disgust faze her. Yes, that's right, I *despise* this woman. And she knows it. Hell, I think that's her addiction to this sick arrangement.

"I wish we could grab dinner tonight, but I'll probably be too late. Tomorrow though?"

"Sure."

I hate her smile now also—venomous and laced with a knowing glint that broadcasts the truth behind our lies. "On second thought. We should stay in tomorrow. I like you just like that." Her slow scan travels from my face to the sheet rippling over my thighs. I've never had a problem being naked until this moment. "I'll be back as soon as I can."

Still no response in my throat. She almost laughs at my paralysis, and every muscle in my body contracts until I hear the front door clatter.

I smash my fist into the headboard.

"Fuck!"

THE CONDO IS empty after I shower and pull myself together. My knuckles throb, and I've been in enough fights to know I'll probably need medical attention for this. It's my pick hand so I should still be able to play. Right now though, I don't give a shit if I never play again.

My search for Hannah only finds her belongings, and I'm relieved that at least her escape wasn't permanent. I don't expect a response from the message I send her and attach myself to the couch to wait for the next shard of my life to explode in my face.

Judge shows are bullshit without Hannah. I try for a comedy, but there's no humor in me. I'm too cynical for a thriller, definitely not a romance, so the TV goes off. Drinking is an okay distraction but becomes a menace when it's a focused activity. After two hours, I'm sure I look as shitty as I feel. I've lost track of the number of shots I've poured down my throat. Then again, I wasn't measuring so the count is irrelevant. The glass slips from my hand just as a scrape at the lock signals the arrival of the only other person with a key. Shit, I don't even remember getting dressed.

"Wes?"

I squint up at the intruder. So beautiful. So tragic. So totally in the wrong place at the wrong time. "Hannah."

"Are you drunk?"

"Um, probably more like wasted."

I follow her eyes down my body and see that I'm in boxer briefs. Barely. One question answered.

"Where's Miranda?"

"Work."

"Are you two still..."

"Yep. Can you grab the vodka? I kicked the whisky." I find this fact hilarious and even tip the bottle to show her the lack of liquid that falls through the opening.

"Not a chance. Come on, rockstar." She grabs my arms, but it's more fun to pull her on top of me.

"Wes," she grunts, pushing against my chest.

"I hate her."

Hannah stops struggling and searches my face.

"Miranda. I hate her so much."

She doesn't respond at first. It's hard for me to read her through the rare sheen in my eyes. Stupid crap like that happens when I'm shitfaced.

"You don't have to keep doing this."

I let out a bitter breath. "What's the alternative?"

No answer again because I'm fucked. "I don't know, but this isn't the way."

"I'm figuring it out."

"You're a mess."

I rock to my feet and stagger toward the bar. My hand waves at the vodka—what I think is the vodka?—until I'm able to wrap my fingers around the bottle. Maybe this is the solution. Drinking my way through Miranda until she's sick of me.

"Holland wouldn't want this, and you know it."

I turn my head toward her double silhouette.

"Break up with Miranda. Let shit hit the fan, and we'll deal with it."

Waves rock in my stomach. I grab the edge of the cart to control the movement and squeeze my eyes shut. The waves become visual behind my eyelids. Swaying then circling into a hurricane of nausea. Oh god, I feel a hot, salty wave escape through my lashes, collect in the corner of my eye.

"What the hell is wrong with me, Han?" I turn on her, demand an answer.

She doesn't flinch. Good. I want her to destroy me with the truth. Sucker-punch the sickness right out of my rotted gut.

"Honestly? You don't give a damn—until you do. And then you implode." She approaches, angelic steps closing the gap between us. I suck in the emotion as she spreads her palm on my cheek. "Or the shit-storm you created implodes on you."

It's a lot to take. Words like that. Compassion from someone I just wounded. Hannah Drake is too much for me, too much to fight.

"Why did you come back?"

"Because we need each other."

"I'm so fucked up, Han. You know that. You know what I just did."

"Yeah. Me too."

"I might do it again."

"Yeah. Me too."

We exchange a lopsided smile, and I can't take it anymore. I pull her in, letting her hair against my shoulder calm the raging surf.

"It was you in my head," I say.

She squeezes harder, presses into my chest. "That doesn't help."

I close my eyes. "I know, but I needed to say that."

"And I need you to stop sleeping with a woman you hate." She pulls back and searches my face. I let the emotion escape this time, make her understand my other need that goes beyond any of this bullshit. It's a gentle kiss at first. Then the urge to overpower what happened in my bedroom takes over.

Her hands shove into my chest and push me away. "You're drunk. Besides..." She places another soft kiss on my cheek. "I can't. Not now. Not when you belong to her."

"But I don't."

"You do." Full-on stare as she begins her official retreat. "Good night, Wes. I'll see you in the morning."

I watch her every step until I'm satisfied she's in her room and staying with me.

I MANAGE a few hours of alcohol-induced sleep, but once the buzz wears off, I'm screwed. I spend the second half of the night reliving each brutal moment of what happened. Miranda and I are symbiotic assholes, bringing out the worst in each other, draining life-forces. And now our poison has struck someone I care about. Hannah was right when she said this isn't what Holland would want.

She wouldn't, but situations like this are the reason she shed me from her life. I'm a uniting force, the villain, the fuck-up. Frederick Alton called it when I was barely out of diapers. The only thing that's changed? I don't give a shit anymore.

My damaged knuckles throb, pulsate with a searing flame.

Ashes of regret.

Proving scars.

Dammit. This proves nothing.

11

SELFISH

"Hannah, hey. I want to write."

My non-bruised knuckles graze her door again. It's almost noon and I still haven't seen her today. I'm not surprised—I've earned her silence—but I have no intention of accepting it.

"I'm tired," she calls out.

"I'm not asking you to run a marathon with me. Just move to the couch and gush about what an amazing one-handed guitar player I am."

I can almost hear the eye roll through the door. I peek inside to confirm.

"Hey," I say, moving into the room.

She throws an arm over her eyes with a groan. "Why can't you just accept boundaries?" she mutters through her arm-wall.

"Because I care about you."

"Yeah? Well, then care enough to leave me alone for a while."

I take my spot on the edge of the bed. My hand twitches with the need to touch her, to trace the smooth skin hiding her eyes from me. She'd probably touch me back with a fist to the face.

"I'm sorry about yesterday. You know that's not what I wanted. I wish..." What do I wish? Too many things for this conversation.

Her arm slams down to the mattress. "I heard everything, Wes. *Everything* you two were doing, hoping you'd send her away, but I had to be the one to run."

I clench my jaw and study the floor. "She was just putting on a show for you. Most of it wasn't real."

"No? It sounded like she was going for world volume records."

I can't afford a laugh and bite my lip to stop it. "Yeah, believe me. I'm good but not that good."

"I know," she says, totally serious, and this time I can't help it. "Are you laughing at me?"

I chew my knuckles and shake my head, resulting in an arm smack.

"I'm sorry! I am, but..."

Is that a smile sneaking over those perfect lips? "I hope that bitch is sore today."

And I'm done. The snort escapes and draws a grin. The need to taste her smile overwhelms me, and I expect a real slap this time when I lean in. Instead she drags me in for the kiss. Sweet—and painful.

"Please, Han," I whisper, hovering millimeters from her lips. "I'm going to figure this out. Just come write with me for a while."

She pushes me back, and a heavy silence follows, filling the space between us with everything I want but can't have. She does nothing to put me out of my misery, just stares with the reminder of how much I've hurt her. I sigh and start for the door.

"Hang on. I need pants."

Oxygen floods into my lungs. *Thank god.*

"No you don't."

"Perv."

I grin. "I'll get started."

"YOU SHOULD SING THE CHORUS," Hannah says, swallowing a mouthful from her water bottle before leaning back on the couch.

"Really? You killed it though."

"Yeah, but switching to the male lead would be more dynamic. Then I'll come in with a harmony on 'peace offering.'"

I run a quick review in my head and replay the progression out loud. "Damn, you're right."

"Hmm... what was that?"

"I'm not saying it again."

Her smile only widens. "You're such a pushover. I bet that's how you ended up with dragonfly plates."

"A pushover? Please. I have dragonfly plates because I don't give a shit about plates."

Her smile fades as her eyes comb over me. "Wes, I have to tell you something."

I rest my guitar against the side of the couch.

"It's about what happened."

"Okay," I say when she pauses.

Her eyes trace the floor, the wall, the ceiling—everywhere but me. "I didn't resign from the firm. I was fired. I had a complete meltdown in front of everyone."

Shit.

"You're human, Han. It happens."

I reach for her hand but she doesn't react to the pressure of my fingers. Is she still pissed at me?

"I could be disbarred."

"What? No way. I'm sure—"

She stiffens, pulls her hand away. "No, you don't get it." Her eyes are wet now, shiny with a pain that searches for me again. "I want to be disbarred. I want to be nothing. And this thing with Miranda? It just confirms... Ah, never mind."

My heart hammers against my ribs, its echoes roaring in my ears. "What were you going to say?"

She clamps down on her lip. Tears glaze her cheeks. This room is suddenly too loud, too fucking quiet. "Nothing. I mean..."

Dammit! "Hannah, talk to me."

"I don't want to exist. I don't think I need to."

A sob rushes out, and I pull her against me. Tears soak through my shirt, searing their way to my heart. I'm no therapist. But the thought of a world without Hannah Drake is something I can't handle. It forms a cavern in my gut, a void, as I hold onto this beautiful soul.

"Okay, well, I need you so we're going to have to figure this out."

Her head moves in disagreement against my chest, and I hold tighter.

"Think of how much easier your life would be without me," she whispers, and I have to temper a spark of anger.

"No. You know that's a lie. That's not you talking and even if it was, you'd still be wrong. I fucked my life up so badly right now you're the only thing I have left. I can be damn selfish, so we're getting help. Real help."

The slightest of smiles pokes through when her gaze arches to mine. "My viper, huh?"

"Damn straight. Get used to it."

"You just need me for the female lead in your songs."

"That's not true. I need you for the harmonies too."

Her soft laugh fills the void with a dull ache as she settles against me again. "Wow, you really *are* selfish."

I kiss her hair. "Extremely."

A hiss escapes when she takes my bad hand and examines it.

"So do I want to know what happened?"

"Probably not."

She traces the skin around the purple ridges.

"I guess it's too much to assume this is from defending yourself against Miranda's wrath after you broke up with her?"

I let out a dry laugh. "She's vicious, but pretty sure I could take her without a scratch. Well, maybe a scratch."

I feel the disappointment seep from her chest into mine. "You should get that checked out. How did you even play?"

"It's my pick hand. Anyway, I don't think anything's broken. The swelling has gone down."

"At least it wasn't from punching Luke again." Her lips touch my bruises, and I close my eyes. Guilt maybe? I don't know, but it sucks. Everything about this moment, this woman, so wrong and so incredibly perfect.

"A headboard."

"Huh?"

"I fought a headboard."

She laces her fingers with mine. "We'll figure this out. Just don't break your hand. Not a good solution for a musician."

And that's the moment I decide if I break my hand over anything, it will be making sure Hannah Drake finds her way back.

12

RENT

I don't know much about mental illness and even less about searching for therapists. Fortunately, ignorance doesn't have much of an effect on me. That fact gets me in trouble more often than not, but today it has me on my laptop running searches and making phone calls.

Dr. Marla Conner is accepting new clients and emerges as my first choice.

"What's her approach?" Hannah continues studying the ceiling as I hover at her door with my notes.

"Her what?"

"Her therapy style. Psychoanalysis, cognitive, behavioral, holistic...?"

"Geez, I don't know. But she's within walking distance of my place and seemed like a cool person when I talked to her. She has a lot of experience working with depression."

"I prefer cognitive therapy."

"Right." It sounds like an excuse to me, but I have no clue. "Maybe that's what she does. Will you at least meet her? I told her you were free tomorrow at ten."

"I'm not."

"Oh really? Is that when Judge Hamilton's on?"

"The previews looked really good."

"Record it. You're going."

"I probably won't like her."

"Maybe not. I'm just asking you to meet her. Rent, babe, remember?"

"I hate you."

"You and everyone else. You're still going."

THIS ISN'T the first time I've been in the waiting room of a counseling office. Not when you have demanding, authoritative parents who insist you're mentally ill if you'd want to waste your life pursuing music. What they didn't know was that they were paying for my therapist and me to figure out a way to navigate my situation.

Holland Drake and Dr. Gabriel Yates—the reasons I'm a successful rockstar instead of a homeless ex-convict.

The white noise machine whispers beside me as I wait. Am I bored out of my mind? Hell yeah. But Hannah is worth it. It's not hard to keep promises when it comes to that girl.

I insert my earbuds and replay some rough recordings on my phone. Old progressions I've been working on. Music that desperately needs lyrics, and my mind keeps drifting across the dated waiting room furniture to the closed door on my right.

Session in Progress

Session in progress. We're all sessions in progress. Aspiring humans trying to survive a world that rarely gets better. Only we do.

Dr. Yates once told me that forgiveness is about the offended not the offender. He wanted me to let go of my anger so I could break free from the effects of my parents' tyranny. I thought I had. My wall is strong, ironclad when it has to be, but maybe this thing with Holland, Luke, Miranda... maybe my session didn't end as cleanly as I thought. Maybe my mess is still in progress.

> Session in progress
> The hardest journey we take
> Raise a glass to the past, it's the future we break
>
> If all goes well or damns you to hell, it's your
>   story to own
> So tell if you dare, to care about your mess, in
>   progress.

Maybe, just maybe, this monumental implosion means my session has only begun.

I RECOGNIZE the look on Hannah's face when she emerges from the office. I also get her silence on the walk back. I know better than to ask pointless questions like, "How did it go?" She doesn't know the answer yet. You never do until these moments are reclassified as "hindsight" and you're sitting in a waiting room reflecting on them while waiting for someone else.

What I *do* is buy her takeout she can eat on the couch while watching petty criminals face charges of vandalism and debt default. It makes her smile which makes me smile from my creepy vantage point in the kitchen.

"I don't know how you can even watch that crap," I call over to her.

"Why not? It's hilarious."

"Don't you just want to punch your fist through the screen and sort everything out for those poor bastards?"

"Not even a little bit. Do you want to participate in singing competitions?"

"Not even a little bit."

"Exactly."

I drop beside her and hand her a water bottle. "So what's this chick's problem?"

"She claims the defendant's daughter caused damage to her car with her bike."

"And?"

"The car is a fifteen-years-old wreck. No way she can prove it unless she has a video."

"Does she?"

"No, but check out her outfit."

"Is she wearing a toga?"

"People never know how to dress for court."

I pop a dumpling in my mouth and pull out my buzzing phone.

Miranda.

I ignore the call.

"You need to break it off with her."

I swallow my food slowly. "I know, but—"

"No, screw the consequences! This isn't about me. It's not even about Holland when it comes down to it. This is about you."

"She could ruin Holland."

"She won't ruin Holland. My sister is a goddess. She has an

entire team supporting her. She'll recover. It's you who will be left behind. You'll be the one taking the hit for screwing up again and coming out the villain when this blows up."

"Since when have I cared about being the bad guy? Isn't that why you came to me in the first place?"

"You don't, but that's not what this is about."

No way are we having this conversation. I start toward the kitchen.

"You're clinging to the last strand of the status quo you have left," she calls after me. "You'd rather sell your soul to Miranda than face the prospect of starting over. That's what this is about."

"Bullshit," I fire back, fist clenched to keep it from slamming into the counter. "You honestly think I'm afraid of change?"

"No, I think you're afraid of who you are without Holland."

The guillotine drops. We stare at each other across the room. The compassionate look in her eyes is even worse than anger.

"You don't even know who that is, do you?" she says softly.

Fuck this.

"I'm going to the gym."

I PUSH MYSELF HARD, but my head is so jammed with shit right now I lose count of reps and inclines. What I need is escape, a mindless inferno that can consume the rage enough to think clearly for once. I need pain. Shaking limbs from overexertion and streams of sweat tracing every line of my body. I had a trainer once, but we butted heads over my aggressive workouts. *It's not good for your body to push so hard all the time.*

So what? It's good for my head, and probably my soul too if it tames my sins.

By the time I wrap, I can barely wipe the towel over my face. That's when I know it's safe to return to the nightmare that is my life.

I breathe in cold air as I exit the gym, and after a long walk, pick-up a snack at my favorite burger joint. I'm not hungry, but it feels wrong to return to the condo without a peace offering.

My grip tightens on the bag of food I brought the second I enter my condo. "Miranda?" I scan the space for Hannah but come up empty.

"Hannah let me in. She's in her room."

"What are you doing here? What about work?"

"I moved some things around." She eyes my takeout bag like it's a kilo of heroin. "You haven't answered my calls or messages."

"I was working out."

Her gaze lingers too long on Hannah's closed door.

"Know what I think?" Clearly, she doesn't care because she keeps going. "I think you're full of bullshit. I think you do have feelings for that princess in there."

"Princess? Hannah is about as far from a princess as a woman can be."

"You're defending her?"

"Of course I am. She's my friend." So much for the soul-saving workout.

"Wow. This is..." Her hand rests on her forehead, scorned southern belle style. "Just... wow."

I brush past her. "Why are you even here?"

"Pardon me?"

Her indignation pisses me off more. Hannah wanted a fan full of shit? Oh she's getting it.

"Who the fuck do you think you are, showing up at my

place whenever you feel like it? From day one, I've been up front with you. I told you we're not together. And now, you're what? Extorting me? Is this the only way you can get sex?"

She's speechless, eyes growing wide enough to release the fury. "I sincerely hope there's a good explanation for this outburst."

I shake my head and drop the bag on the counter. "Miranda, this is *my* place, *my* life."

She draws in a deep breath, and I can almost see the meditation steps cycling through her brain. "You're obviously having a bad day. Let's just go back to your room and work this out." She tugs at the neckline of my shirt, but I pull away.

"Not happening."

"I moved two meetings around to come see you."

Is she for real? "Guess you wasted your time. Hannah, food's here!"

Her sliver of the room boils. I swear she's wheezing flames as she stomps forward and grabs my wrist. "I didn't come all the way here for nothing!"

"Apparently you did."

Her grip tightens. "You're making a mistake. You know who I am."

I yank my arm away. "Do whatever the hell you want. I'm done with your games," I say, pulling food out of the bag.

"Is this really the choice you're making?"

I glance over at the human lava pile. "Technically, it's already been made. And you can save the 'you're going to regret this' bullshit. I won't. Not for a second."

Miranda's wrath focuses behind me, and I turn to see Hannah frozen in the hall.

"Hey, Han. Burgers okay? I got bacon and pepper jack for you."

"Fuck you, Wes!" Miranda shrieks.

"Just get out of my house."

The door slams behind her.

Hannah and I watch it rattle, and she clears her throat. "You'll probably have to get that fixed."

HANNAH LAUGHS through a mouthful of burger. "Man, when you dump someone, you dump them."

"I'm not usually so brutal, but that woman..." I shudder.

"Woman? Is that what the kids are calling it?"

I snicker and slide off the island stool. "Want anything to drink?"

"Just water."

I grab two bottles from the fridge.

"So now we wait, I guess," she says, taking one from me.

"I guess."

She stops and stares me down. "You did the right thing. You did the *only* thing."

My nod is instinctive. I've given up trying to figure out what that is anymore. "She's going to crucify me. You were right about everything you said last night. My life, who and what I am, it's all about to be obliterated."

"Probably." She reaches for my hand.

13

CONSEQUENCES

We're partway through a terrible gross-out comedy when my phone erupts again. I half-expect another furious message from Miranda, but it's worse.

Jacob.

"I'll be back," I mutter to Hannah, and rise from the couch. "What's up, man?" I say into the phone.

"You tell me."

I glance toward the couch and retreat farther down the hall at the tension in his voice.

"Huh?"

"Let me read you a headline the Label just jammed down my throat. '*Platinum-selling Canadian rock band calls it quits after ten years.*'"

Oh shit.

"The Label is wondering why they're the last to know. I just got off the phone with Holland and the funny thing is, it appears she's actually the last to know. What the hell, Wes?"

"Wait, you think I—"

"'*I heard Wes discussing their issues with his manager. He sounded really tense,' said Mr. Alton's former girlfriend on the condition of anonymity. 'I think something happened on their last tour to cause the split.'"*

"That's all bullshit, Jacob! You know that."

"Do I? Who is this woman?"

"How can anyone even take this seriously? She wants to remain anonymous? What the hell is that?"

"It's a tabloid. They sell stories, not truth."

"Well, then we need to sue their asses. Along with Miranda, because it's not true."

"Miranda? Is that the ex-girlfriend?"

"She was never my girlfriend. I went out with her a few times. I barely knew her."

"And she overheard a conversation with me?"

I lean my head against the wall. "Yeah, maybe, I don't know. I didn't think she could hear me. Still, at no point did I say we were breaking up the band. Miranda made that up. I told her the opposite. That we were working it out."

"Wait, so you had a highly controversial and *private* discussion in front of a stranger? And then elaborated on it?"

"It didn't go down like that. Everyone was hounding me. You, Holland, I don't know! I just answered the damn phone and next thing I know she's stalking me."

FUCK.

"Hold on, what? This woman was stalking you?"

"Look, never mind. I finally got rid of her and the leak is retaliation. Let's just call PR and figure out how to fix this."

The silence on the other end is not a good sign. Jacob only stops running his mouth for one reason. He's too pissed to form words.

"It's way past that, Wes. PR can't fix your broken relationship with Holland. Like I said, I just got off the phone with her. This mess is exactly why she wants protections in place. You've pushed her to the edge. Sign the damn contract or she's moving on."

His side of the connection goes dead this time.

Worst part? I don't disagree with a thing he said.

IT'S the day of role reversals. A tap on my bedroom door is followed by a "you okay?" and my brain scrambles for a believable lie. Sometimes the best lie is the truth.

"That was our manager."

Hannah drops beside me and joins my staring contest with the floor.

"It sounded rough."

"These walls, man. I need to get them soundproofed."

"Or just stop accepting nosey strays into your place."

"You're the only one I accepted. Miranda forced her way in."

Her weak smile doesn't help. "So she got you in trouble? That was fast."

"She got me in a shitload of trouble."

"Like?"

"Like, telling the world Tracing Holland broke up."

"Wow. I bet your Label isn't happy."

"An understatement. I don't know, Han. Trouble just follows me."

"It's an alpha thing."

"Whatever."

She returns my smirk, and we study the floor again.

"You and Holland will figure it out. You always do," she tells the darkness.

I stall my instinctive nod. For twenty years that was true. "It feels different this time. I really screwed things up."

"Maybe."

My lips twist into a smile. "That's it? That's your pep talk?"

"That's all I've got. Isn't this when you go to the gym to blow off testosterone steam?"

"Actually. That's a great idea."

I push myself up and move to the closet.

"Wow. I didn't realize you were so vain," she says as I pull out my running shoes. Funny how my "vanity" doesn't stop her gaze from traveling over my body as I peel off my shirt. I take my time finding a new one, loving how my skin blisters from her stare. A rigid, pulsating blaze radiates from her as well.

"Jerk," she says.

"Diva."

"I hate you."

I finally pull on another tee and wink on my way past her. The truth is, part of me wouldn't mind blowing off steam in other ways right now.

"WHERE ARE YOU, *Wes? Answer your damn phone!*"

I listen to the message from Holland as soon as it deposits in my voicemail. Then, I listen again—just to make sure I didn't miss anything in the four-second clip. No, she's definitely beyond pissed.

I counteract the effect of her voice with extra energy on the weights, but I can't call her back. I learned from the disaster with Jacob that I don't have a workable explanation yet. How do you explain Miranda? How do you explain any of the mess my life has become?

I knew she'd call. I came here to figure out how to handle it when she did. But despite a lifetime of learning opportunities, fixing mistakes still isn't my area of expertise. I ignore another call from my father. One from my brother. And finally, the Label. That comes from one of the private outgoing lines which never means good news.

I add more weight and work another set of reps. Too many, I guess, and I'm forced to drop the bar with an angry huff. I swipe the hem of my shirt over my face and straighten from the bench.

Yes, I see her watching me. She has for days now. Hot as hell and glued to the elliptical every time I'm here. She's never said hi, smiled a few times. I always smile back and this time is no exception. What changes is her approach.

"Hi, I'm Breia."

"Wes," I say, taking a swig from my water bottle. I grab a towel and dry off.

"I know. From Tracing Holland, right?"

Right. "Yeah."

"You're here a lot."

"It's great therapy."

"I've never seen you with anyone, though."

"I like to work out alone."

She shifts her weight, gaze sliding over me. "Me too."

My body's surprisingly uninterested in this beautiful, half-naked woman. "It's a great gym," I say.

"It is. Hey, you want to grab coffee or something?"

No. The answer is actually no.

"Thanks, but I have to get going."

"Oh. Okay. I just thought, with everything going on... You know, if you needed a friend."

I don't even have a response for that. "Thanks, but I'm fine."

"Good to hear. It's just they're saying you broke up with—"

I decide to shower at home. "Have a good night."

EVERY. Damn. Time. I have to stop going to the gym.

"Wes. Um, you remember Geoffrey."

I lock eyes with Hannah, then stare at the man in my condo. Good-looking, I guess. Definite country club stalker.

"Hey, man. What's up?" I force out, depositing my bag by the door.

"He brought more of my stuff." Hannah averts her eyes, lower lip clenched between her teeth.

"Got it." None of my business. I set to work on some coffee while they finish their drama.

"I'm sorry for all of this, Hannah. I'm glad you're getting help now, but I'm just not equipped to deal with this." The douche's lament comes with puppy dog eyes and everything. What a dick.

"I know. Thanks for bringing my stuff back."

"Keep me in the loop, though. I still care about you so much. Maybe when things get better?"

A creamer packet explodes in my fist. Shit. "Broke one," I mutter at their glance and grab a paper towel.

"You know, my aunt had a mid-life crisis," Geoffrey-the-Ex continues. "It was tough for everyone, but she got through it. I can ask her if she has books or anything."

"Thanks, but I'm good."

"I worry about you all the time. You have so much potential. I wish there was something I could do to cheer you up."

"You could leave. That would help," I offer. Two sets of eyes zoom over to me again, and I shrug.

"How about you stay out of this?" His small shoulders square as much as the stiff button-up shirt allows.

"Geoff, we're in his condo," Hannah says, gaze arcing between us.

"Well, you know what? I don't think I like you staying with this guy."

I tense, but this idiot is too ridiculous to pound into the floor. Plus, Hannah's right. It's my place, so my mess to clean up, and blood stains.

"It's none of your business where I'm staying. You dumped me, remember?"

"Aw, Hannah, I didn't dump you. I still want you—*us*—we just need some time apart while you figure yourself out. Obviously, you have issues you need to work on."

"Dude, you dumped her. Thanks for the box," I say, finally stepping between them. The universe has had enough of *Geoff*.

He glares at me but makes no move to strike. I'm not used to frailty, and I'm a tad disappointed when he mumbles goodbye without so much as a taunt. I have to suppress the urge to storm after him. Just one blow to the jaw, that's it. Plus, now we're left to address the bigger problem.

"You invited him over?"

"Are you angry?"

"No, just confused."

Her eyes search mine, and I sigh. "Hannah, you wanted to hide. How many seconds until your ex calls your parents and repeats that crappy speech to them along with your location?"

"He wouldn't do that. He loves me."

"Yeah, and he wants to believe he's important, that this somehow involves him. He absolutely will."

"It has nothing to do with him. He just doesn't get it. None of them do."

"Exactly."

She drops to a stool, and I shove a mug across the counter.

"Here. It's a special blend I found at this little shop on the last tour."

She stares into the dark liquid. "Will you lie again if my family calls? Tell them I'm not here?"

"Hannah, come on. You honestly think that will work?"

"Fine. What if I pay you to eliminate Geoff before he rats me out?"

"You couldn't afford me, sweetheart," I smirk against my own cup.

"He was right, though."

I lower my mug. "I'm assuming you're referring to something he said before I walked in, because all I heard was bullshit."

She quiets and studies her drink again. Then, the slightest turn of her lips. "Maybe I should try his aunt's books."

I snort and meet her grin.

MY DRAKE INTUITION IS FLAWLESS. Minutes, if not seconds, pass before the furious phone call from Holland. I'm not even sure what she's upset about. She's always understood Hannah's struggle with depression better than anyone, so it's not that. I guess it's the fact that I'm involved in her life again. Even worse, her sister's life. I get it. On the outside, I wouldn't want me entangled in my sister's life either.

"She's living with you now?"

"She's crashing here."

"Same thing!"

"Um, very different. Where else was she supposed to go when the jerk boyfriend kicked her out?"

"How about our parents' house? God, seriously? With everything else we have going on right now, you add this to the list?"

"I'm not adding anything. Hannah's battles have nothing to do with ours."

"She's my sister!"

"Yeah, and she's an intelligent, grown woman. Let her fight for herself for once."

"With you in her corner? Right."

"You trusted me for twenty years."

"No, I understood you. I accepted you. I've never trusted you. Clearly, I was right not to."

That one hurts.

"I don't know what you want me to say. I didn't ask her to come to me. She showed up. I took her in. End of story. If this is where she wants to be right now, I'm not forcing her hand. She's had enough of that in her life."

"What's that supposed to mean?"

There's no good answer to that question. "Nothing."

She quiets for so long I think she's gone. "Is this about us?"

"What?"

"Are you trying to get back at me about the dispute? The contract? First the news leak, now Hannah?"

I can barely hold the phone. "Are you serious?"

"Please, Wes. If this is about the band, take it out on me, not my family!"

"Fuck you." And I hang up.

My blood is pounding, slamming my heart against my chest. It's painful as I stand there, staring at my phone.

Two slender arms curve around my waist. The pressure from a head settles against my back, and warmth soaks into my skin.

"I'm sorry. Thank you," are the words that float out. I turn and pull her into my arms.

"We're gonna figure this out, okay? Just, you have to fix

things with Holland. She loves you so much, Han. You have no idea how much."

"I do, but with me staying here and—"

"No. You're not using me as an excuse. You are welcome here as long as you need, but I'm a roof, a friend—not an excuse."

I tilt her head so I can read her response. Blue eyes glisten with unshed tears, pain beyond what she deserves to feel.

My gaze lowers to her lips, inviting in that moment. Slightly apart in an unspoken request for mine. I know why I want hers. I still can't figure out why she'd want mine after everything.

I pull away. "I need to shower."

"I want to come with you."

I freeze as my body reacts with the extra fury it withheld at the gym. I'm not accustomed to this rush. This lack of control.

When her hands slip beneath my shirt it's over. She tugs the hem, and I help her yank it over my head. I'm all hers as those lips become mine. Hard and aggressive they attack, hungry fingertips pressing into my chest, sliding around to my back, gripping my ass.

I shove against her, testifying what I can offer if she wants it. She gasps in a breath, an irresistible sound for adrenaline as charged as mine.

"Yes, now," she breathes, dragging me toward my room. "Right now."

"And the shower?"

"Afterwards."

I PROP myself up to get the perfect vantage point of her drowsy contentment. "I should evict you. You broke the lease agreement."

"Yeah? Go ahead."

I run my finger down her cheek and love watching her eyes close. The peace on her face, security from my presence beside her is such a drug. So many women, and this is the one I can't stop touching. This woman fucking owns me.

"You hungry?" I ask, finally forcing myself up.

Her hands slide over my shoulders, naked flesh pressed against my back as I sit on the edge of the bed. Am I really getting hard again? Dammit.

"Don't go yet." Hot breath sears my neck as smooth arms lock me against her.

"Han, you know I would—"

"And you totally could," she interrupts with a damn enticing invitation. I groan out the rest of my protest as her attack drives me back to the sheets. It's her mission, her creativity steering us this time. Her lips snake down my body.

"Shit," I gasp when she takes me in her mouth, but she doesn't stop. I press my fists against my eyes, Holland's scowl fresh in my head. She'd never forgive me for this. Hell, I don't forgive me for this. It's... "Hold on... Just..." Oh god. Too late again. *Shit!*

My weight collapses against cotton as air makes its way back into my lungs, fists pressing stars into my eyes. I push harder at the risk of permanent damage. I'd deserve it too. But somehow I doubt even blindness would provide me any protection from Hannah Drake.

"I DON'T SEE why you're beating yourself up."

"I'm not beating myself up." A casual lie to go with my casual perusal of the stack of menus. "What do you want for dinner? Indian? Chinese? Thai? Italian?"

"I want to know why two adults who have feelings for each other and insane chemistry can't indulge it like adults."

"Because those two adults also share an inextricable attachment to Holland Drake who currently hates one of them."

"She doesn't hate you. Holland's incapable of hate."

I glance up from my menu search. "I've hurt her which is a million times worse."

"So apologize. Fix it."

"It's not that kind of hurt." I finally have her full attention. "Han, look around you. Look at us! You're turning me into the responsible one here. Me! That alone should be triggering warning bells in your brain."

"What the hell does that mean?"

"It means, our 'insane chemistry' is just that. We have no idea what it is because we're both hurting. We're both fighting to repair each other. We're taking a totally fucked up situation and making it ten times more complicated by adding another layer."

"So you don't have real feelings for me? You just like fucking me? Is that what you're saying?"

"No, of course not. Of course I care about you. You're like my little sister—"

Shit. Her face shatters into the entire category of emotions you never want to see on a woman. She doesn't even bother sorting them before charging from the condo.

I'm quick. Much faster than Hannah because I'm more familiar with the quirks of my building. I know to take the stairs at this time of day and I'm already in the lobby, leaning against a fancy pillar when she steps through the parting doors. I don't say anything as I watch her startle at my presence.

"Not here. Not now," she hisses.

"I totally agree. Let's go back upstairs and figure things out."

"I'm not going back up with you."

"No? Where are you going then?"

She quiets.

"The café two doors over has free Wi-Fi. Then again, you left without your laptop. And your phone. And I'm going to guess your wallet and purse. What was your plan again?"

That adorable pout plumps into something dangerously close to a smile. "I hate you. Have I ever told you that?"

"You may have mentioned it on occasion." I draw in a deep breath. "Han, I'm sorry. This"—I motion between us— "is not what I wanted. I always want you in my life. I always have and I always will."

"As a sister."

"As a woman."

I reach for her and breathe a sigh of relief when she slides into my arms. We don't care that the doorman is probably enjoying the most action-packed show of his day.

"I'm sorry too," she whispers. "I keep asking you to be something you're not." That hurts until she pulls back and meets my eyes. "But that's not what I want either. I came to you because I need what you are. I want what you are."

Her words radiate deep, settle in a void I've been ignoring for a long time. "Hmm... I didn't take you for an alpha kind of woman, Hannah Drake."

"Don't alphas expect every woman to want them?"

I laugh and loop my arm around her waist to direct her back to the stairs.

14

HOME

We've just returned from our lobby argument when the door buzzes. Hannah's wide eyes beg me not to answer but I hit the intercom anyway.

"Yes?" I say into the speaker.

"Wes? It's James and Annie," a male voice announces. Firm, imploring.

Hannah is already shaking her head in furious protest as I let go of the button.

"Hannah, you have to. Just talk to your parents."

She threads her fingers on her head. "I will soon."

"At least tell them you're okay."

"I can't! I can't face them yet."

"Then let me do it."

She stiffens, arms dropping to her side. "You'd do that?"

"I'd do anything for you."

Her lip rests between her teeth as her gaze wanders over the door. "Okay. You can talk to them. Just..."

"I know. Okay? We're going to fix this."

She nods, eyes so round I want to slaughter every single one of her demons.

"Thank you."

I toss a quick smile and tell the Drakes to meet me at the Raine Café two blocks over.

DESPITE THE FACT that they've been surrogate parents for most of my life, their current expressions remind me they aren't. I've now screwed with two of their daughters. They're probably wondering what devious plan I'm plotting for Emma and Sylvie next.

"Hi. Thanks for meeting me." I slide into the chair across from their creased brows.

"Hannah is with you? She's okay?"

I face their concern, prepared for the fight. "She's been staying with me. Physically she's fine. She'll open up to you eventually. She just needs time."

James arches two fingers over his mouth. It's the same reaction I got from Papa Drake when Holland announced our short-lived engagement. I've needed their family in my life way more than they've needed me, though the Drakes are too generous to ever balance the equation. They accepted me because I was important to Holland. Now...

But why you? It's all over their faces. Why Wes Alton? Why did Hannah go to the one man who keeps disrupting their close, happy family?

"Hannah is strong. She's just figuring some things out," I say, folding my hands on the table.

"And you think you're the person to be guiding her through this?" Annie's voice is little more than a whisper.

This one hurts because there's no anger in her tone. No

resentment, just the love of a mother who desperately wants her daughter back.

I can't speak. I don't have an answer that will work for this conversation. I'm not right for this. God, I know I'm not.

"She doesn't want to put you through it all again." It's not an answer, and only hurts them more. I can't even look at their faces now.

"She's our daughter, Wes. Please, send her home."

A server slows his approach, probably sensing his intrusion. He's going to get water while we decide, he tells us with an awkward smile.

"I'll be back in a minute. Washroom," I add, taking advantage of the opportunity for escape. My lungs are heavy, my brain overwhelmed with the encounter.

They nod slowly, and I have to swallow the emotion as Annie's head finds James' shoulder when I look back. He whispers something against her hair and deposits a kiss.

I splash cold water on my face, and watch my eyes glisten from the drops. Hazel irises almost glow beneath the sheen, making me look like a different man. A person who might actually care about someone more than himself. Someone who can make a good decision. A selfless one. Beads form in the corners of my eyes and slide down my cheeks. Is this what I'd look like if I cried?

I wipe my sleeve across my face and lean into my reflection. Fuck it.

I RETURN from the washroom resolved. I've been fighting on the wrong side, and Hannah's war is too important for me to be selfish.

"We ordered a sampler platter. Hope that's okay," Annie says when I return to my seat.

"Sounds great." I won't be here to sample food anyway. I take my napkin and ask the Drakes for a pen. I expect their confused expressions but remain silent as Annie searches her purse. She hands me one, and I scribble a name on the napkin. After scrolling through my phone, I add a phone number beside it.

They're still staring at me when I look up and slide the napkin across the table. "I'm sending Hannah home. You're right. She needs you more than she needs what I bring to her life. She's going to hate me for it, so all I ask is that you make sure she keeps up with the new therapist we found. She has a standing appointment at 10am on Fridays."

Annie's eyes soften as they connect with mine.

"Thank you, Wes."

I offer a stiff smile and leave before they can see my eyes.

HANNAH GLANCES over from the couch when I enter. "That was quick. How'd it go?"

"Really well. Pack up your stuff. You're going home."

"Hilarious." Her amusement fades as she reads my face. "Wait, what?"

"Hannah, you're going home to your family. You need to be with them right now."

"What are you talking about?" She's on her feet now, following me through the condo toward her room.

I grab her suitcase and throw it open on the bed.

"Hey! What are you doing?" She clutches my arm as I reach for a drawer.

"You're going home."

"What the hell? What did they say to you? I don't want to go home!"

I stop and spin toward her. "Nothing except show me how much they love you. How much they are going to be exactly what you need right now."

"I thought we agreed *you* are what I need," she snaps, yanking a handful of clothing out of the suitcase.

I narrow my eyes and shove more back in. "No, we've been pretending I'm what you need because it's what we *want*." I hold her arms in a loose grip. "Hannah, we both know this was temporary. I will stand by you through the rest of it, but not alone. I will not be your excuse to disappear."

Her eyes darken. "This is bullshit."

"And non-negotiable."

Vipers measure their venom too. Yep, they control how much they want to release into their prey.

Letting her go will fucking gut me.

HANNAH'S PROTESTS fade into somber acceptance as we pack her belongings. Once they're secured and ready for transport, she casts a last scan of her hiding place. I let her process the moment in silence. I hope she sees it for what it's been—a cave, not a hospital.

We move her stuff to the lobby and get a cab. After loading the trunk, I slide into the seat beside her.

"We're doing the right thing." I tuck my arm around her shoulders. She burrows against me, and I stare past her at the tall buildings.

"I hate you."

"I know." I kiss her hair.

"What about our music?"

"What about it?"

She adjusts against me, and I meet her look with a smile.

"Wait, you want to keep writing together?"

"Of course." I pull back so I can cup her face. "I'm not leaving you, Hannah. I'm forcing you to accept as much love and support as you can get right now."

She plants a light kiss on my lips, then snickers. "That's so not an alpha line."

"No? What if I say it with your hand on my—"

"Shut up!" She laughs, and slaps my arm away.

TWO FIGURES BURST from the porch at the approach of our cab, and Hannah's hard expression melts at the sight of her parents. It's a strange feeling being on the side of a right decision for once. I tell her to go while I take care of the fare and luggage.

"Thank you," she whispers, then ventures from the cab toward her parents' waiting arms. I'm paralyzed as I watch her folded in love, tears streaming down three faces.

"Hey, man. You good?" the driver interrupts. I clear my throat and count out some bills. "You need change?"

"Keep it. Can you wait for a second?"

I exit and stand by the trunk. We remove the bags, and I start transferring them to their new home. Three sets of eyes remember me at the same time, and I manage a hard swallow. "Where should I put these?"

"On the porch is fine," James says.

I stack them by the railing, onstage again beneath their

stares. With a grim twist of the lips, I pass their cluster of affection, this time with nothing to distract me.

"Wes, wait!" The voice calling me back is more mature and tremulous than Hannah's. I turn just in time to receive a tight hug from Annie. "Thank you, sweetheart," she says against my chest.

I clench my jaw. "No problem."

15

GAMING

I can't go back to an empty condo after dropping Hannah off, so I do something I haven't done in months. Not all disasters are accidents. Some I just invite.

The Leafs have a three-day break, so I take a chance that rightwing Dany Carle will answer his phone.

"Dude! Where ya been?"

I cringe and separate the phone from my ear at the voice exploding through the receiver. "Touring, then dealing with some shit. You in town?"

"Until Sunday, why?"

"Want to hit a club or something?"

"For sure. Me and some of the guys are on our way to Harem, then maybe Sultana. You in?"

"Absolutely. I'll meet you there."

"Hell yeah! Hey, Meyers. Alton's joining us tonight."

"Nice! Tell him he's paying."

Yep, exactly what I don't need and exactly what I want.

STRIP CLUBS AREN'T my typical scene, and I haven't been to Harem in over a year. Seems irrational to pay women to remove their clothes when you have a line of volunteers. But tonight isn't about my brain, so I shut off all avenues to its whining the moment the bouncer waves me in.

"Carle here yet?" I ask him.

"Yeah. Brought the whole team tonight."

"Great, thanks."

The vibe is different than I remember. Or maybe I'm just more forgiving tonight. This place is definitely more 1800's burlesque club than seedy strip joint. I suppose that makes sense since no guest leaves with less than three zeros on their bill.

It's not hard to find half of a professional hockey team. My grin is unavoidable when an entire section of the venue erupts at my arrival.

I'm greeted with a slew of punches, backslaps, and *what the fuck mans*. Dany clears a spot beside him.

I throw back the shot he shoves at me. "Fuck, yeah," I say, slamming the glass down.

He laughs and signals for another round. "Glad you came out, man."

"Thanks. Nice win last night."

"Damn straight. Heard you played our house on your last tour."

"We did. I made sure to jack off in your locker before the show."

"I wouldn't have it any other way. Oh shit, Damiana is up. Check this out."

I do. I guess I shouldn't be surprised my mind chooses that moment to flood me with images of an ex-lawyer on my couch in baggy sweats. Hair twisted up and falling over itself, wry smirk blasting the idiots on my TV screen. She's the type of woman who'd march into a strip club with me and conquer this table of testosterone. It kills me that she's the only person who doesn't see that.

I gladly accept another shot.

Damiana spots our table and tosses plenty of extra attention our way throughout the performance. Her tips tonight will buy her a decent used car. Dany seems to think he'll be the one driving it. To be fair, history has taught him he's often the one guy a stripper actually does want to take home.

"That ass, though," he hums, smacking my arm.

"It's her paycheck, dude."

"Yeah, but... Shit, she's coming over."

Our table shrank as the guys were peeled off for more expensive investments. It leaves little competition for Dany, and based on the layout of our corner, that competition is basically me.

"Dany Carle," she purrs, running a pink nail over his jaw. "I've missed you."

Her gaze travels to me, perfect eyebrows arching to remind me she owns these tables and everyone in them.

"This is my friend, Wes," Dany says. "Wes—"

"Damiana," she interrupts, attention locking on me. "You a hockey player too, Wes?"

"No."

"He's a musician," Dany adds.

"Really? A famous one?"

I grin in spite of myself. "Nah, not really. Just a few gigs here and there."

"Fucking liar," Dany smirks. "Is that your new game, Alton? False modesty?"

I make some crack about *him* being the "player" and feel the intensity change in Damiana's stare.

"Hold on. Wes. Alton. Tracing Holland?"

I lock my gaze with hers in confirmation. Dark red lips curve into an enticing smile.

"Dany, how dare you not bring Wes by before now."

Dany rolls his eyes. "He's been on tour. Wait, why are we talking about this?"

She giggles and scoots past me to reach Dany. Yes, that move was for me as much as him when that perfect ass lands inches from my face.

"You ready for more?" she directs to my friend. Her hands slide up his arms and latch around his neck. He lets her tug him up from the booth and sends me a bold grin. Dany Carle is known for his appreciation of women and their admiration of him.

And suddenly, I'm alone. The few players left acknowledge me from the other side of the table, but I don't know them well enough to have an interest in conversation. My gaze flickers back to the stage again.

I wonder about Hannah, how she's settling into her parents' care. It has to be hard for someone as independent as she is. I can't imagine doing the same thing. Then again, my parents would never let me through the door with anything resembling a suitcase.

A gorgeous blonde hates that I'm alone and offers her companionship. I thank her and send her on her way. A few other offers don't tempt me either, and finally I'm starting to regret this after all. I glance at my phone and actually consider checking up on Hannah. *From a strip club, you idiot.* I put my phone away and turn to shots instead. Most of the latest round has been neglected, and I horde several to my section of the table. Three? Four? I lose track because I've had at least that many already. The burn starts to feel really fucking good, and the best part? My brain finally does what it promised hours ago —absolutely nothing.

I have to piss and push myself up in an aggressive burst that leaves the room a wavy blur. Shit. Gotta love how you're always more drunk standing than sitting. I use the table to settle the floor and finally start maneuvering toward the washrooms. I can't tell if I'm handling my stagger well. I'm a practiced drinker, so I'm hoping my skill is hiding the fact that I'm wasted.

I'm confident I'm headed in the right direction until a tug on my jeans alters my course. Soon I'm moving down a dim hallway toward a private room.

"Wes Alton." My name slips past too-full lips resting dangerously close to my neck. "I've been waiting for your turn."

I blink to clear the image of Damiana's dark hair and eager eyes.

"Where's Dany?" I ask, scanning the room.

"Not here."

I shake my head but soon find myself anchored to a couch by bare thighs. "Okay, I think—" She shushes me—actually shushes me!—with fingers on my lips. The other hand presses down my torso and discovers my natural reaction to any beautiful woman when I'm hammered. Her hand starts an intoxicating rhythm, and the spinning room adds streaks of bright sparks. I grab her wrist but can't get my brain to decide between shoving it away or guiding it.

Walking cliché, Wes Alton, soothing his pain with alcohol and strippers. That was my sober brain.

She must sense her new advantage because suddenly rules are breaking right along with my will. Her teeth sink into my lip just hard enough to earn a groan when her grip slides past my open zipper. Expert hands tighten and release. Expert lips suck and invite.

"You want to let me call the shots? I'll take care of you, baby."

My abs contract at her tongue traveling over the dense muscle. It feels so damn good with the matching rhythm of pressure on my dick—and expensive.

You're paying for sex now?

Dammit, it's a practical decision.

I straighten, resting unsteady hands on her shoulders. "Thanks. You're a beautiful girl," I mutter. With a gentle push I separate her from my body. It takes more effort to remove my drunk ass from the couch.

Unaccustomed to rejection, she launches into a tirade instead of making another attempt. I'm grateful for her pride. I just need... to find a door. The walls swirl and climb at impossible angles. The smell of expensive perfumes grind my stomach into a pool of nausea. My pocket starts to buzz, and I almost lose my balance. I steady myself against the wall before pulling out my phone and squinting at the text. The sober half of my brain can't interpret the words, but the drunk half starts inching to the door again at their command. Dany. Sultana. *Where the hell am I?* people want to know according to letters on my screen.

Damiana is rationalizing my bizarre rejection in a distant world behind me. According to her testimony, I'm the first drunk patron to haunt this establishment which is why I'm turning her down. I ignore her because she seems like an okay girl, and I don't give a damn. I just want to go home. Plus, I still have to piss. I fumble with the lock, the handle, and finally lurch into the dark hallway. My legs start moving again, carrying me... away. Somewhere. Washroom. Three wrong turns later, I finally find sinks and stalls. And Dany.

"There you are! Dude, bus is leaving. Let's go."

I grunt. "Give me a sec."

"Yeah, like, exactly a second." His warning look slides to

the door. "Guys are already loaded. *Loaded.*" He belts a laugh at his own pun.

"You're an artist. I'll be right out."

I'm rinsing soap off my hands when the door swings open to expose a tree trunk of a man in a black t-shirt. He zeros in on me and crowds way too close for comfort.

"Need something?"

"Yeah. The money you owe Damiana for your private dance."

"Huh?"

"You heard me. Go take care of your tab."

"Okay, I don't know what she told you but—"

"She didn't have to tell me anything. I saw you go in with her. I saw you come out. Pay. Your. Tab."

We confront each other in the alien washroom lighting. This isn't the first time I've stared down a precipice of violence in a public restroom. Images of my clash with Luke Craven come barreling back. I was the asshole wearing black in that one. Then again, he was too when he had his hands all over Holland in a public place where rumors could have wrecked her.

"You want a broken nose?" he asks.

Kind of, but then, suddenly I don't care. This whole night is about not giving a shit. Besides, it would piss Dany off if I make them wait any longer. My fist releases at my side. "Fine."

"Fine?"

"I'll take care of it."

His stance shifts with an unsteady nod. I'm sure he didn't expect this to go down without blood. I certainly didn't and take some solace in the fact that at least I still *look* like a dude who wants to kick someone's ass.

I have no interest in another encounter with Damiana, so I leave a stack of bills and an explanation with the hostess. The bouncer glowers at me from his perch beside the stage, and I toss over a taunting thumbs-up. Even new Wes can't totally walk away from an encounter without a fuck-you. His thick chest puffs through a too-tight shirt but he doesn't move toward me. I'm kind of disappointed, regretting the lack of bloodshed.

But the night is still young, and so far, a complete bust as I shove through the exit and climb into Dany's chauffeured vehicle.

DANY'S "BUS" is actually a modified, totally obscene SUV that fights its way through the maze of lights in downtown Toronto. Bottles circle and slosh expensive liquid on expensive leather. Dany doesn't care. I'm not even sure he notices. They're singing the national anthem now, but my buzz has degraded from pleasure to pain. Nausea rises with each sway and bump of the vehicle. I just have to make it to Sultana where I can retreat to my new favorite hangout: toilet stalls. It would be nice to *not give a shit* without puking my guts out one of these days.

We ignore the line snaking from the club's entrance and march toward the bouncer who waves us in. The group disperses on individual campaigns the second we're assaulted by flashing lights and powerful thumping, which leaves me free for my own mission.

I feel much better after clearing my stomach of its contents, and rinse in the sink. After popping a mint, I'm a different man when I leave the washroom—upgraded, confident, and ready to finish what Damiana started. My body still hasn't recovered from her seduction and is now on the hunt for relief.

I settle at the bar and order a drink beneath the watchful eyes of two barely legal fangirls. They can't be more than twenty, but I'm hungry for inane drama. They oblige with chatter about sparkly shit on cellphone cases, university gossip I don't understand about people I don't know, and the shortest skirts in existence. The girls are so sorry about my band break-up. They can relate because their sorority... I throw back a couple more shots, and let them gush while they slurp a few rounds of the fruity crap cramming up my tab.

"There are private rooms in the back," the curvy brunette informs me.

Her friend's eyes widen in agreement. "So private," she adds.

I know. I've spent many hours in those rooms and appreciate that these girls know the game. How many celebrity conquests have they lured into their web, how many free drinks have they collected? It's going to save me a lot of time and post-party angst.

"You are so much hotter in person," the brunette says once we're settled in our new hangout. I wish I remembered her name. It had a poetic quality that would work nicely in a song. Daphne? Danica?

"What was your name again?" I murmur against the strawberry-scented flesh of her neck. She's climbed on top of me, her fingers already working their way up my chest.

"God, you must work out all the time," she says, ignoring the question. Her friend whines from above my head and reaches down to fight with my shirt. I push up to help free it and give the blonde access as well. Heat spreads through my blood at their combined efforts, pooling in my crotch. A groan leaks out as the brunette's mouth moves along my hips to the button on my jeans. I don't usually like threesomes, often more awkward in reality than they're worth in fantasy, but right now, the only place I want to be is here. I want to forget that smartass, complex woman who can stop a guy's heart with baggy sweatpants.

Omigods draw me back to the present. A chorus of oohing and ahhing over my body and every reaction it makes to their attention. So many dirty words meant to cement their legacy on my list of lays. And shit. I'm bored. Horny as hell, and fucking fed-up. I've come pretty far to back out now, but my efforts are definitely aimed more at completion than enrichment. Soon both are writhing over me, a maze of limbs and hair, grunts and moans. So many sounds they think a guy wants to hear, but there's nothing these two sirens can do to stop me from glancing at my phone when it buzzes.

I stiffen at the name and leave a swell of bare female flesh protesting on the lounge.

> Thought you should know, this "loving support" thing is torture. Mom still believes grilled cheese is an accepted form of therapy. Dad won't stop apologizing for storing his fishing crap in my closet because obviously that's why I'm depressed. This is your fault. SAVE ME!

I grin and tap out:

> On my way.

HANNAH IS in my arms the second the cab drops me off, and we retreat to the Drake's finished basement.

"I already miss you," she mumbles into my chest.

"I miss you too," I reply against my better judgement. She pulls back, eyes broadcasting everything I was afraid I'd see. Then she grimaces.

"You smell like a drunk women's locker room."

"I was at Sultana."

"Alone?"

"I wasn't there long."

"Groupies?"

"A couple."

"At the same time? You're such a stud."

Her head settles against me again, and I kiss her hair. "They were boring."

"And naked, I bet."

"Yeah, but not nearly as hot as you eating cereal on my couch."

My next song is going to be an attempt at capturing the poetry of her laugh.

"Sure, whatever."

"It's true. They've got nothing on you, babe."

"I should be pissed," she mumbles.

"Are you?"

"A little."

I brush her hair back for a better view of her eyes. Damn. No wonder they haunt me.

"If you were in the middle of something, why'd you come?" she whispers, those blue orbs sucking me into her universe.

"You asked."

She breathes a heavy sigh. "I couldn't get you out of my head. I tried."

I grin. "You didn't try very hard. It's only been a few hours."

"It was enough to know I was better with you."

"I'm still here. I'll be here whenever you want me."

Her nails press into my back.

"Thank you. Sorry, I ruined your wild night."

"My night's just starting."

"ARE you seriously planning on sitting here and watching TV with me for the rest of the evening?"

"Sex would be weird with your parents upstairs. They already hate me."

Hannah swats my arm.

"I just thought you'd have better things to do."

"Like?"

"Gym. Some groupies."

"Ha."

"Were they good?" By her tone, I'm not off the hook.

"Enthusiastic."

She folds her arms and shifts her attention back to the screen.

"Han..."

"No, I get it. God forbid a rockstar keeps his dick in his pants for two seconds."

Shit.

"I hope you were safe," she says, entirely unconcerned about my health. The quiet pain on her face—damn. There's a look I'd do anything to avoid.

"We didn't get that far."

My phone buzzes. Who invented these annoying things anyway?

"Jacob again," she says, reading the display.

"Yeah. They want to set up a meeting this week. Ultimatum Time."

I feel her stare, her search for signs. I'm careful not to give any away. This is not her problem and won't ever be as far as I'm concerned.

As if that's ever worked on Hannah. "What are you going to do?"

"I don't know yet."

"So what, either you sign the contract or the band is done?"

"Nah, not the band. Just *my* career."

Those ocean irises are still digging into me as I wash away that sentence with a swig of beer.

"So that's it then? End of story."

There's no critique in her tone so I can't be annoyed.

"What about your own implosion?" I ask my adorable black kettle.

She takes the hint and grunts. "My situation is different."

"How so?"

"I..." Her argument transfers into a slow smile. "Okay, yeah. Same thing. Are we strong, weak, or insane to throw everything away?"

"Probably all three."

She turns my hand and traces the lines in my palm. I study her graceful fingers as they explore mine in a pattern that tries to make sense of a world her head can't.

"I couldn't do it anymore, Wes." The words come out too quietly for the way they fill the room. "I couldn't live someone else's life. I had to blow it up."

"And start over?"

"I have to figure out who I am and embrace it no matter what that looks like. I'll let the pieces fall where they will, but it has to be real. That's the prison. That's the hopelessness: being the person you think you should be instead of the person you are. I'm a fraud."

"You're a viper."

Her eyes glisten as they gaze up at me. "I don't know what I am anymore."

I brush a light kiss on her forehead. "I do. We'll figure the rest out."

We're interrupted by a shriek. The basement door swings open, footsteps pound on the stairs.

"Hannah? Are you down there? O.M.G., Holland just asked Shandor to play their January shows! He's..."

Sylvie freezes on the landing.

"Wes."

"Hey, Sylvie."

"I..."

"I should go," I say to Hannah. Her heart is broken for me. It's the worst part of Sylvie's news. "Have a great night."

16

FIRED

"Fuck!" I slam my door shut and stalk to the minibar. A generous pour burns its way down my throat. Then another. And another. The shot glass smashes against the wall, and I shove my hands through my hair. Important meeting, my ass. Apparently we're past the ultimatum stage, straight into the "auditioning a replacement" phase of the band feud.

> Thanks for the heads-up.

I manage to delete the "you dick" before I send my text to Jacob. The phone rings a second later. I slam my finger on "accept."

"What the fuck, man? You're replacing me and didn't even give me notice?"

"Hang on. What are you talking about?"

"Sylvie fucking Drake is freaking out because her boyfriend is playing the January shows with Holland."

He's quiet. Dammit, it's true!

"The promoters are panicking, Wes. We needed to put

their fears to rest and assure them the shows would happen. Of course the spot is still yours if you want it, but you've been refusing to talk. What were we supposed to do?"

He's still a dick. I shouldn't have deleted that part.

My thoughts are too all over the place to come out.

"You still there? We were going to talk about this at the meeting next week. I'm sorry you found out the way you did."

"Yeah? Me too," I hiss.

"Shandor Xodyar is a fantastic musician. He will do the songs justice. He's been in the industry a long time. He knows the game."

"Oh, well in that case."

"All you have to do is sign the contract, Wes. One signature and you're back on the bus."

"But not *her* bus," I say.

He doesn't get the joke. "No, she'd have her own, per the contract. But you would—"

"You can tell Holland I wish her and Shandor the best. If I wasn't going to sign the damn contract before, I'm sure as hell not signing it now."

SPENCE CALLS. Hannah calls. And finally, Holland. I ignore all three and turn off my phone. I feel like punching someone and decide to take my aggression out on gym equipment. Then my bar, because this is worse than getting kicked out of my parents' house or watching my first guitar splinter all over a driveway. I can stand betrayal from the people I hate. It's being broken by those I love that leaves me paralyzed on the couch. There's no hope for peace by targeting the enemy with my anger this time. No, because the target doesn't deserve it. My adversary is Holland Drake and that's all my brain needs to accept that I'm in the wrong. Holland is always on the side of right.

So where does that leave me?

Am I strong, weak, or insane?

I'm not a hypocrite. I also have no idea who the hell I am without Holland.

I WAKE with a start to a familiar smell. Flowery, but in a fresh clean way.

"Hannah?"

"Thank goodness! I'm glad you're here. I was so worried about you. Your phone was going to voicemail. Holland called us and said you had it out with Jacob. She wanted someone to check on you."

"Yeah." I close my eyes again. Not nearly enough time has passed since my make-out session with the whisky bottle for this, or any, conversation.

"You're wasted again."

"Maybe?"

"Okay, then we'll talk later. I'm getting you some water."

I grab her wrist. "Go home, Hannah."

"Right." She smirks. "I'm not leaving you alone."

"I'll be fine." That protest was all I had left in the arsenal.

By the time she returns, I'm half-asleep again.

"Here, drink this." Liquid slips past my lips and cools my stomach.

"You've met this Shandor dude, right?"

"Not now, Wes. We'll talk about it in the morning."

I push myself up. "No, I want to know. What's he like?"

She shrugs. "Dark hair, mid-twenties. He's cute."

I shake my head. "Not girl shit. Is he a decent guy?"

"Seems like it. My family approves of him for Sylvie."

The Drakes approve of him. If he's good enough to date one of their daughters...

"He's worked as a guitar tech and crewmember for a while," she says.

"So he knows how to take care of people and keep his head out of his ass."

"I've only met him a few times, but he doesn't seem like the diva-type. He'll listen to Holland, respect her. He'll have to if he wants to keep dating Sylvie."

I try for a smile, but it comes out as a nod.

"It's pretty late. Slide back," she says, pushing me against the cushions of the couch.

Now, I do manage a twist of the lips. She stretches out along my body, and I slip an arm around her to secure her to me. She wraps her hand around mine.

"Good night, Wes."

"Good night, Han."

WHEN I WAKE UP, Hannah is out cold. My head is in a vise and my stomach flips through raging waters. The light is so damn bright. The traffic outside deafening. Hangovers suck.

She stirs as I climb over her but sinks back into sleep when I tuck a blanket around her. I study her soft features for a moment, still in disbelief that she's here. That after everything I've put her and her family through, she understands me enough to accept my flaws. How did I miss this growing up? How did I miss her?

Oh right. Holland.

My chest constricts as I study the complicated woman on my couch. It wasn't Holland who haunted my thoughts last night, even while I tried to erase her with other women. It's not Holland I'm desperate to protect at this moment or who I was relieved to find in my arms this morning. No, it's Hannah. Somehow the snarky ex-lawyer has crept into the void I'd given up on.

There's no Holland anymore when I'm with Hannah Drake. It's a terrifying thought, and I escape to my bathroom before it comes to life.

HANNAH'S MADE coffee and looks like she's showered and cleaned up as well when I venture back to the living area.

"Morning, sunshine," she says.

My lips curve in an ironic twist. "Morning." I pour myself a cup of coffee and lean across from her at the island. All she's missing is a newspaper and she'd be the picture of breakfast leisure.

"So what's on the agenda for today? Looking at MBA programs?" she asks.

"Huh?"

"Well, now that you're not a musician, I just assumed you'd get yourself a tie and go work for Daddy."

"Ha. Actually, I figured I'd follow your career path and watch judge shows for a living."

"Speaking of that, did you know Judge Stanton is retiring?"

"Isn't he like a hundred?"

"Well, yeah, but still..."

"Shit, what will you do with your extra half-hour each day?"

"Annoy you. Oh, I know! We can meet up at Hanover Deli on your lunchbreak."

I raise my brows. "You mean my lunchbreak from this fictitious job at my father's company I won't have?"

"I bet he'd hire you."

"I bet he wouldn't."

"I'm willing to be a reference."

"Awesome, thanks. Hey, aren't your parents freaking out right now?"

She passes her mug across the counter. "Can you fill this up?" I do while she says, "No, they know I'm here."

"And they're okay with that?" I carefully slide the full cup back to her.

"They sent me. Sylvie and I told them what happened."

"Wait, what?"

She shrugs. "Now that they know you didn't kidnap me as part of some malicious plan to tear apart my family, they trust you."

"Even with the Holland thing?"

"Eh, I'm pretty sure they've realized you hurt yourself more than anyone else at this point."

"And she gets clinical on me."

"It's called honesty. You should try it."

"I don't know. Doesn't really fit my badass mystique."

She grins and lets her gaze roam over my body. "Nor does your shirt."

"You don't like my shirt?"

"I don't like any shirt on you."

Fuck yeah. "Funny, because I love my shirts on you."

17

VIPER RISING

I'm late. They're waiting. An entire conference room of suits watches me as I stand behind an open leather chair. By their expressions they're not as impressed by the fact that I showed up as I am.

"Wes, good of you to come. Have a seat."

"No thanks. This won't take long."

The room shivers in an almost audible gasp. Lawyer, lawyer, lawyer, label exec, lawyer, label exec, and Holland. Jacob whispers something to her, but her eyes don't leave my face. An apology for the pain in her gaze claws at my tongue. I manage to shove the lump back to an ache in my chest.

"You haven't brought representation?" one of the suits asks.

"I don't need it." I zero in on Holland. "I'm not going to fight you on anything, Hol. It's yours: the band, our songs, everything. Take what you want; give me what you think is fair. I trust you." I swallow as the ache starts to swell into my vocal chords. "Send me whatever I need to sign to make it official."

And then I'm gone. Life exploded, field of nothing surrounding me. I feel free and completely broken. Beginnings, ends. There's poetry in there somewhere, but right now I'm a mess of fragments.

Once outside, I pull out my phone and dial the only person left that matters.

"Wes? It's over already?"

"Yep."

"How'd it go?"

"How do you feel about grabbing lunch with an unemployed musician?"

IT'S a strange feeling being nothing. No expectations, no plans, no identity other than who I used to be. I thought it would be terrifying. God knows, coming to this decision took an extraordinary amount of angst, especially for someone who relies on instinct for most of my functioning. But now that it's done?

"What's the smile for?" Hannah asks through the crunch of her salad.

"I'm a blank slate."

"I've been telling you that for years."

"Hilarious. You know what I mean."

Her smile fades as her eyes rest on mine. "Yeah, I do. I'm a blank slate too. Together we're practically a sidewalk."

I laugh and dig into my sandwich. "How about a blank canvas then? That's less—literal."

"Artistic too. I accept your metaphor, Wesley Alton." She reaches across and grabs a chip off my plate. "You know they won an award for these?"

"A potato chip award?"

She nods and steals another. "Best house-made snack chip, Province of Ontario."

"You're making that up."

She shrugs into a devilish smile. "Now you're gonna look it up."

"At least I'll have plenty of time."

She brushes her fingers on a napkin. "Seriously, though. What's next for you?"

It's a great question. I just turned the page an hour ago and have no idea how to answer it. There's only one thing I know with certainty.

"For now, I write."

Her features relax. "Good."

I stare through the window at a bird exploring something on the bench. "I have to find my voice without Holland."

My gaze ventures back to Hannah and meets empathy.

"You need to find your voice, period," she says.

She's not wrong, and I search for the bird again. "I was always defined relative to someone else. The son of Frederick Alton. The backup to Holland Drake. Now what?"

"Try being the little sister of Holland Drake," she snorts, and I shoot a grin.

"No thanks."

Her forehead creases, head tilting in concentration. "So this is it for both of us, right? The start of chapter two?"

"Time to figure out our own spotlights." I reach across the table and grab her hand. She squeezes back.

MY FIRST DAY of nothing doesn't go well. Unfortunately, you can't broadcast the beginning of new chapters, and my phone explodes with reminders of the last one. I check a few of the messages, but only the last catches my interest. I hear the ache in Holland's voice as she pleads for a one-on-one to talk this out. My chest tightens in response, and my finger finds its way to the call back button, but I manage to crush the rebellion. If I call her, I meet her. If I meet her, I cave and we're right back where we started—where neither of us belongs anymore.

I have faith in Holland. She will rebuild her life the way it should be. With Luke. With her bright star shining into the lives of everyone around her, making them better. Now I have to figure out how to function without being the shadow to her light.

It's a monumental task, but I'm going to try because there's a girl with long brown hair and a wicked sense of humor. A fucking brave girl who challenges me, excites me, and right now, needs a traveling companion on her own journey. You know what? Fuck it.

I pick up my phone, and she answers on the first ring. "Hey. What are you doing right now?"

"Not much. Just trying to avoid my mom's desperation sandwiches."

I snicker. "The basement free?"

"I think so?"

"Good, I'm coming over."

"Um, okay..."

"With my guitar."

A smile colors her voice when she says, "I'll have the beer waiting."

"WHAT DO you think about changing the third chord in the progression to a seventh instead of the minor?"

I run the idea through my head. "Hmm. I'm game. Let's try it." I strum through the chorus again with the new chord, and we both cringe in unison.

"Okay, no." She laughs. "Keep the B minor."

"Yeah. But I like where your brain is going, Drake. Wait, I know." I launch into the bridge and throw the seventh in there instead.

"Yes! Love that," she says. "Can we run it again?"

"From the top?"

"I want to hear it all together now."

"You got it, babe."

Her grin lasts through the entire intro. And yeah, so does mine.

As the song wraps up and I play through the outro, I can tell by her expression that something's up. She's quiet as the last chord fades out.

"What's going on?" I ask while her fingers tap a rhythm on her knee.

She peeks over at me and resumes tapping.

"What is it?"

An inhale freezes her for a moment before she pulls out her laptop. "I've been working on something too."

I can't read her expression when she diverts to the computer. "You've been writing on your own?"

"I know! I'm sorry, it's just—"

"Sorry? Why the hell would you be sorry? Let's hear it."

She scans the screen, fingers still drumming. "Well, I don't have music yet, just lyrics." She turns the display toward me. "I was hoping you'd be willing to help me."

"Willing? Are you kidding? Let me see that."

"Argh, I'm going upstairs," she groans, and I drag her hands from her face.

"Not a chance. Sit."

"Wait. Maybe this is a bad—"

"Quiet." I press my fingers against her mouth and tuck her to my side. She resigns into a stiff monument while I read.

Coil of strength wound tight
to hide
to lie
to wither and writhe
In its prison it cries, 'Coil of rage!'

Dirty secrets revealed
The bed
I made
Was never the place
To trap this broken soul, It's over!

Stand back, you're gonna want to stand back

I'm breaking free to strike
Fangs bared, spring out,
out
Of hell, don't tell
Me what I am
I'm not, not your pet
I'm your hidden regret
So hear me, you should fucking fear me!
As I rise

It's a lot. Too much maybe as I read through her words, once, twice, and a third time to make sure I'm completely immersed in the story of this incredible woman beside me.

"Hannah..." is all that comes out.

"Is it bad?"

"No! It's..." It's *daaamn.* "What's it called?"

"'Viper Rising.'"

18

HADES

My flimsy condo walls don't protect me from the blast of headlines over the next couple of weeks. I'm accustomed to the villain role but not on a such a public scale. It's a relentless wave of hostility that I can't erase with a swift blow to the jaw. The speculation about our band breakup ranges from a royalty dispute to a surprise pregnancy. That one makes me laugh. I can only imagine how Luke feels about his girlfriend's phantom bundle of joy. Theories vary on the father.

For the most part, Holland is supposedly the victim of this mess. The unfortunate angel whose only crime was partnering with a plague like me in the first place. There's even a classic Frederick Alton *I told you so* in the form of an Alton Media campaign to distance them from me. I guess I should be honored that my father finally used his vast PR resources to impact my career.

Everyone has different opinions, but they all agree that Wes Alton is done. No band in its right mind will ever touch him after this.

I shove my phone away and opt for a drink instead. Whisky, my faithful ally. Never judges, never uses stupid words like "reportedly."

Reportedly, I can spout whatever bullshit I want because I used the word reportedly. You can't give "reportedly" a bloody nose either, which frustrates the hell out of me.

I've just filled my glass when the damn phone erupts again. For once I don't hate the thing.

"Hey, Sophia."

"You answered!"

"I'm surprised you're still talking to me. Dad let you call?"

"I'm twenty-four," she huffs out like she's so not. "He doesn't get to boss me around anymore."

"...once he's paid for your wedding."

"Shut up. Actually, that's why I'm calling."

I swallow the unexpected knot in my throat. "Okay?"

"Dad doesn't want you there. He told us we should all distance ourselves from you as much as possible."

The pressure sinks to my chest. "I'm not surprised."

"He's an asshole."

"Don't feel bad. I get it. You can't have me there."

"Huh?" I picture the pink splotches spreading over her cheeks. "No, that's bullshit. I'm calling to see if you'll perform at the ceremony."

My grip tightens on the phone.

"Wes? What do you think?"

"You're serious?"

"You're my brother and the most talented musician I know. I wouldn't want anyone else."

"Your wedding is in a few months."

"Exactly. Plenty of time. I'm thinking a couple songs during the ceremony and a longer set at the reception."

"Um..."

"You can pick the songs, but I want an original for the processional."

I laugh. "Oh really?"

"Yep."

"What kind of song?"

"Surprise me."

"You know I don't do fluffy love songs."

"Duh. That's why I'm asking you. I want something kickass that'll make Mom crap her pants."

"Ha! Okay, I'll just whip that right up."

"Good. Hey—"

"Yeah?"

"I love you, big bro. You're going to survive this. You always do."

MY NEXT CALL is to an ex-lawyer on the outskirts of town. Her voice is thick with the nap I just interrupted.

"Ugh. What do you want?" Hannah groans.

"Hey, sunshine. I need the lyrics to that song."

"'Viper Rising?'"

"Yeah."

"You're going to work on it?"

"Better. We have a gig."

"What?"

"We're going to finish that song and perform it."

"We?"

"Yes. *We.*"

"But—"

"Not interested, Han."

"In?"

"Excuses."

"Okay, but—"

"It's for Sophia's wedding."

"She wants me to sing at her wedding?"

"She wants me to sing and I'm not doing it without you."

"But—"

"I'm hanging up now. Send me that song, then get over here so we can work on it."

HANNAH WAVES her hand halfway through the bridge. "Do you think we can take the song up a step? It would have a lot more power in E."

I glance at her in surprise. "You think you can sing it in E?"

She shrugs. "Won't know until we try."

"Damn, if you can hit the end of that bridge in E, do it."

"You're going to harmonize lower, right?"

"The last time through, yeah."

"Let's take a break first, then run it again." Damn, she's bossy. I smile to myself as I rest my guitar against the coffee table.

Two hours into rehearsal and I realize how much I miss having Hannah Drake in my guest room. I've always preferred being alone, so this revelation doesn't sit well with me. I don't like that I have to find excuses for her to stay after we wrap. Her gaze doesn't help when it keeps wandering over my body, triggering hot memories.

Her perfect curves have been taunting me all afternoon. Hidden in a retro band tee that's cropped just enough to make me think I'm supposed to look. And hell if I don't. Look. Over and over, my optic nerve singes with her.

"Want to watch a movie or something?" I ask.

"Not really..." Her gaze locks on mine, then travels to my lips before resting on the open v-neck of my shirt. Her touch sends spikes of electricity through me as she traces my ink. She's waiting for a reaction, inching closer the longer I go without rejecting her. I should push her away.

Her hand spreads farther now, contracting beyond our line of sight. I hiss in a breath at the pressure of her body as she removes the space between us. Aligning in all the right places, securing her grip around my neck so I have no choice but to...

I groan at the movement of her hips. It's not even me, just my fire that consumes her mouth. It rips that fading band image right over her head. She's ready, so ready. Arching from the aggression of my mouth that travels over her body, her hands threaded in my hair to lock me where she wants me.

"Is this what you want, babe?" I flip her on her back.

She gasps at my desire digging into her hips and tears open the zipper of my jeans. "You've been my wet dream since I was fourteen."

"Ha. I knew it."

"Shut up, you—"

I cut her off with my lips. My tongue. She moans, and...

We're screwed.

"HAVE I ever told you how much I love Hades?" Hannah says, grin as mischievous as her hands exploring my chest.

"You may have mentioned it."

"He tastes good too." She proves it with a trick that already has me hard again.

"Dammit, you're impossible," I gasp, eyes clenching as she works her way down once more.

"You don't want another round?"

"Never."

"Liar."

She has me paralyzed. Fuck, I'm obsessed. She's ruined any chance I have with finding satisfaction in other women. Are my groupie-days over? I have no idea what to do with that.

As always, my phone takes a perfect moment and makes it crack.

"Holland," Hannah says.

"Really? That can't be good."

Hannah hands me the phone and slides off so I can adjust.

"Do you mind?" I ask.

"I need a drink anyway. You want something?"

"Sure."

She clears the couch while I accept the call.

"Holland, hey."

"Hey."

"Everything okay?"

"With me? Not really, but I'm getting there. Thanks for what you did at the contract negotiation. You didn't have to do that."

"Yeah I did. I want you to be happy, Hol. That's what I've always wanted."

She quiets. "I know. Anyway, that's kind of why I'm calling. I just wanted to say that I'm sorry about the Mila Taylor thing. I don't know where she got that information, but my people are working on fixing it."

My heart stops. "Mila Taylor?"

"You don't know?"

"Um..."

"Crap. Wes, I'm sorry. I thought... I mean, everyone's talking about it."

"Yeah, that's exactly why I've been trying to avoid *it*."

"I figured at least Jacob would have called you."

"Well, he hates me more than anyone right now."

I can almost hear her bite her lip through the phone.

"What's going on?"

She sighs. "I'll send you the link. Mila Taylor got involved and posted about you yesterday."

"Shit."

"Yeah. It wasn't good, Wes."

"Does that bitch ever have good things to say about an artist?"

"She liked our last album. Remember? We went platinum after her stamp of approval."

"I'll never understand her power in this industry. She's not even a good writer."

"I know, but she's popular and makes and breaks people."

"I'm guessing I've been broken?"

"I told you: it's not true, and I'm going to figure out where she got the info."

"What's not true?"

"She... just read it? I'm sending you the link now."

"Okay. Thanks for the heads up."

"Wes?" She stops.

I wait.

"I wish..." It's all I get, but right now, it's everything.

I barely hear Hannah return as I open the link and read.

Alright people! Everyone's talking about the breakup of Tracing Holland, aren't they?! Turns out, it's looking more like a massive cock-up if you ask me. I've heard that lovers-gone-sour Holland Drake and Wes Alton haven't only had enough as a band, but will be scrap-

ping it out in criminal court. Apparently, Canada's rocker bad boy has also buggered it up to the point of felony charges. OOPS. He might have to live off royalties from the film version of his life after he gets out of nick! Ta-ra, Wes. Your pretty mug is going to be a hit in the slammer!

- Mila Taylor, over and out.

"Fuck!"

This time I really do smash the damn thing.

"The Mila post?" A voice interrupts, and I twist toward Hannah who lowers herself beside me.

"Wait, you knew?"

"Everyone knows. It's all over the news."

"And you didn't tell me?"

"I figured you didn't want to talk about it. I wasn't going to bring it up. It's bullshit."

"Like that matters," I mutter, resting my head on my fists.

A squeeze on my arm reminds me that one person in this universe hasn't abandoned me. I reach over and take her hand. Cling to it while what's left of my world crumbles around me.

"I'll never work again, Han."

"But it's not true."

"Doesn't matter. When Mila Taylor says you're out, you're out."

"That's not fair."

I shrug, and push myself up from the couch. Water isn't going to cut it anymore.

"What are you going to do?"

Her question digs into my chest. "Write the shit out of 'Viper Rising.' Let's get to work."

WRITING IS A GREAT DISTRACTION. Unfortunately, it can't block freight trains.

The criminal charges turn out to be assault related to my now infamous fight(s) with Luke on our tour. Holland assures me he didn't press charges and won't. I believe her since typically the perp is included in the process. Apparently, that fact is irrelevant in the world of pop "reporting." If I still had a label, a manager, *anything,* we'd be working on a publicity stint to clear this up. I don't, so all I have is Hannah's concern. Must be a slow news season if my collapse is the most remarkable topic in Canada.

"You have to do something," Hannah says, marching from one side of the living room to the other. I must look particularly bad today if she's willing to take up arms on the one subject I insist is off limits.

"What am I supposed to do?"

"I don't know. Did you see the thing about the strip club and those girls?"

"Yeah. They just want their fifteen minutes. I don't do drugs."

"I know but what if the spotlight isn't enough for them? What if they escalate their claims?"

"What, like harassment?" Apparently you can't turn off lawyer brains. "They pursued me. Not the other way around."

"It doesn't matter, and you know it. Just an accusation is enough to hurt you."

I suppress a laugh. "What's left to hurt, Han?"

Her gaze hardens, and I clench my jaw. I haven't told her yet. Honestly, I didn't want to, but she seems intent on fighting battles that don't matter anymore. "I'm officially banned from the Alton estate."

"What?" Her lawyer-face melts into compassion.

"Frederick didn't even give me the message himself. I was informed by security this morning."

"Oh my... I'm so sorry." She lowers herself beside me, but the heat of her presence isn't enough this time.

"No violent felons in his house. Definitely no drug addicts. Makes sense after spending a fortune on the ad campaign to cut ties with me. The editorial in *The Star*? Genius."

"Wes..."

"He's been waiting fifteen years for this moment." I squint at an imperfection in the white paint. Scuff? Small crack? Hard to tell from this distance.

"How can he believe those lies about you?"

I don't answer at first. She hasn't spent a lifetime picking through my father's hatred. To her, family is more than a stigma.

"Hannah, he was probably Mila's source."

I'm relieved that she doesn't respond. She's too intelligent and I'm too serious for some pointless declaration about how that can't be true. We both know it can. We both know it probably is.

"Kick 'em when they're down. The key to Frederick Alton's success." There's an edge in my voice that scratches deeper than intended. What do I care about this final betrayal? He's been trying to erase me for as long as I can remember. Well done, Frederick. I'm annihilated.

Hannah tucks her arm around mine, rests her head on my shoulder. She reaches for my fists and smooths my fingers in hers. The violence in my stomach is no longer directed outward, and it fucking aches with the weight of failure.

"You know the worst part? I always figured I'd end up here at some point. This last decade has been a fight against the inevitable. Holland blocked the walking shit-storm that I am."

She squeezes my hand. "That you were."

I glance down at her. *That I am, babe.* "I need food. You hungry?"

19

SISTERS

Amazingly, Sophia still wants me to play her wedding. The plan is to use Limelight as a cover, so I crash on the couch and give Jesse Everett a ring with my brand-new phone.

"Hey, man. How's life since the tour?" I ask when he answers.

"Better than yours. I don't have a rap sheet."

I smirk. "Yeah, well, I don't either. Mila Taylor, man."

"Is any of it true?"

"Just that I left Tracing Holland. The band is still intact. Holland is hiring Sylvie's new boyfriend."

"Wait, Shandor?"

"You know him?"

"Yeah. Met him at the Bahamas gig. Cool dude. Guy can play. Total flamenco vibe."

"Flamenco? Holland will have fun with that."

Jesse laughs. "I'm sure if he can play like that, he can manage the rock thing. Plus, she's got Luke and NSB behind her." Apparently cringes are audible. "Shit. Sorry."

"It's cool. I'm over that. Bigger shit on my plate right now."

"Obviously. What's your next move?"

"That's why I'm calling."

"You want in on Limelight?"

"Ha! No, dude. I wouldn't do that to you. Remember my sister Sophia?"

"How could I forget? Did she like the swag?"

"Loved it. Listen, I'll save you the background drama, but can you pretend you're playing her wedding in April if it comes up?"

"Um... sure?"

"I know. Totally messed up, but she wants me to play and our family would freak. Everyone would with what's going on right now. Better that they think it's you, then we show up last minute."

"Makes sense. We got your back. Hey, does she want us to play it for real?"

"Seriously?"

"Wouldn't that be better? You can still do your thing, but we'll play too. Then we're officially booked."

"I'll ask her. I have a feeling she will lose her shit."

"In a good way?"

"In a 'never mind, big bro, I only want them' kind of way."

"Sweet. We're in. I'll talk to the guys."

"Dude, you're the best."

"You got it, man. Mila Taylor is on my shitlist too."

"Wait, did she go after you too?"

"Eh, we'll talk about it another time. Let's just say, right now your sister's wedding might be our biggest show this spring."

"Fuck. I'm sorry, Jess. You guys are legit."

"Whatever. Hey, I've gotta run, but it's been good catching up. Send me the details."

"You got it."

I swear, the universe is confusing as fuck sometimes.

I'M REWARDED with an ear-splitting shriek for my announcement that our Limelight lie is now the truth. It's going to be the "best wedding ever," according to my sister, although the band's instant availability isn't as much of a surprise to Sophia as it was to me. She's aware of Jesse's clash with Mila Taylor. Apparently, it's now a public feud since he made the rookie mistake of fighting back. I'll have to address that with him at some point.

"You're still doing my processional, right?" she asks.

"Is that what you want?"

"Duh."

"Then I guess that's a yes. Hannah and I are working on something."

"Hang on. Hannah Drake?"

"Yes."

"Wes... really?"

"What? I thought you liked Hannah."

"I freaking love her. It's just..."

"Just what?"

"I'm not sure it's a good idea for you to be spending so much time with her."

"Why not?"

More silence. "Well... gah! I can't tell you."

"Tell me what? Come on, Soph."

"Fine. Wes, she's had the biggest crush on you for, like, ever."

The snort escapes before I can stop it.

"That's not funny! I'm serious. She's an amazing person and... Don't say anything. She'll kill me."

"Sophie, relax."

"This is serious, Wes. She's not the kind to play around."

"I know, okay? I know."

"You know? About her feelings?"

"Yeah. Look, enough good people have been dragged into my thing. Just trust that it's fine if Hannah and I perform together at your wedding."

"Wait, are you *dating* her?"

"Sophia..."

"What? Are you?"

"No." I clear my throat. "Not officially," I add because by her silence, she doesn't believe me anyway.

"Oh my gosh. Have you *slept* with her?"

"Sorry, gotta go. Oven's beeping. My brownies are done."

"Bullshit!" she laughs.

"What? I bake now that I have so much free time."

"You bastard!"

"I wish."

"Fine. Keep me in the dark. I'll just have to get it from Hannah."

"You better not. She's going through some major shit too. She doesn't need more drama. I'm trying to protect her."

"Of course you are."

"What does that mean?"

"It's what you do, Wes."

"Huh?"

"It's your excuse."

I shake my head and consider hanging up on my sister for the first time in my life. "Excuse for what?"

"Excuse to ignore your own issues. You define yourself by pouring all your energy into other people. The problem is, it's not your job and it blinds you. It's why you cross lines."

"How the fuck did we get to this?"

"Don't get mad. I'm just being honest. Hannah is my friend, and you're my brother. I love you both, and I just don't see this ending well. You're going to go all superhero on her perfect ass."

"I'm hanging up now." Although her ass *is* perfect.

"You know I'm right. All I'm saying is you need to keep your head on this time, okay? Don't do anything in her name that she wouldn't want you to do."

"Like?"

"Punch her boyfriend in the face?"

I let out a grunt.

"I love you, bro. I want you to be happy. But that's not going to happen if you keep wanting to control everyone around you."

"Wow. You're welcome for booking Limelight for you."

"Oh, stop. Go brood and punch something. Later tonight, you'll think back on this and know I'm right."

Whatever. "Are you inviting Luke?"

"No, but I'm sure he'll be Holland's plus one."

I sigh. "I swear, that dude ..."

"That dude could be your brother-in-law one day at the rate you're going. Ever think of that?"

"Shit."

"Yeah. Exactly. You better figure it out."

ONCE AGAIN, the universe decides to screw with me. I've barely had time to process Sophia's speech before I get a message from Holland. She's in town. She wants to meet. Is Luke with her? Yeah.

I almost call Sophia next to see if she had anything to do with it, but it's Hannah's number that I dial.

"Holland's in town?" I ask.

"Yeah. For a couple days before the winter tour."

"She wants to meet up. Why didn't you tell me?"

"Didn't know I had to."

I'm pacing my condo like it's an Olympic event. My hair is a mess from shoving my hands through it.

"Do you know why she wants to meet?"

"No. I didn't even know she contacted you."

"Does she know about us?"

"What's there to know?"

"That we've been hanging out."

"Hanging out, huh. Naked?"

The smile in her voice finally draws one from me. "You know what I mean."

"And if she does?"

"Then that explains why she wants to meet up."

"And if she doesn't?"

I lean against the wall and force my fingers into a steady rhythm against the paint. "Be my date for the meeting?"

"Are you serious?"

"I need you." Ah that sounds so permanent.

I can't tell if she sighs with relief or something else. "Okay. Should I just get a ride with my sister?" she asks dryly.

Another quirk of the lips. "Not a bad idea."

"You know this is nuts, right?"

"This whole situation is messed up."

"Well, yeah... Where is it?"

"My place."

"Yep. Totally messed up."

I TEXT Hannah right after we hang up and ask her to come early to make sure she's here first. I don't even know why I invited her. Am I planning to disclose our relationship to Holland and Luke? Why the hell would I do that? And now of all times? We haven't even figured out what we'd be announcing yet.

But there, in the heat of the moment, I couldn't imagine fighting my way through this situation without Hannah. We've been through too much together to start compartmentalizing our trials. She's given me everything; I'm still holding back so much. Maybe Sophia's right. I'm not giving Hannah enough credit by assuming she can't handle my shit. And there it is: the truth my subconscious understood without me. It's time for her to understand what she's getting into. She thinks she wants me, but she needs to see the real Wes Alton, the asshole who deserves the destruction in his wake.

She must have left right after my message because there's a knock twenty minutes later. She's back to knocking again, and something constricts in my chest.

I buzz Holland and Luke in fifteen minutes later.

"THANKS FOR LETTING US COME OVER."

Holland is as beautiful as always. Luke wears that scowl he reserves especially for me.

"Luke."

"Wes."

"Come in." I wave them toward the couch, and Holland stops cold.

"Hannah?"

"Hey, sis."

"What are you doing here?"

"I invited her," I say, accepting the eye darts.

"I thought you moved back in with Mom and Dad." Suspicion drowns her words, and Hannah's, "We're friends," doesn't help much.

"Can I talk to you for a second?" Holland directs back to me.

"You can talk in front of me," Hannah says. "I already know everything about the band stuff. Unless this is a 'don't mess with my little sister' kind of talk. In which case, he's well-versed on the topic."

A snicker is completely inappropriate at the moment so I bite my tongue to stop it.

"So you two aren't...?" She can't even say it.

Hannah taps her chin. "Dating? No. Sleeping together? Sometimes. Unless you want to date and make it official?" This one is a direct jab at me and comes with a coy smile.

Really, Han?

"You're sleeping together?" is apparently all Holland heard.

"Okay, hold on. Back up." I step between them. "Why are you here, Hol? It's not to talk about Hannah."

"I didn't think we'd have to talk about Hannah," she shoots back.

"We don't," Hannah and I say in unison, which definitely doesn't help.

Even Luke is staring at us like we're some strange museum exhibit. He's unexpectedly silent, however. For a brief second I suspect he actually gets it. After all, I know he doesn't think he deserves Holland either. And he's right about that. Shit, no wonder we hate each other.

"We're writing together." All eyes rest on Hannah, whose tone has changed. Softened with the significance of that statement.

"Music?" Holland asks. I brace for a rant, unprepared for the release that settles over her.

Hannah seems just as surprised. "Yeah, it's been really good."

"Oh, Han!" Holland rushes in for an embrace. We can barely hear her voice muffled against her sister. "I'm so happy you're creating again."

Hannah's gaze flickers to mine over Holland's shoulder. "You can thank Wes for that. He also forced me back into counseling."

Holland pulls back, expression confused instead of accusatory now. This new universe doesn't make sense to her either.

"He sent me home, Hol. I didn't want to leave."

I feel two sets of eyes on me now. Luke's face is stone, but Holland's confusion has morphed into curiosity. Something else. We have to end this before it becomes something it's not.

"So what's up, Hol?" I move to the fridge and grab a few bottles of water. I hand one to Luke who stares at it like I've just tried to hug him.

"Thanks," he mumbles. Holland cracks the lid of hers, and I have to admit the quick twitch of her lips when I take a sip of my own feels damn good.

"Can we sit?" She's already moving to the loveseat. Luke leans against the wall behind her, arms crossed, gaze warning me that he's not as easily impressed.

"I wanted to meet with you alone," Holland begins. "No lawyers, no labels. Just us."

I lower myself beside Hannah. Far enough away that we could be just friends. Close enough that she could change that impression.

"About the Mila thing?"

"About everything. I hate the way things are. Where they're going."

Her blue eyes hold compassion. Even her pissed-face isn't very convincing and had lasted all of ten seconds just now. Luke once gave me permission to fuck him up if he ever hurt her. Dude's brave to take the risk. I'll give him that.

"I heard about you hiring Sylvie's boyfriend," I say. Another sip of water because *what do I care?*

She tosses Luke a glance for support. Maybe I'm cool with how he squeezes her shoulder, how she reaches up and laces her fingers with his. Guess their connection is sort-of natural for them.

"I didn't want you to find out that way."

"No? What was the better way to tell me you replaced me?" My voice is even. After all, it's done. I'm just curious at this point. I wish Holland didn't seem in pain about it.

"We weren't intending to replace you. We just needed someone for our shows until we worked everything out." She quiets, gaze shifting to the floor. "And since we didn't..."

"But we did, Hol." She flinches, and I try to give her as much sincerity as a guy like me can muster in situations like this. "We did work it out."

The declaration hangs between us, heavy in its finality. This is news to her. My acceptance. She doesn't seem to know what to do with that.

"What's next for you then?" she asks instead.

I stretch my arm across the back of the couch. "I don't know. I'm thinking real estate license?"

Hannah swats me on behalf of her sister, and I grin.

"Seriously, Wes. What are you going to do?" Her expression is all concern for the man who's made her life miserable.

"I don't know." *Let you go.*

"He's going to finish writing 'Viper Rising' with me,"

Hannah announces. She shifts closer and pulls my arm around her shoulders. Air siphons from the room as it absorbs Hannah's demonstration, waits for Holland's reaction. Even Luke's frown tenses.

Holland stares. Then she takes a long swallow of water. "Can we hear what you have so far?"

"Um, sure."

I squeeze her knee as I push myself up. "I'll get my guitar."

Eyes press into my back on the journey to my Martin. I remove it from the case with extra care.

"You ready?" I ask Hannah. It's everything I can do not to put my guitar down and draw her against me at the look on her face. So much hope. So much fear. This moment began long before now. It's eternal for her. Maybe for me too if my future is truly being rewritten.

I start to play. In E. Because I believe Hannah Drake can hit that bridge like a fucking fiend.

THERE ARE TOO many types of silence. I've never been great with any of them, but the ones saturated with emotion are the worst. They drip and ooze and fill a guy's chest with a mass of sentiment better left untouched. This one though. God, it's painful against my ribs as tears cloud hypnotic blue irises and trickle down soft cheeks. When the shoulders of two sisters lock against each other, I need a distracting inspection of a scratch on my guitar. Luke watches from his perch, hard set of his jaw loosening slightly.

"I can't even tell you," Holland whispers. "That was... Hannah!"

Hannah doesn't respond with words. She has a solid grip on her sister's back, face mercifully hidden from me. How did I get that scratch again? Oh right, I have no idea because there's a dozen on this piece of wood I carry around.

"Those are your words, aren't they?" Holland again. She knows her sister's story better than anyone. Better than I do no matter how much I like to act otherwise.

"Wes wrote the music."

"Great tune, man." Luke.

We all stare. His arms are still crossed, eyes still daring me to try something, but Luke Craven was not being sarcastic. He genuinely likes our song.

"Thanks."

"Might want to think about adding a second turn after the bridge. Maybe the same as the early one but with the 6 instead."

Luke Craven is now giving me, Wes Alton, songwriting input. Bathroom combatants to cowriters. This Twilight Zone, I'm telling you. I can't look at Holland. I'm positive her face will make me do something stupid like take his advice. Damn, it's good advice.

"Yeah? We'll try it out later," I say. Meanwhile, my brain is already playing through the progression and imagining a killer drop after the bridge followed by an epic build—on the 6. Shit. It's fantastic advice.

"We're going to perform it at Sophia's wedding," Hannah says.

This news is clearly a harder pill for Holland. Her gaze passes between the two of us, and I can almost see the headlines forming in her brain. It's one thing to be couch buddies with her sister. Public performers?

"Wow." Her gaze settles on me. "Your father is okay with this?"

"Ha, no way," I scoff. "He doesn't know. Limelight is booked to play."

"Really?" Luke's stance tenses again. Ah, that's right. Jesse and Luke are besties as well. Damn, I'm never going to get rid of this guy.

"Yeah. Jesse's a lifesaver."

"Jesse's in a shitload of his own trouble. Didn't he tell you that?"

Holland shoots Luke a warning glance, and he shrugs.

"Just that it involved Mila Taylor," I say.

Luke grunts. "That's an understatement."

"Okay, we're not here to talk about Jesse either," Holland interrupts.

"Why are we here, Hol?" I'm not trying to be a dick, but right now we're wasting some seriously valuable talent on small talk.

"I told you. To patch things up."

"They're patched though, right?" Me again, sounding like a jerk.

Luke agrees and shoots daggers across the room.

I swallow and focus back on Holland. Even lean forward for extra sincerity. "Holland, I'm serious. No hard feelings. I get why you wanted the contract. I get why you hired this Shandor dude. I get it, okay? I'm not upset. All I ask is that you try to understand why I have to walk away."

"From our friendship, too?"

"Only if that's what you want."

"I don't."

"Good."

We exchange a smile. She fidgets with a folder, and I sigh. "Ah. You also brought the contract."

She seems nervous and I can't really blame her. "I was hoping maybe you'd change your mind today." The folder stops in midair between us. "You're sure. Absolutely sure you want out for good?"

No. Pressure floods my knee, and I glance down to find painted black nails sinking in.

"I'm sure." I reach out and take the documents. "It's better for both of us."

Luke Craven actually shakes my hand when they leave.

20

DENIAL

The silence echoes through my foyer when they leave. Phantom screams about finality and regret. I'm not wired for this shit. When you rule your universe there's no standard for reactive beginnings. No, life is a map and you fucking plot your course and own it.

Now my life's map is just a stack of lawyer jargon.

"Wes?"

I'd almost forgotten about Hannah. She studies me from the vacuum of her sister's absence by the door, strands of dark hair wisping around her face as they slip from the pile on her head. Only Hannah could wear imperfection so perfectly. Her eyes are heavy with sadness, for me, for her, for all of humanity because that's what she does—takes on the burden of universal existence. Depression, man. I've never wanted to kick anything's ass so hard in my life.

"Come here," I say, arm extended. She slides into my embrace, and I lock it around her. Fresh, clean, floral vapors wind through my head as I bury my lips in her hair. "We got this, Han."

She burrows into me, fists clenched on the back of my shirt. Damn, if that doesn't make you want to stand in front of a freight train for a person.

My fingers slide over her neck, trace the outline of the skin beneath her collar. So soft, so delicate, so the opposite of everything I love about this woman. Love?

Shit.

I breathe in more of her, closing my eyes to absorb her scent, the power it has over me. I don't just want to protect her. I want... what? Forgiveness? Redemption? Or maybe pain because that's what it is to love a Drake. Sweet, cleansing pain that inflames vipers and saturates leeches.

"I can't believe you just did that," she murmurs against my heart. *Thud. Thud. Thud. Thud.* I don't remember other women ever triggering this click track that reverberates through my body.

My hand travels farther down her back. *Thud-two-three-four.* Blood pools in a punch between my legs. I need her to recoil, but she dissolves into heat instead.

Her grip tightens on my shirt, lifting the hem to invite cool air on my back. It does nothing to tame the raging inferno. She tugs the shirt over my head, hair falling into my eyes. It's her job to smooth it back as she grasps my face with a jerk toward her. I take her mouth, let that internal metronome beat my tongue to hers. My prey writhes with each shove of my hips. I want her to gasp, beg for more of my venom.

I lower her jeans and strike, loving how her thighs tense with each bite toward my goal—*thud—thud—thud—thud.* Her entire body flexes into my pursuit and...

I need you to be my viper.

Blood thunders through every artery, but it's not lust that it fuels now. It's fear, terror, for this soul I want to protect beyond all reason. Hannah is not my prey; she's my responsibility because fuck if I don't love this woman. Fuck if her pain doesn't make mine irrelevant. No, I'm getting my shit together because this ends now.

Hannah Drake will shine.

"What's wrong?" she asks when I lean back and pull her jeans up her legs.

I grin. "Absolutely nothing."

Her eyebrows crease in skepticism. "Really."

I soften the pressure of my hold and clasp my hands loosely behind her back. "You want to practice our song?" *Instead of sex?* She doesn't have to say it. I read the confusion just fine.

My veins pulsate. I ache for her when she loops her fingers in my pockets to pull me back—*thud—thu-ud*. Smooth palms surge up my chest, across my pecs. Fingertips sink into the ridges of my biceps.

And I step back.

Reach for her hand.

Interlace our fingers in the gap between us.

Yep, it's damn well possible I love Hannah Drake enough to suffer the *thud* when it's not what she needs.

"Do you still play keys?"

BEAUTY IS SKIN DEEP; to watch a woman find herself is fucking hypnotic. A radiance leaches through the cloud surrounding Hannah as she loses herself in the music. Her words, her art—I'm just a voyeur now, stalking her private journey. Maybe that's why I've fallen silent from my stretched-out position against the armrest. Stalker Wes with his body reacting to each sigh and twitch of hers.

It's a funny thing, self-denial. I'll admit it's a game I've rarely played. Always seemed selfish to me, because that's what it is, an exclusive event: me versus me. What could be more selfish than that?

But there's something freeing about each *thud*. It's a reminder of what this woman is to me. It's torture the way she gathers her hair in a lazy clump with one hand and runs the tip of a pen along her bottom lip with the other. Torture, yes, and rewarding because she's lost in something other than masking her pain.

"You need a new keyboard," she says, finally joining me on Earth. "You know they make them with the knobs and faders actually built in now?"

"Whatever. There's nothing wrong with Bessy. She likes her little nanoKONTROL companion."

"Bessy? Also, her *companion* is a parasite."

Parasite? Okay, that was funny. "Hey, how about you figure out what you're playing on the chorus while I go make coffee."

"Gonna be a long night, eh?"

"At the rate you're not working? Probably."

There's the playful glare I've come to crave. She lets her hair drop from the makeshift bun, and I have to look away. Self-denial is hard when the person you're denying tears through your clothing with a gaze that rages over hot flesh. *Thud-thud-thud.*

"Cream?" I ask.

"Black today."

"You hungry?"

"No."

"You sure? I can order something."

"Not hungry."

I don't believe her.

My hand shakes from restrained need now. I grip the bag of beans to settle the tremor. Knuckles white, the last thing I can tolerate is her approach, so of course I turn to find that searing gaze inches away. She tugs the hem of my shirt. Warm fingers that play with hair and piano keys now work their way over my abs.

They slide down, and I hiss in a breath.

"That was amazing," she whispers. "Know what else would be amazing right now?"

I close my eyes.

"What's that?" I manage. She has to know what she's doing to me.

Her hands trail back up my chest, massage the taut muscle beneath my shirt.

"I would. Absolutely love. Ice cream."

My eyelids snap open to find a volcanic grin that burns straight through my lust. My lips spread into an equally wide smile because, my god, she's serious.

"Is that so. What flavor?"

The corner of her mouth quirks up as she squints in thought. "Chocolate, I think. Wait, double chocolate."

Those lips are begging for a kiss. Sure it's dangerous, but she's left me no choice. I lean in to brush my response against her mouth.

"Fine. But you're going with me."

"Like a date?" she asks, eyes hooded with expectation.

"Exactly like a date." I skim another touch on those addictive lips.

"I want sprinkles."

"Fine."

"And whipped cream."

"Done."

"Chocolate chips."

"Of course."

"And banana. Oh, and a soft pretzel."

"You know I'm unemployed now, right?"

I DON'T WANT to look away from the spoon sliding between her lips, along her tongue. Who needs booze when you're two feet away from Hannah Drake eating ice cream?

Too bad my phone has to erupt and ruin it all.

"Give me a sec?"

Hannah's eyes follow me with her nod.

"Jacob," I say, shifting in the booth to face the window.

"Holland told me about your meeting."

"Yeah."

"Did you sign the papers?"

"Not yet. I will."

"Well, don't bother."

Fuck. "Why not?"

"The Label is contesting the terms."

"What do you mean?"

"They think Holland is being too generous and they want more of a cut for damages. The contract is dead."

"Damages? Are you kidding me?"

"And... Mila posted again."

"No way."

"Says you're in a relationship with Holland's sister? Please tell me that's not true."

"What if it is? Hannah has nothing to do with this."

I cast a look across the table, and the seductive spoon has stalled mid-air.

"She's Holland's sister! She has everything to do with this." He quiets as I work on my breathing. "Look, I'm doing my best with the Label, but this thing with Hannah is not gonna fly. You've put her in Mila's crosshairs. Holland too."

"I didn't even—"

"You know what? It doesn't matter. I'm not interested in

your drama anymore. I represent Holland and Tracing Holland. I'm calling because your shit is blowing back on my client and it's got to stop."

Did he steal that line from my father?

"Fuck you, Jacob. I took myself out of play. Gave my blessing to the guitar tech. What else do they want?"

"A public apology."

"Not happening."

"At a formal news conference."

"I said—"

"They'd accept a high-profile interview too. As long as it comes across sincere enough to repair the damage you've inflicted on the band, they won't sue."

"Sue? What—"

"Find yourself a lawyer, Wes. We'll be in touch with more details."

"WHAT'S GOING ON?" Hannah asks when I hang up.

I stare at the device I now hate with a passion. It's a fucking grenade.

"Just a second." I pull the pin on my phone-bomb and search for Mila's latest attack.

Well, well, well. Have you heard the latest on everyone's fave disgraced rocker, Wes Alton?! I've had a whisper that he's copping off with Holland Drake's little sister, Hannah. If you want to get your own back, diddling your exes sis is one way to slap her in the chops. Mate, can you sink any lower? Or is it Hannah running after big sis' sloppy seconds? If his performance on stage is anything to go by, I wouldn't be queuing up to test out his skills in the sack...

I close my eyes, fingertips pressing into the planes of my face.

"Wes? What's wrong?"

I can't look at her, this girl who's about to see her world destroyed because of me. I don't have an explanation, no magic to soften the blow, so I just hand her the phone and let it burn.

Her face drains of color as she reads. Eyes glossy, her head remains bent over the phone for longer than necessary. In silence, I watch as she absorbs what I am: the snake she should have run away from.

My lungs struggle against the weight.

Run, Hannah.

She will. I see it in the way she shrinks against the backrest of the chair. The cloud we've been shoving away has settled over her again with its full force.

"I'm so sorry, Han." My voice is raspy.

She nods, teeth pressing on her lower lip. The tear that slides down her cheek fucking slays me as she places the phone beside her bowl and rises. With each pause in her escape, I straighten with hope. But she never lapses. Never even glances back.

I stay with her half-eaten double chocolate ice cream until it's nothing but a sick puddle.

21

WHISKY THEATER

It's whisky for dinner that night. Phone off, TV off, fucking *lights* off, it's just me and my bottle on the guest room bed.

It still smells like her. Girl scents cling to everything in their rooms with all those ointments and sprays they toss around. I breathe in the flower-scented pillow pressed against my face. How long will her scent last? Soon her essence will fade back to just an extra bedroom in my condo. Stale, untouched. At some point, someone will crash here again. They'll comment about the renaissance crap I brought back from one of our European tours. Try to impress me with knowledge I don't give a fuck about. Holland liked it. That's why it returned on the plane with me. It's not a story I bother telling anymore.

I've already abandoned the long list of "should-dos" that piles up when your life goes to shit. Somewhere there's a lawyer I should be hiring. A new agent. I have a processional song to rework now that I'm a solo act. But it's impossible to move when you're clinging to the last remnant of Hannah. What if she's gone when I come back?

Poof.

I snicker at my fingers that wave above me in this drunken theater. She's evaporated. *Bravo, you inspired thespian.*

I'm well-versed in this whisky dialect that draws out pain in long syllables until it hurts less. My Martin forgives; my bottle forgets.

> "Her darkness is mine
> Desperate to hide,
> In the lie of
> Breathing hard.
> Igniting skin, she sins in the betrayal of lust
> She just, needs a sign that she's alive and
> Free to fly."

Whisky sings too. Constructs lyrics that will stay locked in its protective oblivion because I'll never remember them sober.

Fly, my angel. My fingers dance through the air again, this time as streaks of movement in the dim light.

> "...lie in wait, hold tight, let them fight
> Until you strike
> Them dead."

The "Viper" melody is nearly unrecognizable in my stuttered, drunken performance. I burst out laughing, doubling over on my side because *shit.* Irony, man. I wrote that song to help her kick the world's ass, and *I'm* the one she sent to the grave.

My stomach cramps from amusement, then dries up in a painful rush.

I'm in the grave.

The next shot straight from the bottle trickles down my

chin. Pungent drops soak into the pillow, and I spring up in alarm.

"Fuck! No no no." I'm frantic, scrubbing at the amber liquid staining the linens. I pull it to my nose for a desperate inhale and recoil in horror. "Fuck!" Tears burn my eyes. Something snaps deep in my soul.

I slam the whisky-scented pillow into the wall. *Poof.* Hannah is gone.

IT'S THURSDAY, I think. Friday? Who cares. I haven't looked at my phone in days. Haven't even turned it on. The TV stays fixed on food channels. I eat... No, I don't eat. I drink. And piss. And sometimes sleep when I drink enough to forget.

I finally changed my underwear this morning, but couldn't be bothered with anything else. Boxer-briefs and cooking competitions—my new legacy.

The whisky doesn't talk much anymore, definitely doesn't sing. It's just a tool now to make me numb and survivable—sometimes sick. But the nausea is worse today.

I stagger to the bathroom and drop in front of the toilet. The white porcelain isn't in good shape since I turned the cleaning people away yesterday. *"Come back next week,"* I'd said through a laugh because I'll probably be just as fucked up then. It was the highlight of my day.

Now, maybe I regret it as I launch the latest stomach-full of alcohol into the toilet. Impressive aim this time, so points for that.

Hand braced on the wall, I force myself back to my feet. The shower comes into sharp focus, and I hesitate. Maybe my new routine could use a shakeup.

Seconds, minutes tick by as I hover under the hot stream.

Too hot, really. I keep cranking the controls until my skin hurts enough to drown out the agony beneath it. Eventually, it's too much, and my survival instinct kicks in to stop the torture.

I don't know how long I stand in the resulting steam cloud. Drops of water gather and slide down my body. I watch a few, then close my eyes to see if I can feel them. Touch. Such a strong ally I've been missing in my war against feeling. That's what I need.

I shuffle back to my room and pull on real clothes for the first time in days. Thanks to my pre-shower cleanse, I'm also more lucid than I've been, maybe even hungry. Progress.

Once I'm ready, I buzz down to the doorman and ask for a cab. Then I'm off. Touch. Food. Forgetting the shit-fest my life has become. *Harem, I'm on my way.*

I'VE NEVER BEEN to a strip club alone before. It's hard to believe it's the same place where I partied with Dany. It's seedier when you're by yourself, darker, which suits my mood just fine as the hostess leads me to a booth. I order food, no drinks this time because I actually want to see if I can fill my stomach with something besides booze.

I don't recognize any of the dancers from my last visit, and suddenly it hits me. I'm not here for them. I skim the floor until my eyes catch the familiar gaze of the bouncer manning the VIP section. A spark of life shudders through me at his glare. It feels so fucking good. So *real,* and everything else fades around me.

I push myself up and beeline for his post. I'm a VIP, right? I smirk. Maybe two weeks ago.

"Need something?" Tight Black Shirt asks as I approach.

"Yeah, a table." I say it loud enough to draw the attention of the guests behind him. The higher the stakes, the better.

"Looks like you have one already," he says, pointing to the booth I left.

"Nah, I'm thinking I'd like something more private."

His eyes narrow. Check.

"That booth looks pretty private to me."

"Yeah? Then maybe it's the view that sucks."

"It's right in front of the stage."

Thick arms cross over his chest. Check.

"Exactly. That's the problem. Where do you find these hags?"

Face flushed, cheeks puffed, muscles flexed in restrained fury. We're in business.

"You need to leave. Now." His voice is that perfect hiss of animalistic threat.

"I'd rather just have a table. That one will work." I motion to the first one I see behind him.

"Not gonna happen. It's time for you to go."

Ready.

"You know, I would, but the cab isn't scheduled to pick me up for another hour."

"Then you can wait on a fucking bench." His pretzeled arms bulge as he closes the gap between us.

Aim.

"No thanks. It's pretty cold out there."

Veins protrude from his neck.

"Not my problem, asshole."

Fire.

"Hey, just a suggestion. Maybe ask your supervisor for a bigger shirt? The man-boob thing isn't a great look."

His arms shoot out to me, but I'm prepared enough to duck away. The resulting flail only pisses him off more, and he lunges again. My planning doesn't help this time when I misjudge his reach. A steel fist smashes into the left side of my face.

Hell yeah!

I laugh and straighten, savoring the iron taste of blood. "Wow, that's quite a punch you've got there. You learn that at the Bouncer Academy?"

"Fuck you," he growls. "Get the fuck out."

"What about my table?" I take a step toward the rope, and he shoves me into another giant body behind me. Bonus points for attracting the other bouncers, but these guys are pros. I'll have to work harder. I didn't come here for just a permanent ban from an establishment I hate.

I twist right and smash my elbow into Brute 2's side, causing Brute 1 to jolt forward in defense of his partner. I'm faster, though, and land a solid strike to Brute 1's nose. He staggers back, blood streaming from the broken appendage.

I get a decent gloat in before a rib-crushing blow sends me to the floor from behind. Brute 2 is quickly on me, anchoring my arms back. I struggle enough to earn a sickening kick to the stomach from Brute 3 who must be standing in for his injured friend. My laugh is more subdued this time with no oxygen to fuel it. I can't see much with my cheek pressed against the floor, and watch a set of expensive leather shoes and perfectly tailored suit pants approach.

"Get him out of here," Tailored Suit says to his Muscle. He must make a motion I can't see because the grip on my wrists adjusts from painful to damaging. My suspicion is confirmed when they yank me to my feet and start pushing me to the back of the building instead of the front.

"We're not done," Brute 2 hisses with hot breath against my ear. It smells like the breath of someone who's had a long day and is ready for a workout.

Congratulations, Wes Alton. You finally get to hit rock bottom in a dark alley.

I HAVE no idea what time it is when I come to. Every joint and muscle in my body aches. I can't see through my left eye, and my shirt is stiff with dried blood. Even my nostrils burn from the stench of garbage and piss.

My wallet!

It's there. Those guys are pros. No phone though because I left that useless piece of shit at home.

"Fuck," I mutter as I force myself to my knees. The gravel swirls below me, and I brace my trembling palms on a carpet of debris and broken glass. My left hand is a mess. My right hand isn't much better, and I stare at swollen evidence of the damn good defensive blows I got in before they leveled me. Two-on-one, then three-on-one. Not great odds.

I reach for the concrete wall and stagger to my feet. Hunched over, I wait for air to sift back into my lungs while the commotion of downtown Toronto hums just meters away. It burns to breathe. They must have cracked a few ribs. I rest my forehead on the arm pressed against the building. The mangled remains of my other hand clutches my side in support of my lungs. More air. I'll need a lot more to make it to the street. Damn it's cold.

The alley stops spinning after several seconds, and I lurch toward the main thoroughfare. It takes several long breaks and a shit-ton of willpower to make it back to the safety of civilization.

Safety? No. Civilization fucking sucks.

The first three cabs ignore my signal—not surprising given my state. Who wants the burden of a criminal or dead body at this time of night? I've almost given up when a brave driver finally pulls to the curb.

"Fuck. Hospital, eh?" he says as I ease into the back of the cab.

"No, Spadina and Lakeshore."

"Seriously? You look like—"

"Spadina and Lakeshore."

He shrugs with a *must-be-fun-to-be-nuts* look as he shifts back to the wheel. The car jerks into the flow of traffic, and I clench my teeth to keep from groaning. I swear this dude goes out of his way to brake late and accelerate early at every stop. By the time we pull up to my building, I fear I'll be leaving several body parts in the back of his vehicle.

Oh well, he deserves the mess.

I tip him anyway, a reward for being willing to pick me up, and do my best ninja impression through the main entrance, past the security desk, and onto the elevator. I don't need any commentary from Lawrence, the doorman. Ninja skills are severely lacking when half your body doesn't work, but with no wait for the elevator, I'm gone before he can interfere.

The elevator has never been so slow. I slump against the wall, shaking so hard I'm afraid I'll knock the car right off its cable. Will I die of blood loss or hypothermia? It's an interesting question I ponder until the elevator finally stops. Six stumbles later, I'm at my door.

I curse at the stove clock when I manage to get inside. 3:37am. I was in the alley for at least seven hours. *Shit*. Yeah, I probably should have gone to the hospital with a concussion like that, but fuck it. Maybe those dead brain cells will prove to be an upgrade.

With ginger movements, I strip off my clothes and step into the shower for the second time in twelve hours. My injuries force a much cooler temperature with this one, though. God, it hurts. Fire everywhere. Stabbing pain pierces through dull aches, and the more I see of the damage, the more relieved I feel. Each wound is a badge, a fucking neon sign that I'm alive and broken and exactly where I should be.

Wes Alton's soul is visible. *Here you go, world. See what I am.*

I turn off the water and by some miracle I make it to my bed, still dripping with pink streaks of water-blood. I fall to the sheets and close my eyes, praying that this time I don't wake up.

22

PHANTOMS

"Wes?"

I swat away the phantom. Must be new casting by my whisky theater.

"I object," I mutter, because this ghost reminds me too much of Hannah. I'm also too weak to fight it when it pushes me on my back and scans me from head to toe.

Her gasp sounds painful. "My god! What happened? I'm calling for help." She reaches for something, and I grab her wrist. Shit, it really is Hannah. I thought I took her key back. Didn't I? No. I'd never have the strength to do that.

"I'm fine." Yeah, not exactly a solid argument. "No hospital."

I flinch when she touches my face. "I'll be right back," she says, voice quavering. She returns with first aid supplies, and I try to move out of reach.

"No. Go home." Funny how I sound drunk even though I'm not for once. Drunk on pain, I guess. I like it. Have to remember that one in case I'm ever able to hold a guitar again.

"Not happening," she says, and positions herself next to me on the bed.

I close my eyes. "Just leave. I don't want your help."

"Yeah? Well, I don't want to help."

I look at her then. I have to because it's Hannah and she's the most beautiful, amazing woman ever created. "Hannah." Just breathing her name settles a peace over me.

"Don't. Not now." She's angry. Of course she is. But is it new anger or old anger? It's a question I face often in my relationships.

"So why are you here?"

"Because I have to be." Her hard tone lies through tears when her eyes meet mine. "Because I hate you, and I love you, and I hate loving you, but I do." She cups my face. "So much."

I'm shaking when she starts tracing the evidence of my pain. The cuts on my face, the bruises on my chest, each seeping wound should be scaring her away to the safety of someone who's not poison. I've exposed my demon for her. How is she not running?

"Hannah..." Her flower-scent overwhelms me. I can't think anymore. I just want to drown in that smell. That would be the sweetest death. Sweeter than sex, music, fame. A flower-scented pillow that never fades.

"I'm here."

She is. Fuck knows why, but she is. I close my eyes, the pain finally taking more than I can withstand. Still, I feel the tug of a smile on my cracked lips. "Hannah..." I whisper, and everything goes dark.

THE FLOWER-SCENT IS GONE when I wake. This time it's disinfectant and chemicals wafting over me in a nauseating greeting. Beeps, hums, distant voices. The sterile glow of hospital lighting seeps through the swollen slits of my eyelids.

My first attempt at movement fails. So does the second. By the third, though, I'm able to lift my arm enough to see an IV extending from a vein in my hand.

A rattle at the door reveals a sandy-haired woman in scrubs. Her smile is bright and mischievous. "Well, hello there, Mr. Alton," she says in a chipper voice. "Nice of you to join us."

"My pleasure," I mumble, although it doesn't come out as words. Damn, I must be drugged up. That would also explain the floating walls and lack of pain.

"You got yourself into quite a jam, eh?"

"You could say that." My syllables form better this time.

"Want to tell me what happened?"

"Just a fight."

She winks. "How are the other guys?"

"There were more of them, so they're fine."

"I see. Well, I'm Linda if you need anything. I'm going to let Dr. Smyth know you're awake. She'll have some questions for you."

Yep, exactly the reason I didn't want to come to the hospital in the first place.

"What about Hannah?" The nurse raises an eyebrow, and I grunt. "The girl who probably called the ambulance. Did she come in with me? Is she here?"

Linda's apologetic look does nothing to soften the blow. "Sorry, I'm not sure about any of that. Dr. Smyth may have a better idea. She'll be right in."

DR. SMYTH DOESN'T REMEMBER a Hannah either. She *does* have a lot of questions about what happened. I downplay the incident and refuse to involve law enforcement. I know the Brute Trio will keep it to themselves as well, so no need to waste taxpayer dollars on more headlines I don't want.

Her updates on my injuries are encouraging, though. No internal bleeding or brain trauma. Just a crap-load of superficial wounds and fractures that will take some time to heal. But they *will* heal, she promises with a smile that indicates I should be happy about it. I smile back because there's no way in hell I'm having a forced conversation with a psychiatrist while I'm here.

Her confidence fades when she learns I'm *that* Wes Alton. We both stare at my bandaged hands in thoughtful silence.

"You should be able to play again," she says finally. It's the same tone my mother used when she promised maybe one day we'd get a dog. I never got a dog.

"When?" I ask.

"I'm not comfortable issuing an exact estimate. There are many factors to consider."

"Then give me a non-exact estimate. Will I be playing by April?"

She doesn't have to give me *any* estimate with that expression. No. I won't be playing for my sister's wedding. The last thing I had left is gone too.

I shut my eyes and rest against the pillow.

Dr. Smyth launches into backtrack mode, and I don't have the energy to stop her optimistic lies. In rare cases this, that, *fucking everything* happens, but I stopped believing I'm one of the lucky ones years ago.

I'm also not interested in self-pity. "Sounds good," I say, cutting her off. "Hey, doc, I have trouble sleeping. You know, the pain..." is bad, but being conscious is worse.

"Of course. I'll have Linda get you something after we draw blood."

"Thanks."

She rests her hand on my forearm. "You'll play again soon, Mr. Alton. You just need to have hope."

I manage to suppress my laugh.

WHEN I WAKE AGAIN it's dark outside. The gleam of parking lot lights sprinkles in through the slotted blinds, and a clock on the wall tells me it's 7pm. A sign next to it reports that visiting hours end at nine. I guess that's relevant information for some patients.

I briefly consider calling Sophia. At the very least, she should know about my hands so she can make other arrangements for her processional. But I don't want to freak her out with a call from the hospital and I don't have my cell. Besides, the thought of turning on that digital monster after all this time is more painful than anything that happened in the alley.

A light knock on the door draws my attention, and I turn to face Linda who's probably doing another of her vitals checks. That would have been helpful at the moment because my vitals nearly crash when the dark hair of a younger woman pushes through instead.

"May I come in?" Hannah asks.

I'm too stunned to answer. She smiles at my dazed nod and closes the door behind her. My gaze is glued to every flex and sway of her body as she crosses the room. There's a glow around her, I swear. The chair beside me creaks as she lowers herself and balances a small duffle bag on her lap.

"Sorry I wasn't here sooner. The nurses said you were sleeping when I came by this afternoon so I went to your place to get some stuff for you."

"Thanks" –is what I say to the woman who makes my heart explode.

She clears her throat and holds up the bag. "So here. Um, I wasn't exactly sure what you'd need but I brought some clothes, a toothbrush..." She looks at me again with a tortured expression, and something cracks in my soul. "Nine empty liquor bottles," she says quietly, eyes heavy. "Is that all you've done since that day?"

"Not all." I raise my messed-up hands, but she doesn't smile.

"I brought your phone too." It's a warning, a question, and a critique all-in-one.

"You turned it on," I guess, and she nods. *Shit.*

"Take it from the expert. Hiding from the storm doesn't make it go away."

"Is that why you came back?"

She adjusts in the chair, focusing on the floor. "I was worried, yes. You weren't responding to any of my messages. Then I found out no one had heard from you." She bites her lip as tears fill her eyes. I've never hated myself more. Her pain is on me. "When I saw you there, all bloody and not moving—" A sob cuts her off, and I instinctively rock forward. The strain hurts like hell, but it's worth it when my fingers reach her shoulder and she slides onto the bed. I pull her in and bury my face in that intoxicating flower-scent.

"I need you, Han," I whisper, my voice cracking. "I can't do it without you." Tears, *my* tears, burn in protest but I don't want to move. I *won't.* Not when I have her in my arms again. "I love you."

Another sob leaks out, and I lock her against me. My rock. My goddess. My kickass viper.

"You should have stayed away," I say through a kiss on her hair.

"I know."

"It's going to be even harder now."

"I know."

She pulls back and grips my cheeks. *"I'm breaking free to strike. Fangs bared, spring out, out. Of hell, don't tell. Me what I am..."*

I silence her beautiful song with a kiss. That voice. That smell. That magic we have together—I want it in my world forever. *"I'm not, not your pet. I'm your hidden regret. So hear me, you should fucking fear me. As I rise."*

23

HOT DATE

I'm released from the hospital the following morning. Hannah helps me home, and everything feels different when I limp across the threshold. I won't be tossing potpourri around or anything, but it's damn nice to watch my girl use *her* key.

"Do you need more meds?" she asks as I lower myself to the couch.

Shit, yeah. "No, I'm fine."

"Okay. Want some coffee?"

"Sure."

She sets to work on the beans, and I absorb everything about her as she moves around the kitchen. Even her coffee skills make a guy think in lyrics.

"How's therapy going?" I ask before the crazy in my head goes public.

"Good."

"What about with your parents?"

"Really good." She leans on the island to face me. "You were right to send me home. I never would've confronted my illness hiding here."

"That's great, Han." *Except I miss you like hell.*

"Ah, and I forgot how awesome it is having Emma and Sylvie around."

"They're like manic supernovas."

I crack a grin at her laugh.

"You should have seen Sylvie yesterday. Shandor is coming into town to rehearse for—" She stops and the laughter drains from her face. "Shit. Wes, I'm so sorry."

"To rehearse for the spring tour?" I settle against the armrest. "I bet Sylvie is excited to have him around."

Hannah remains silent, her gaze creeping over to me. "Yeah."

I offer an encouraging smile, and feel my own muscles release when her light returns.

"She spent four hours on hair and makeup to meet him at the airport."

"Only four?"

"Dad pulled the plug a half hour before arrival time and said if she didn't get in the car, she wasn't going."

I laugh and lean back as she returns to the coffee-prep.

"I'm glad you're here, Han," I say. "Your parents can't be thrilled that you're helping me."

Her hand stalls on the carafe. "It doesn't matter what they think. Besides I used the Drake Guilt Whip on them."

"Wow, brutal."

"Exactly. I went all out. 'You raised me to be strong, loyal, and compassionate. My friend needs help.'"

"Damn."

She tosses a mischievous grin over her shoulder. "What were they going to say to that?"

"You sure you don't want to be a lawyer anymore?"

WE'VE JUST FINISHED our coffee when Hannah glances at her phone.

"Wow, it's late. I should get going."

My heart cramps as I force a nod.

She shifts closer to my end of the couch. "I'll check your dressings like the doctor said before I go."

"You don't have to. The visiting nurse will be here this afternoon." I leave out the part where I don't want to see her reaction to the damage I inflicted on myself.

"You sure?" She hesitates, eyes squinting in doubt. "Do you need anything else?"

She doesn't want to leave either. *Think!* There has to be something.

"Hot date tonight?"

She chuckles. "I wish. No, I promised my parents I wouldn't be long. They want to take us all out to some new hibachi place."

"Us all?"

White teeth sink into her lip. "Uh, well, the six of us, plus Shandor and Luke. It's not often we're all together."

My lips twist... into something. "I see. Sounds fun."

Yeah, that didn't go well.

"I shouldn't have said anything."

"Don't worry about it," I say with much more finesse. She'll still worry. Her fingernail is already lodged between her teeth. "Hey, Han, there's something else before you go."

And that intro did nothing to ease her anxiety. *Really, Wes?* "My hands, you know?" I hold them up in case she forgot why she was here. "I'm not going to be able to play." I clear my throat of the emotion. "I'll call Soph in a bit so she can make other arrangements, just wanted to fill you in."

She stares at me in silence. Is she angry?

"Han? You okay?"

She shoves her phone into her back pocket and moves toward the door. "I'm fine. Gotta jet. Also, that's total bullshit. We're playing Sophia's wedding."

I can't even shove myself off the couch before she's through the door.

I BRAVE my phone the following morning and immediately wish I hadn't.

My dear readers. You'll never guess what juicy goss just found its way into my grabby mitts.... Oh, Wes. Take my advice. When you're already in bother with the old bill for being handy with your fists, maybe take it down a notch and lay low? It seems our wannabe boxer didn't come off too good this time and landed himself in a hospital room. Fingers crossed you didn't do any damage to those pretty hands. Oh, hang on. It's not like you'll be needing them anytime soon... Mila Taylor out

---

A smirk spreads across my lips as I shake my head. Amazing. The woman is swift and omniscient, I'll give her that. I scribble "Mila Taylor" on the list of shit I need to deal with. It's right under lawyer, wedding, and business manager. And just like the others, it's scrawled in almost indecipherable hieroglyphs. Today's visiting nurse praised my ability to hold a pen. I told her I'll look for a career that only requires kickass pen-holding skills. She didn't get my humor and suggested "guest-book attendant." Good thing my sister's in the market for one. Are things finally swinging my way?

I text Hannah for law firm referrals and send a message to my business manager about the pending suit. Then it's on to the litany of missed calls and voice messages. I cross Hannah off the list. Fixed that, although I save her messages because I refuse to be without her again. Jacob has updates and questions. Holland is worried. Sophia is worried. Freddy Jr. wants to have lunch, as do Raymond and Pamela from the Label. Four messages are bullshit and not worth finishing. Two more are from the hospital, and the last one is a tabloid that got my private number somehow. Shit...

I add "*get new number*" to my list.

I straighten on the couch and study my handiwork. Not half-bad. Guess I can rock responsible after all. Time for the e-mails.

I open my inbox and let out a long breath. Yep, no. Think I'm good with the voicemails and texts for now.

"*Check Email,*" I write.

HOLLAND IS COMING over for coffee. No Luke this time because he's finally been called back to the part of his life that doesn't involve his girlfriend. I was beginning to wonder how the dude could do the international superstar thing when he always seemed to be hovering around here.

I'm prepared for her reaction when she sees my damaged face, but it still stings. She says nothing as her gorgeous smile fades. I can't look anymore and step back so she can enter.

"I've got that breakfast blend from Rienti's brewing that you like," I say, suddenly aware of my heavy limp.

I reach for a mug and clench my jaw to suppress the wince from the burning in my ribs. She doesn't need to see that too.

"You still have some left?" she says, voice small. I smile over at her.

"I bought a few bags when I saw how much you loved it on tour. I thought..." I stop and turn back to the mug. *I thought we'd be using it a lot on our next one.* I clear my throat. "How are rehearsals going?"

"We don't have to talk about that."

I add a splash of cream and one ice cube, just the way she likes it. "I want to. Is this Shandor guy getting it? Does he need help with anything?"

She stares at the cup I push toward her for too long. Shit, she's going to tear up. I can't handle that right now and turn back to the coffeemaker.

"He's doing great. He's a fantastic musician."

"Good. What about the riff on 'Acrobat'?"

"He's got it. Even the effects."

I nod and lean on the island across from her with my own cup when it's safe.

"Is it true about what happened to you? This was another fight?" she asks.

"Ah, Mila. Damn hospital staff must have leaked it."

"Or your opponents."

"Nah, they were pros."

She returns my wry smirk. "Clearly."

I let out a breath. "I don't know, Hol. I just needed... Yeah, I don't know what I needed, but I went looking to get fucked up."

"You were successful." We exchange another smile, and suddenly we're fifteen-year-olds in my basement again.

"What's going on with the album? Is it still dropping next week?" I ask.

She shrugs through a sip of her coffee. "Supposedly, but the Label is pretty sure it'll tank. There's even talk of canceling the fall tour."

The look on her face is too much. "Hol, I'm..." I close my eyes and force in air. "I'm sorry." When I open them again she's blurry through a thin sheen of liquid. "I didn't want this. Everything I've done, it's all been to protect you and give you everything you've wanted since we were kids."

She shakes her head, tears gathering in her own eyes. "I *had* everything I wanted, Wes. I *had* it."

Oh god. The hot drops slide down my cheeks when I clench my eyes shut, and a ragged breath rattles beneath my broken ribs. I wonder if she can hear it in the silence. "I know." It's barely more than a whisper, and soon she's next to me. My Holland. My friend, my world, takes me in her arms and holds on with twenty years-worth of compassion.

"Let's fix this," she murmurs. "You want me to be happy? Then let's put our lives back together."

———

HOLLAND and I spend the rest of our coffee date talking, laughing, and planning.

"You're gonna kill it," I say. "How much of the new stuff are you doing?"

"Hmm... most of the set will be from the new album. We'll still do 'Acrobat' and 'Perfect Storm,' of course." She quiets and gives her coffee an unnecessary stir. "You sure you're cool with all of this? You really don't want to come back."

I smile and hold up my hands. "Couldn't if I wanted to."

She rolls her eyes. "You know what I mean."

I nod and grow serious. "We were great together, but I think we're stronger apart. I know you will be. I'll always be here for you though."

A sad smile settles over her lips. "I know you're right. It's just..."

"Hey. I was thinking, if you want, we could still write together. For *your* band?"

My heart bursts at the light opening up on her face. "Seriously? You'd do that?"

"It would help the Label's PR team, right? Put the fans' fears to rest?"

"Hell yeah it would."

"Might even save the record if we come out that the rift is repaired. Everything is good, it's just our last album as a band?"

"You'd do that?" Shit, the viper-killing expression is back in her big blue eyes.

"Of course. Raymond and Pam want to have lunch. Why don't you come with us and we can lay it out with them?"

"I'm in." Her grin imprints itself on my soul.

"What are you doing tomorrow?"

24

SOLUTIONS

It's disturbing how much I miss Hannah when she's not around. Whenever she's scheduled to arrive, I sit here, staring at the door. She said eleven, after her counseling session, and it's already over fifteen minutes past. A knock rushes through me in a wave of relief.

"Just come in," I call out from the couch.

The door clicks and opens to my heart-stopping viper.

"Hey, beautiful," I say.

She grins. "Hey, yourself. Those meds must be taking their toll."

I laugh. "Why's that?"

"Because you've got a goofy smile on your face."

"Is that so? Or maybe it's the girl in my foyer." Totally worth it when she skips to the couch and launches into my arms.

A groan leaks past my grin, and she gasps.

"Oh, crap. Sorry!"

"Don't worry about it. They're already broken."

She delivers a playful swat, and I draw her in for a long kiss.

God, I missed those lips, the fire of her skin. My need becomes more desperate, and she melts against me.

"You sure this is okay?" she breathes. "You're not in pain?"

I thread my fingers in her hair so she can't pull away. "Not anymore."

Her lips crash against mine, and by the hunger in her kiss I know she's missed me just as much. I search for the soft skin under her shirt, and she clutches my hem. She starts to pull, and I secure her wrist.

I will never be able to stomach her disappointment.

"I want to see you," she says, eyes pleading. "It's been so long."

"It's not something you want to see."

"There's nothing about you I don't want."

Fuck. She's straddling my hips and feeling my response.

"Show me," she continues, firmer this time.

I let out a heavy breath, but don't stop her when she slides my shirt up. I adjust so we can pull it off, and she settles back into position.

We're silent as her gaze wanders over my body. It can't be pretty with its rainbow of blues, yellows, and greens. Delicate fingertips trace the lines and touch gentle brushstrokes over each imperfection. Every so often she hits a particularly damaged area and triggers an involuntary hiss. But I never stop her. My body, everything about me, belongs to her.

"Are these wounds the end or the beginning?" she whispers finally.

I remove her hand and bring it to my lips. "Both."

A breathtaking smile spreads over her face as she leans in. "Good."

I'M NOT THRILLED about meeting the Label brass when I look like the loser of an MMA fight, but it's time to own up. I promised Hannah an end to Old Wes and that means laying down my sword to fix things for Holland.

The others are already seated when I limp to the table and extend my hand. Two firm shakes and a kiss on the cheek later, and we're ready for battle.

No lawyers present. Beacon of Hope Number One.

Raymond and Pam are still staring at us after I take my seat, and I can't tell if it was the affectionate kiss I gave Holland or my messed-up face that's derailed their agenda for lunch.

"You two appear to be getting along," Pam says.

I look to Holland and I'm blasted with Drake-sunshine.

"Yeah, we're good. Really good," she says, sharing it with the Suits as well.

"That's wonderful." Pam's tone is more "recovery-mode" than anything. I'm not sure why they wanted to meet, but I already see that their plan has changed.

"We're going to keep writing together," I add. Might as well stack the deck early. "Shandor can continue performing with them at the shows, but Holland and I will write for the band."

It's a good thing we haven't started eating yet or they'd be choking right now. More headlines we don't need.

The server interrupts for our drink orders, giving our stunned companions time to regroup. Hopefully they enjoyed that brief moment of stability because I'm already working on the next bombshell.

I cast a quick glance to Holland before facing the execs. "I also wanted to talk about a public apology and what I can do to fix things for the band." Even Holland's eyes widen in shock.

Raymond clears his throat. Pam reaches for her glass. Holland—yep, still gaping.

"I see. Well, okay," Raymond says after a pause. "What did you have in mind?"

I shrug. "Whatever you want. You tell me what you need me to do. I was thinking Mila would be a good start."

Pam nearly drops her water. "Mila Taylor?"

"Yeah. Think you can get me an interview? Might as well go to the source. If she's going to attack me, it should be with the truth."

"You want to sit down with Mila Taylor?" Pam asks. I'm not sure she heard the rest.

"I think that makes the most sense. If we can do it now, then maybe we can get the hype going in time to save the 'Swan Song' release. We frame it as our *planned* final album together before I *planned* to move on to other projects." I check Holland's reaction and love the look on her face. *Yeah, sweetheart, I've been working shit out in my head too.* "I mean, the album is freaking, 'Swan Song.' Who's not going to believe it was meant to be the end of an era?"

"And all the rumors out there about the split?" But Raymond is just checking off boxes now. His brain is already making love to my plan.

"Eh, those were just rumors spread by my vengeful ex, Miranda. She spun the truth to get back at me. A few public appearances with Holland and no one will question it."

"In fact, we'll be playing together soon," Holland announces, and all gazes shoot to her. My heart hammers at her mischievous grin. *What the hell is she talking about?*

Pam verbalizes the question first, and Holland's response is so casual, I almost believe I'm forgetting something. Was I that drugged up from pain meds?

"Wes's sister is getting married in a month and the band has agreed to back him up on a new song he wrote with my own sister, Hannah."

"Tracing Holland is going to perform at Wes's sister's wedding?" Raymond says it like there's a hidden camera somewhere ready to expose our prank.

Or maybe that's my expression. Holland gives me an encouraging nod.

"Um... yeah," I stammer. "Hannah and I have been working on it for a while. She'll be performing it with us as well."

"What's this song called?" Pam asks, nearly salivating now.

I'm still in disbelief as I glance at Holland. "It's called 'Viper Rising.'"

"Do you have a work tape?" Raymond asks.

I nod and pull out my phone. I scroll through the recordings and settle on the best one Hannah and I put together from our rehearsals.

"It's rough. Just a live scratch in my condo."

Yeah, they're not listening, so I just push play.

I set the phone on the table, mostly so my shaking hands don't drop it. I've never been so nervous in my life. I don't remember the song being so long or the recording having so many pitchy notes. I don't remember my B-string being a little sharp. I definitely didn't remember the thud of the icemaker dropping its latest creation in the reservoir right after the drop in the bridge.

Just when I think my lungs are about to explode, Holland reaches over and squeezes my knee. I swallow hard to keep the emotion inside and allow my fingers to creep over to brush hers before she pulls away.

As soon as it's over, I take my phone back and watch as the jury leans into their chairs.

"The first time we heard it, we knew we wanted to support him. It's amazing, eh?" Holland says, grin bright with expectation. "Luke liked it too."

Raymond crosses his arm and studies me. "It's fucking brilliant. You have more like that?"

"A few finished. Several others in the works."

Holland didn't know that, and I suppress a smile. Her sister is one kickass songwriter too.

"They as good as this one?"

"I believe they are," I say.

They exchange a look, and I hold my breath.

"You've caused us a lot of headaches the last couple of years," Pam says, eyes slicing into me.

I let the air out of my lungs and nod. "I'm sorry for that. I had a lot of shit twisted up inside me, but I'm working hard to straighten it out."

"I'll vouch for him," Holland says.

Beacon of Hope Number Two.

"What's the name of your duo?" Raymond asks.

"My duo?"

"Yeah, you and that girl who's singing. Her voice is haunting. Recordable for sure. She as much of a hothead as you?"

Holland snorts a laugh. "Hannah? Please. She's the only one who can control this landmine right here. Probably the reason we're even having this conversation."

"Really..." Raymond draws the word out, eyebrows high as his brain works on this puzzle. He checks with his companion and turns back to me. "That true?"

"Pretty much." I say through a smirk.

They release a slow nod. "So what's the name of your new group?"

"Uh..." *Shit.*

"Viper Rising," Holland cuts in. "Their first track is also the name of the band."

"Viper Rising," Pam muses. "Hmm."

"I like it," Raymond says. "Pam?"

She nods. "Me too. Let's get you two in for a conversation and see what you've got. Bring your guitars."

Wait, what? "Sure, sounds great. I can't play yet, though." They study my hand, and I swear their disappointment matches my own.

"I'll play for their audition," Holland says, and I'm officially out of words.

"Well, okay then. Let's set something up after the release. For now we'll work on getting the media situation ironed out."

"You got it, boss," I say, and take the hands they offer.

"Good. Thanks for the, uh, meeting then," Pam says.

"Thank *you*, ma'am," I reply. "Looking forward to turning the page."

"We are too, son," Raymond says. "What do you say, time for some food? The sweet corn crème brulee at this place is criminal."

Wow, that does sound amazing.

Also, what the fuck just happened?

WITH ALL THE wild events of the day, watching Hannah's reactions to the recap is my favorite part. I find myself searching for more reasons to make her smile and force those gorgeous eyes to ignite with excitement. When I get to the part about "Viper Rising" she just about collapses on the couch.

"Wait, are you serious? They liked me?"

"They loved you, Han. They want us to go in for an audition and talk details."

Mouth open, she moves her head in slow arcs. "I don't... I just..."

"Looks like maybe you have a new career. Hope this doesn't interfere with your judge-show gig."

"What? Wes!" This one is a shriek that sends her crashing against my chest. I let out an *oomph* as she settles against me.

"What do I say? What do I wear? Wait, how are you going to play for an audition?"

I laugh and kiss her hair. "Don't worry about that stuff. It's just a formality. They're already interested. As for playing, that's the best part."

"A possible record deal isn't the best part?"

I shake my head with a grin. "Not for us. Holland is going to play for the audition and the whole band will back us up at the wedding."

I'm worried for her poor jaw after its violent drop. "No."

"Yep."

Blue eyes narrow and cut into me. "No! You're lying."

I laugh. "Why would I lie about that?"

She screeches again and suffocates me in another embrace.

"Ahh! I love you!" she sings, then pulls back, expression changing. "I mean... you know what I mean."

"I hope you mean you love me because I'm pretty sure I love you too."

Her teeth sink into her lip as tears collect in those bright, wide eyes. I didn't think it was possible for Hannah to look any more beautiful.

IT'S NOT until we get to the Mila interview portion of the play-by-play that Hannah returns to Earth. I regret saying anything the second she deflates.

"Do you think that's a good idea?" Based on the severe tone, she's in lawyer-mode. I'm no match for Hannah Drake in lawyer-mode.

"Probably not, but if I'm going to set the record straight, she's the one I need to convince."

She must really love me. I can see the retort she's holding back bashing against her tongue when she straightens on the couch.

I study her face. "Just say it, Han."

She lets out a long breath and relaxes against me again. "The problem is you're approaching this interview as if Mila Taylor is a serious journalist. She's a blogger, Wes. She's loved for her wit and caustic personality. Honestly, half her fans probably follow her because she's popular. The truth has nothing to do with the equation."

She's right.

"I can still try to change her perspective."

She nudges closer, and I tighten my arms around her.

"When's the interview?"

25

INTERVIEW

Thursday. I find out the interview with Mila Taylor is Thursday. I never stressed over these things before. The person on the other side of a conversation was just one more acquaintance in the long parade of personalities I dealt with. I treated them the same as everyone else. If I liked them, they got charming, witty Wes Alton. If I didn't, they got smart-ass Wes. I didn't give a shit either way; it was their call how they wanted to play the exchange. Plus, there was always Holland to smooth things over and my volatile reputation to hide behind.

This is different. This is the first public exposure of New Wes, and I have no idea how he handles interviews.

I stare into my coffee mug, elbows resting on the cool granite of the kitchen island. So much rides on this moment. It's a lot carrying two souls I'd protect with my life, in addition to the scrap that's left of my own.

My healthy fingers tap a disjointed cadence, waiting for my phone to ring. This device I've come to despise is now going to decide my fate. Fucking irony, man. Just one joke after another.

I startle at the shrill eruption and draw in a deep breath when I see the foreign number. Yorkshire, England I was told.

Here we go.

"Hello. Wes, here."

"Hiya. It's Mila. How goes it?"

Her clipped accent makes me smile, especially the soft tone I never saw coming. I guess I figured she'd speak in ogre grunts.

"Thanks for agreeing to this."

"A cozy chinwag with the infamous Wes Alton? No way was I missing that chance."

I force a chuckle. "Yeah, well, thanks for making me infamous."

"Nah, mate, that was all your doing."

Deep breath. *New Wes.*

"Actually, that's what I wanted to talk about. I'm not sure who your sources are but I have an idea. They have a personal vendetta that has led to some bad information."

"Ooh, how intriguing. Tell me more." She doesn't sound intrigued. At all. Why exactly did I think this was a good idea?

"Look, here's what's really going on, and you can do with it what you want. Yes, I'm leaving Tracing Holland, but Holland and I are on great terms. I'm pursuing another project we're all really excited about, including Holland. We're still going to write together, and we'll even play together on occasion. 'Swan Song' is our last album as a band, but we're still going to work with each other."

Her silence leaves me drumming broken rhythms again. Shit, and you can't read body language over the phone. I have no clue what's going on over there in Yorkshire.

"Also, you should know no criminal charges are in play. I'm going to guess you got that from my father? He hates me and owns the world of PR so be careful with anything you get from him. Same with Miranda Rivenier. We went out a couple times, and I broke it off. She didn't take it well."

Still no response. Did we get disconnected? I swear this is the worst interview ever, and now I'm babbling like a teenager to his school newspaper.

"You there?" I ask.

"Yep, I'm here."

Am I bombing or killing it?

"As for Hannah Drake, she's an amazing woman. I have a ton of respect for her and would appreciate it if you left her out of this."

"I see."

Shit.

"Okay, well, any questions for me?"

"Nah, mate. I think I have what I need. Thank you for clearing things up."

Things are clear? That makes one of us.

My fingers resume their song from earlier until my phone lights up with a message. Hannah.

> How did it go?

I unlock my phone.

> No clue.

MILA POSTS THE NEXT DAY.

Peeps, have I got news for you! You'll never guess who came begging at my door. It seems our vicious little pitbull, Wes Alton, is just a toy poodle at heart wanting a pat on the head.

There there, Wesley Boy. Put your lip away. Don't let those meanies spreading nasty rumours see you cry.

You see, he claims the rumours aren't true. He's still on good terms with his bessie, Holland Drake. They're even going to continue working together. Do I believe him? Maybe. Did I laugh my arse off as I listened to the legendary bad boy snivelling into his phone? Abso-friggin-lutely.

I'll tell you one thing, though. As much as I wanted to hate their final album "Swan Song" when I previewed it, I didn't. It was actually bloody good listening and Tracing Holland fans are in for a right treat.

So for those of you that are about to lose the plot, Wes style, take a leaf out of his handbook. This is the way to do it.

Well, good luck with your new "project," Wesley. Still sounds like shite to me, but you never fail to entertain. –Mila out

---

Well, fuck.

I grin and lean back on the couch.

PAM CALLS FIRST. The Label is thrilled. They must have been watching for the post as well, and they're shitting their pants at the way this hype should skyrocket interest in "our final album together." The article was only up for an hour when promoters were reaching out to book the band, and other publications wanted details on "the real story." She also praised me for what she called "forgoing my ego." Whatever.

Holland is next.

"Did you see it? Mila endorsed the record!"

"It's great." I drop to the couch and settle my head against the armrest.

"Seriously, it couldn't have gone better. I just... Thank you, Wes. And sorry she said those other things about you. I know there's no way you came off like that."

"Ha. It's Mila. Can't expect anything different. Enjoy the ride." We quiet under the weight of my words. I'm happy for her. I meant every syllable; it just happened to be a ride we always assumed we'd take together.

"No matter what happens, Tracing Holland will be your legacy," she says finally.

I let it sink in, but it doesn't quite feel right. "Well, part of it. I have Viper Rising to build now."

"Right." I hear the smile in her voice. "Speaking of which, Hannah is on her way over there now."

How does my heart still react to that fact after all this time? "Sounds good."

She's silent again, and I imagine the irresistible purse of her lips when she's pondering something. "You really like her, don't you?"

Oh boy. "I do. A lot."

"She likes you too."

"I know. Hol?"

"Yeah?"

"I will die before I hurt your sister."

"I know."

My breath escapes with relief. "Good. She's special."

"I know that too."

"I guess," I say through a laugh. "She's your sister."

"No, it's not that."

My humor wanes as I wait for her to continue.

"You and I have been close for most of our lives. Inseparable for a lot of it, but I feel like I was a crutch for you. It wasn't me; it was *Hannah* who pushed you into the man I knew you could be. No matter what happens, remember that."

It's true. And it's Hannah I'm dying to have in my arms right now.

I DON'T HAVE to wait long. I'm not sure why she didn't tell me she was coming, but I figured she wanted to debrief over the events in person. When the door clicks, I'm glued to the opening like the little dog Mila says I am.

I take her in my arms and plant a kiss on her forehead, then... I step back in surprise. Her face. A frown. Concern. Why is there concern?

"Geoff called."

Fuck no!

"He misses me and feels bad about what happened between us. He wants to make it up to me."

Brute Two's fist struck me with less force than that blow.

"Really."

She lets out a dry laugh. "Yeah. He's booked us a cruise and everything. Can you believe it?"

I'd take you anywhere. I thought you knew that. "Wow. You going?"

Her pause cuts deep. "I don't know."

Nothing moves from my head to my mouth while she waits so she continues.

"Things haven't been good with Geoff lately, but we've devoted three years of our lives together. Hell, I thought I was going to marry him at one point. How can I not hear him out? Then again, we have that Viper Rising audition. And you... God!" She locks her fingers on her head, pain flooding her eyes. It's too much, and I have to look away.

Ahh!

I can't breathe. I should be screaming a defense, it's right there, but that was Old Wes. New Wes wants Hannah to be happy, hates the distress on her face. He wants her to go on a fucking cruise with a douchebag if that's where her heart will shine. The fact that we're even having this conversation tells me what I thought we had was a warped fantasy in Selfish Wes's head.

Even as the words come out they sound foreign to me. "We can always push the audition. They're not going to be in a hurry to move on things while I'm injured and we're still sorting out the Tracing Holland drama."

"True."

I can't tell if it's the answer she wanted since she won't look at me.

My heart is pounding. Impressive considering I'm pretty sure it's in a dozen pieces right now. "If you really want to go with this guy, we can make it work."

If he's the one you want, I will let you go.

She watches me, eyes round, waiting for... I still don't know what, but I'd do anything to give it to her. My blessing? *Fuck!*

She searches my face. "It's just... You said we're fooling ourselves with this—whatever it is. You said we're wasting our time, that it could never work between us, and I can't afford to pretend anymore. I'm twenty-six. If I'm going to start over with a new future I have to get serious."

I did say that. I've said a lot of stupid things in my life.

"I love our friendship and I don't want to hurt you, but I was thinking about it last night. What are we doing? Am I just going to keep playing around like a teenager. And then Geoff calls. First the Viper Rising opportunity, then Geoff comes back out of the blue? It has to be a sign that it's time to move forward, right?"

Has to be the universe fucking with me again. "I did believe that then, Han. But..."

But what, Wesley? But I love you so much that if you leave with this guy I'll implode? "I was wrong. I see things differently now. I think we can make it work."

Her smirk slices into me. "Yeah? With the groupies and strippers on the side? Right."

I feel sick. Even worse when her eyes fill with pity.

"Crap. I'm sorry. You're serious, aren't you?" She sighs and covers her face. "I... I don't know." Her beautiful features come into view again, and I swallow the urge to beg. "I'm afraid of you, Wes. Of us. What I feel for you is so... It's not safe. Not stable."

Blood rushes to every part of my body.

"It's so much. It's like, I do things without thinking. Every time we're within a few feet of each other, my brain shuts off."

I close the gap and tip her chin. Fine. I'm a dick. I'm not losing this woman to fucking *Geoffrey*. "No it doesn't. You just open yourself up to the part of you that's been cut off for most of your life."

"I become a rebel."

"You become a viper."

I kiss her then. I have to if this is the last chance I'll have to show her that she's better than who she thinks she should be. I part her lips with my tongue and find hers. She groans as her body responds to my demands.

"This is real," I breathe against her mouth. I reach for her top and pull it off. Even with the splints on my fingers there's no fumbling with clasps and straps. She's mine. *Mine,* and Geoffrey better be ready to fight his ass off.

We're on the couch now. I have Hannah pressed into the cool leather. Every muscle is tensed and ready for battle. I move against her, enjoying the way the reservation slips from her guard at each push of my hips. Her fingers spread over me, sinking into my flesh.

"I want this every day," I say. My lips trace down her neck to find her breasts. She's delicious, especially when she arches in unison with the pressure of my mouth. I don't stop until her hands are threaded in my hair, guiding me with an urgency that would make any man hard. Me? I'm granite.

"Wait, ahh!" She cuts off with a moan.

"You want me to wait?" I work my way down her smooth stomach and caress the skin along the edge of her jeans.

"No, don't wait. Just..." Another jerk of her body when I run my hand up the inside of her thighs.

"Just, what?" I free the button, slide down the zipper to expose the most mouthwatering black satin I've ever seen. This is viper fabric not country-club fabric.

I tug the elastic with my teeth and let it snap back with a playful grin. Her gasp is everything a guy lives for.

"Still want me to stop?" My lips come down hard on the soft material.

"No," she breathes.

I nibble harder with each shift down.

"No, because this is..." She's panting now. I can barely understand her through the short breaths. Until, "This is my point."

I pull back, eyes locking on hers. Her expression softens into a brutal plea. "You make me crazy, Wes. I lose control. Do you have any idea how scary that is?"

I live my entire life on that precipice. "That's living, Han," I manage, even as I watch her slip away. Her gaze drops to the floor.

"For you, maybe. For me..." She shimmies back and straightens on the couch.

Panic sets in. Fear that's not remotely eased by the sympathy on her face.

"For me, I need control. I need to let my brain make decisions. There are rules, Wes. An order. There's a way things are supposed to be."

"Yeah? Like locking yourself in a career you hate? Or dating some dude for his trust fund? That doesn't sound safe to me. That sounds like a recipe for lifelong depression."

What the fuck is wrong with you, Wes?

She bolts up from the couch.

"Han, I'm sorry. Hannah!"

I reach for her, but she backs away, throwing on clothing and shoes with careless fury.

"Will you just..."

She spins around, gaze searing into me. "Thanks for making this easier. Tell the Label we can do the audition in a few weeks when I get back."

And I've lost.

26

BLOODY HEARTS

To say I'm a mess over the next few weeks is inaccurate. I'm too numb to be anything. I'm an answer to interview questions. A signature on contracts. I'm a physical therapy patient and Holland's guide through our rehearsal, but I'm not Wes. Thanks to the pre-release hype, "Swan Song" kills it on the charts, and their tour gets off to a hot start. Critics rave it's our best yet. The Label freaks, the band celebrates, and I... crack a smile.

"Have you heard from her?" I ask Holland when we take five after several run-throughs of "Viper Rising" in my condo. She has a three-day break from the road and is devoting one of them to this song.

I get the *sister-look* I've come to dread and focus an intense stare on my water bottle.

"She planned to unplug while she was away. Take a break, you know?"

"Yeah, of course," I force out. "I get it."

She's not buying it. I see it in the way her gaze locks on me. "She just needs to figure things out. She cares about you."

"Cares, yeah. Great," I mutter. My fucking dentist *cares.* "When do you want to rehearse with the other guys?" No way I'm getting a pity talk from Holland about her sister.

"I'll check with them. We'll have to wait until Hannah is back."

Right. Our lead vocalist who I shoved away. "You should be prepared to sing her part."

Holland crosses her arms and shoots me another *look.* "Hannah won't back out. She has a problem with too *much* commitment to things, not the other way around."

"Yeah? Well, you didn't see her face when she stormed off."

"What did you say to her?"

"Something stupid I didn't mean. She won't respond to my messages now."

"Like I said, she—"

"Yeah, she unplugged. Have *you* heard from her in the last three weeks?"

She's suddenly very interested in her own water bottle.

"Holland, come on."

"I don't want to get involved. I can't, okay?"

I clench my jaw and struggle not to send a foot into the guitar stand. Then my heart collapses in my chest. "Wait, you know something," I say. "What has she said?"

"Wes, I can't. Don't put me in this position."

"Please!" God, I hate begging, but for all I've lost throughout my life, I've never suffered the black hole I'm in now. "What is it?"

She runs a hand over her flushed face, and I'm finding the air in this room less breathable by the second. "The cruise," she says finally.

"With the ex?"

She nods and huffs a breath that ruffles her bangs. "Geof-frey, yes."

"He wanted to work things out with her," I say. I don't like the way her lips thin into pale strips.

Her eyes suddenly search for everything in the vicinity except me. "Not exactly."

"What does that mean?" Is she trying to torture me?

After a long pause, she levels the most empathetic sister look I've ever seen. She hasn't said a word and already I'm spiraling.

"Holland, please. What's going on?"

She groans and rests her hands on her head. "Okay, fine, but please remember I didn't want to tell you this." I wait when she pauses. I wouldn't have been able to speak at this point anyway.

"Before Geoffrey talked to Hannah about the cruise, he had a long conversation with my parents."

I feel the blood draining from my face, probably pooling in my feet since suddenly I can't move.

Holland reaches for my arm, squeezing lightly as she says, "He asked for permission to propose to Hannah. That's what this cruise is about. That's probably why you haven't heard from her. I'm sure she wants to tell you in person."

The room is spinning. I drop to the couch as the walls crash down around me. "You *think* that's why she hasn't responded or you *know*?" I say finally. Tears. Yeah, that didn't sound like me because Wes Alton doesn't cry. But fuck if learning you've lost a woman like Hannah Drake doesn't make your eyes malfunction.

Holland wraps her arms around me, and it's everything I can do not to break down. I won't. I've lived almost thirty years without Hannah. So what if I have to live the next thirty? We'll still have our new band. We'll be friends. We'll be fucking *coworkers*. My shoulders shake from some foreign emotion as Holland holds tighter.

"I *think*," she says. "I don't *know*."

"God, I love her, Hol. I love her so much."

She nods against my chest, and I bury my face in her hair. I don't want to see right now. I just know I'll be staring into a rainbow of gray.

"I fucked up."

"You didn't."

"You don't understand."

She pulls back and forces me to look at her. "No, *you* don't. I'm not sure what you said to her, but that's not what changed her mind. I love my sister more than anything, but she doesn't choose with her heart. She chooses with her head and Geoffrey makes *sense*. They've been talking about marriage for a while."

"But she won't be happy!"

"You don't know that," she says, eyes full with my pain. "And even if she's not, it's her choice. She does what she's *supposed* to do. The easy, safe road. It's who she is."

I jump up, fingers tangled in my hair. "What can I do? Tell me, Hol. I'll do it. Just help me. Please!"

"Stop." She reaches out, but I duck away to keep pacing. My world is moving so fast and yet completely dark at the same time. Nothing makes sense. No, *everything* makes sense except for me. I'm the one who doesn't fit anymore.

"When's she coming back?" I ask, voice raspy.

"Two days."

I nod.

Her eyes... "It's too late, hon," she warns. I shake my head, and she sighs. "What are you going to do?"

I press my fists into my eyes.

"Wes, talk to me."

I draw in a deep breath and meet her gaze. "I'm going to find a way to give her my heart and force her to give it back."

DAY One of my mission starts the second Holland leaves my condo. I pick up my guitar and stare at my stiff fingers. The physical therapist said I'm not ready. He's probably right, but time isn't the only parameter that matters. Most of the damage to my left hand was to my ring and pinky finger, so tuning the strings doesn't present much of a challenge. With a little extra effort, I'm able to tighten and release the pegs enough to bring the pitch into an acceptable range.

My right index finger got pretty jacked up, however, so holding a pick is a problem. I drop it on the first two attempts, and the third results in one successful strum before the pick ends up in the body of my acoustic. I curse and jiggle the guitar with a gentle shake upside down until the pick clears the opening. I decide just to strum with my fingers for now. Even that is no easy task since I can't get my right thumb and index finger to meet. So no fingernail strum either. Oh, wait, the only chord I can form with my left hand is an awkward Em anyway. Shit. I lay the worthless instrument on the couch and set up my keyboard instead.

After a few passes of the keys, I'm more confident. I don't have the dexterity I'd need to perform, but for writing, this will do. I open a new file on my laptop and set to work.

For three hours, I'm glued to my couch. Eventually, my back and ribs ache to the point of watery eyes. My fingers barely move. Just as Physical Therapist Jeff warned, I wasn't ready for this, but I push through until the pain and stiffness is so bad I can't press a key or type a letter no matter how hard I struggle.

I shut my laptop in disgust and fall back to the cushions. Staring at the ceiling, I try to gather the strength to move to the kitchen, but everything has become a lot more difficult without

Hannah. Even weeks after the fight, I feel my injuries more now than those first few days when she was my rock. Who knew broken ribs and fingers hurt so much?

My phone buzzes, and I yank it into view. I force a smile to mask the disappointment in my voice when I answer. Holland wants to know if I'll meet up with her and the guys for dinner. I ask her to tell the rest of the band I'm looking forward to playing with them again, but now's not a great time because... I'm busy? She pauses long enough to tell me that she *gets it*. Twenty years with someone make their silences as expressive as their words.

My gaze journeys to the mini-bar when we hang up. I study the beautiful tapestry of glass and color arranged on the marble top. I haven't touched it in weeks. I knew if I was going to get her back I'd have to put my life together, and I couldn't waste time on oblivion. But I had hope then. It was an argument I had to overcome, not a fucking marriage.

What's left of my hope now? A song. A string of notes and words that has to convince a viper that the life she chose is not the life she wants.

I curse and drape my arm over my face.

DAY TWO DOESN'T GO any better. This time I have to start off stiff, sore, and discouraged, and there's no improvement from there. No lyrics are striking enough. No melody haunts with the passion and desperation I need to convey. Nothing is good enough for my Hannah.

I spend hours deleting what I type, rearranging chords until they start to blend together in a squall of sound. I've said "my ears are bleeding" many times in my life. This is the first time I'm actually concerned it's true. Then again, maybe it's just my brain exploding after two days straight of this torture. Hours of non-stop effort and what do I have? Six words I hate.

Bloodshot eyes scratch through the veil

I lost track of which revision this is. I must have attempted a hundred opening lines. This is the latest, probably because I've reached the point where words are blurring and the physical becomes lyrical.

I'm definitely ready for a break when my phone rings. Not Hannah this time either. I sigh and connect with my sister.

"Hey, big bro!"

"Hey, bridezilla."

"Whatever. Are you still good for the processional? It's like two weeks away. How are the hands?"

"All good. Holland and I have run through the song. We'll do a full rehearsal with the band in a little bit."

"That's so great that you're playing with them after everything."

"Yeah."

She seems to want more, but I have nothing.

"Do I get a preview?" she asks finally.

"No way. You need to be surprised along with everyone else."

"Ooh, so mysterious. This is going to be epic!" I can picture her *epic dance* on the other end of the line.

"Hope so."

"And I can't wait to see Hannah sing!"

"Yeah." Maybe I'm being rude but I can't do this right now. "Hey, I've gotta get back to work, but you concentrate on being an awesome bride. We got this."

After we hang up, I use the break to shower and force some food down my throat. Then it's another longing glance at the bar before I grab a bottle of water instead. Hannah comes home soon, and I'm not giving up without a fight.

IT'S LATE, too late for a knock. My gaze springs to the door, and I force my stiff legs to straighten. Cops? Building security? Pranksters? Who assaults someone's residence at this hour?

Hannah Drake.

I stand in shock. Hand gripping the doorframe, I can only stare at the most gorgeous person—*thing*—I've ever seen. Her eyes radiate with the glow of a woman in love, skin golden from the caress of the sun. It's painful how beautiful she is.

The ache knots in my throat, but I refuse to give in. No, I'm fighting. I will fight until the ring on her finger is a gold band instead of a diamond. My eyes drop in search of the evidence, but she has her hands tucked in her back pockets. On purpose? Probably.

"Sorry, it's late. Can I come in?"

I nod and shift so she can pass. The fresh and flowery scent I've come to crave washes over me as she brushes by. I have to clench my fists to keep from taking her in my arms for a taste. Just one touch. I concentrate on locking the door instead.

"We need to talk," she says, and my limbs go numb.

"Wait. Before that, can I just..." I scrub at my face. "Can I just play something for you?"

"Wes, I—"

"Please. I'm begging you, just listen?" I *am* begging. Desperation seeps from my pores, fills the space around us. I move to the keyboard before she can argue and start playing.

The signature rasp in my voice is almost a croak as I make my way through the song, but I fight on. I need her to understand. Even if she walks out of here to become Mrs. Country

Club, I need her to do it with my heart in her hands. So I play. The concert of my life, I pour out my soul for this woman.

> Bloodshot eyes scratch through the veil and
>   find you, find you
> Truth locked beyond my reach
> You flood in, addictive fangs, sink deep
> So deep I bled
> For you,
> Fled, for you
> Chased the moon, I died and came back for you
>
> Wrapped in you
> Trapped trapped, before I knew
> How to survive the loss
> When you find me too, those hidden parts
> I blocked, beyond your reach
>
> Your perfection is
> My rejection, burns
> Hot through the bloody heart you own
> Until the beat, beat, beat
> Stops.

I look up at the abrupt ending that I left purposely unresolved. It's her song to finish, not mine.

Her eyes are glossy when I find them. The emotion has to match mine as I wait in agony, and she reaches up a hand to clear the tears. It's then that I see it on her left hand: Nothing. Fucking *nothing!*

"Geoff proposed on the cruise... I said no."

My empty chest fills with flowers and hope and a soul-crushing love as I constrict her against me before she can utter another word.

"Thank god," I whisper against her hair, and her own arms tighten around my back. "Thank god."

HANNAH IS SETTLED into me on the couch as we talk. I stroke my fingers over her arms, her neck, her cheek. Anywhere I can reach, I want to touch.

"Frankly, I was shocked by the proposal," she says. "I don't know what he was thinking. And how awkward is that? Stuck on a boat with someone for two weeks? I said I'd think about it because, can you imagine sharing a cabin with a guy you rejected? Geez," she laughs.

I swallow my jealousy at the thought of her sharing a cabin with *any* guy and rest my lips on the side of her neck.

She squirms against my hold. "That tickles!"

"Yeah?" I go in for another taste. She reaches back to swat me away.

"I'm trying to talk!"

"I'm listening."

"No, you're not. You're horny."

"I'm always horny for you, babe."

She bursts out laughing and twists to give me a look. "Whatever." After a sigh, she leans into me again. For someone who finds my horniness funny, she doesn't seem to have any issues feeding it with her own exploration of my body while she talks. "Anyway, you know what he said after I told him I needed to think?"

"I would have jumped off the boat."

"I know." She pulls my hand to her lips, and I feel the tingle spread with irresistible urgency. "But not Geoffrey. No, he smiled—actually *smiled*—and said that was smart. Not even in a 'just to be polite' way. He meant it!"

"Fucking idiot."

"Don't be mean. But yeah, that's when I knew without a doubt."

She shifts so we're chest to chest now.

"Knew what?"

"That's not the kind of love I want. I want a burning, bloody heart I can own."

And I kiss her. I inhale her. I claim her until she has no choice but to hand over her burning, bloody heart as well.

27

REHEARSAL

The gang's all here, including a new face I don't recognize. Dark, mysterious, and exuding solemn confidence, he's the exact opposite of his girlfriend, Sylvie Drake. I would have known this was Shandor even without the blond energy-ball fawning all over him.

"Wes!"

The entire room zeroes in on me when Spence comes rushing over for a vicious man-hug. Okay, so maybe I missed the guy. He's no longer my drummer, but he'll always be a good friend.

"Hey, dude. Good to see you."

"Been a minute. What's with the drama?" he says with an arm-punch.

"Why, you been bored without me?"

The others have joined us now too, and we exchange a variety of greetings. Even Luke—Shit, Luke?—gets a hand-shake. I feel Hannah's amusement behind me before she goes in for a full-on hug with the guy. Not blowing a gasket when my girlfriend hugs my nemesis—fucking weird. But here we are. All greeted, smiling, and ready for me to meet my replacement.

"You must be Shandor." I offer my hand. He returns a firm grip that doesn't suck, and I point to the rack near where he was before. "That yours?"

"Yeah."

"A Starplayer, huh? Damn." His severe expression breaks into a grin at my admiration of his baby. "May I?"

He nods, and I remove the guitar from its stand. I inspect the shiny black finish and gold pick guard. Not brand new, but in good condition. This dude takes care of his shit. His pedal board is impressive too. Pretty sick, actually.

"I also use my Les Paul on tour," he says, amber eyes testing me right back?

"Yeah? Sweet." I return the guitar to the rack and slap his arm. "Heard good things, man."

When I turn back around, everyone is staring like I'd just done an arabesque. I swear, everyone wants you to be a decent person, and when you are, they go all cross-eyed.

"Shandor used to live in Slovenia," Sylvie announces, throwing her arms around his waist.

"Romania, babe," he mutters. "And I've lived in a lot of places."

"Duh, that's what I meant." She rolls her eyes and flips multi-colored strands of hair over her shoulder. Blue, pink, purple (is that a feather?) are scattered over her long blonde locks the same color as Holland's. Hannah is the outlier in the family with her smooth chocolate waves that I can't stop running my hands through. Even now, I refuse to move on until I pull her against me and plant a kiss on those flower-scented curls. She twists back to give me a smile, and I have to taste that too.

"You ready?" I brush her lips with mine.

Holland shoves me toward a mic. "Ugh, get a room."

I laugh and begin adjusting the stand. It's then that I notice the other is still vacant. Hannah hasn't budged.

"Come on, Han. Right here." I point to the microphone beside me.

A terror fills her eyes that sucks the humor out of me. "One sec," I direct to the others and duck around the wedges to meet the girl stationed by the equipment cases.

"What's going on, babe?" I lift her chin. "You ready to do this?"

Her gaze shoots to the makeshift stage setup and back to me.

"I don't think I can," she whispers. "I..." Her ragged breath burns my own lungs, and I draw her into me.

"Of course you can. You're my viper," I say against her ear. "You're going to go over there and kick this song's ass. *Your* song."

Her nod contains zero conviction, and I raise her face again with a stern expression.

"Okay, look. See that guy playing drums? That's Spence. He agreed to sub-lease his apartment to Shandor. Shandor claims that he paid Spence a security deposit, but now Spence refuses to return it."

A smile starts to lift the corner of her lips, and I grow even more severe. "The lessee claims that Shandor broke the agreement by moving his pet alligator in, when clearly that wasn't allowed per Article Four of the lease."

"Lessor," she mumbles, burying her face in my shirt.

"Huh?"

"Spence is the lessor. Shandor is the lessee."

"Smart-ass." Her laugh vibrates through my chest, and I tighten her to me. "Fine, whatever. What's your ruling?"

"Depends. Was it a service alligator?"

I snort a laugh. "You ready, babe?"

This time I believe her nod, and after a long, stabilizing breath, I lead her by the hand to the stage.

"Ladies and gentleman. May I introduce the incomparable, Hannah Drake."

Cheers and applause ring out from our little audience, and my heart bursts at the grin that spreads over my angel's face.

"Thank you, thank you. Please hold the applause until after the performance," she says before being swarmed by her two sisters in an explosion of Drake-affection.

"We doing this or what?" I tease, and shrink at the triple death stare. "Just asking."

Hannah smiles over to me as she breaks away and approaches the stand. Her fingers wrap around the mic clip, and Luke adjusts it for her.

"That good?" he asks. "Make sure it's... yep, there you go."

I nod a thank-you in his direction, and he steps back to observe. Sylvie is... oh, seated on Shandor's amp. He whispers something to her, and she scurries over to stand by Luke.

"Okay, well, you've all heard the song?" I ask, scanning the others.

"We've run through it a couple of times," Holland says. "Shandor has a pretty sick riff you're gonna love."

I glance back at my replacement. "That so?"

He shrugs, intense yellow eyes alive with excitement. Okay, yeah. I like this guy.

"Just a couple progressions on the bridge."

"Dude, and that chorus thing," Spence calls over from behind his kit.

"Oh yeah. There's a lead line on the chorus I thought would be cool."

"Sounds good, man," I say with a smile. "Can't wait to hear it. Count us off?" I direct to Spence.

He nods and taps his sticks in the air. One. Two. Three. Four.

THE FIRST RUN-THROUGH is good considering we've never played it together before. They were right. I love Shandor's leads and make a couple of suggestions that he rocks like a pro. Spence kills it on drums, adding an edge our living room acoustic version couldn't touch, and then there's Holland. Playing with her again, it's like coming up for air after being sucked into a riptide. Even though she's changed up her part from our solo rehearsal, I know what she'll do when she does it. The tone of her guitar is as familiar to me as her voice, and the way she makes it sing—pure magic.

But in a room full of rockstars, it's ex-lawyer Hannah Drake who leaves a reverent silence in her wake when the last note rings out. We all stare at the stranger before us, this soul who came alive for five minutes and transformed into something of another world. She's human again when we exchange a grin and her face flushes with a mix of embarrassment and euphoria. I know the feeling. It never goes away; you just learn to mask it better.

"Damn," I say, breaking the spell before things get awkward.

"Wow," Holland adds.

"Can I have an autograph?" Luke calls over, and Hannah snorts.

"Stop it, guys."

"Better get used to it, Han," I say, enjoying the way her nose scrunches in response.

She straightens and whips back to face the band. "Are we running it again or what?"

———

THE UNIVERSE FEELS RIGHT for the first time in a long time when Hannah throws herself back on my couch. I lock the door behind us and move to the kitchen.

"Wow, that was intense," she says through a long breath. She sits up to peer over the backrest. "Are you getting water?"

"Want some?"

"Please."

I grab a couple glasses and open a bottle of seltzer.

"Ooh, so fancy," she gushes as I hand her the fizzy drink.

"Figured we should celebrate."

"It *was* a pretty good rehearsal." She inches forward and holds up her glass.

"Nah, not that."

"To the first official performance of Viper Rising?"

I shake my head. "Close."

"Ugh, just say it," she groans, flicking water at me.

I laugh and wipe the drops off my cheek. Finally, I raise my glass and touch hers. "To me."

Her entire body participates in the eye roll. "Seriously?"

I smirk and silence her with a kiss. "I didn't finish," I breathe against her lips. "To me. For having the sexiest, smartest, most talented girlfriend on the planet."

Two blue pools widen and melt as they search my face.

"My god," she whispers before leaning in and brushing her lips against mine. "You're so... Freaking... Ridiculous."

She shrieks through a shower of seltzer water.

28

WEDDING

A pair of arms slither around my waist from behind. I lock them in mine as I stare at my reflection in the floor-length mirror.

"Wow." Hannah pokes her head to the side for a better view. "Although most guys button their dress shirts for formal occasions."

"Working on it," I mutter. "Can't believe she talked me into a tux."

Hannah's hands wriggle free to climb my bare chest, shooting electricity over my skin. "Sophia will change her mind when she sees what you've done to it. Here, let me."

She tugs the open sides of my shirt to turn me, and I suck in a breath.

"Holy shit." My gaze spreads over the goddess before me. "That's what you were doing in the bathroom all day?"

"You like it?"

She spins so I can appreciate every seam and strap of the black slip that makes her look... Stunning? Exquisite? Ex-boyfriend-slaying? Geoffrey would crap his pants.

I groan and shake my head. "There's no way in hell I can spend an entire day being good with you looking like that."

Her lips spread into a sardonic grin I feel in my bloodstream. "You'll manage. Let's work on you. Those buttons must be complicated."

"I have a better idea. Let's release some of these pre-wedding jitters." I raise my eyebrows and nod toward the bed.

"After all the time I spent on hair and makeup? Not a chance, hot stuff. Keep it in your pants."

She swats my hands away and continues working on the buttons.

"I mean, there are options that would leave both in pristine condition," I point out, sampling the skin on her shoulder. Yep, tastes as good as it looks. I move up her neck.

Her snort-laugh isn't very encouraging. "Oh yeah?" she purrs, fingers moving into my hair. She forces my face up and deposits a solid kiss on my lips. "Here's the problem," she says. So innocent.

"Damn, woman."

She turns my head to the mirror. "Red lipstick isn't a great look on you."

"Hmm... But *you* are."

She giggles. "You're impossible."

MY MOOD CHANGES the closer we get to the venue. Security has been instructed to watch for me, so the plan is for Holland to let us in through a loading door in the back. I get the word from Jesse that Limelight is onsite and set up. We'll be using their equipment, which is in place for the rest of the ceremony.

"It's going to be like a Processional Flash Mob," Hannah whispers, eyes alive with excitement.

I force a smile, but my mood is less forgiving. Truth is, what seemed like a no-brainer months ago now seems unforgivably stupid. It's a new status for me: concern. Suddenly, I want Sophia to have an amazing wedding more than I want to piss off my parents. This caring-thing sucks. Makes things complicated.

"You okay?" Hannah asks as we hover outside the locked door.

"Fine," I lie.

"You look... Wait, are you nervous?"

Her worry is too sincere for me to handle right now, so I focus on the scars etched into the steel door. "If I get kicked out, don't follow."

"Wes..."

"I'll be fine. Just promise me you'll stay and support Sophia." I finally meet her eyes and watch her soften with compassion. Makes no fucking sense, but there she is. This goddess-angel melting for a snake. I press my lips to hers in the lightest of touches. Reverent so as not to disturb perfection.

A scrape at the door sends lightning surging through me. We step back as Holland pushes through and waves us inside.

"I feel like an accomplice to a crime," she whispers, successfully looking the part with her furtive peeks around each corner and open doorjamb.

I huff a wry smile. "I don't think there's much of a punishment for accessory to trespassing, but I promise to keep your name out of it."

She shoots back a mock glare before continuing to guide our covert team. We pass a few witnesses on the way, mostly catering and facility staff. Despite the looks, no one says a word, and I'm sure they wouldn't have thought twice if we weren't creeping around like bandits in our formalwear.

"Here," Holland whispers, pulling to a stop. She knocks on a door, and Spence's head appears through the crack.

"Hey, man! You showed."

"Shh!" Holland hisses at him as we sneak inside.

"Of course I showed," I say once we're safe and I scan the room. It's not the elaborate green room I'm accustomed to. Audio equipment, stacks of mismatched chairs, and piles of I-couldn't-begin-to-guess cram the perimeter of the space. We're practically standing on top of each other to fit. Sucks being the fake band at an event. Jesse and the gang are probably sipping champagne and snacking on caviar while we pack into the storage closet next door.

"I spoke to Sophia when we arrived," Holland whispers. "Here's what's happening: Limelight is going to take the stage as planned. When it's time for Sophia to enter with your father, Limelight will move off, and we'll go on." She quiets when my jaw tightens. "She's hoping that your parents will want to save face and not make a scene."

I nod. "She always was the more optimistic of us."

Holland squeezes my arm. "It means the world to her that you're even trying to do this. If it fails, you've still won."

"Minus the prison thing."

She rolls her eyes, and I smile. "See that door there?" She points to the opposite wall from where we came in. "That leads right onstage. Jesse is going to shoot a text when it's time, and then we go out."

"Dude, the place is jammed," Spence says. "How does your family know so many people?"

"They probably don't," I mutter. I swear a colony of ants is crawling over my nervous system. Each second is torture on my patience as adrenaline displaces the fear. I'm ready, fucking primed to fight and take this conspiracy public. I hope my father detonates. I could use a good confrontation. My fists are already clenching in anticipation when a soft hand slips into mine and the ants go still. Everything calms and becomes a moment in the present instead of a vision of the future. I'm here. Now. With the woman I love, about to do something completely stupid and amazing. This isn't Hell; this is paradise.

I toss a smile at her, and she squeezes.

"We're on," Holland whispers and points toward the door.

THE MURMURS about the bride's appearance at the back of the aisle shift to a different tone when we take the stage. Jesse nods as we pass, and I return it.

I see my mother first. Pale, she grips the back of a chair for support.

That's right, Mom. Faint. Your friends will love it.

I search down the aisle for Sophia and find the second most beautiful woman in the room. She's glowing when our gazes connect. Frederick Alton? Not so much. He flinches and steps forward, but Sophia pulls him back and tucks her hand in his elbow. She whispers something that slows his boil to a simmer. He gives me a look that promises future pain, but for now, the show's on.

At center stage, Hannah is rigid, knuckles white as they choke the mic stand. I've seen naked fear like that before, scanning a canvas of strangers as though they hold power over your existence. *I* had those eyes once, still do at times, and I will Hannah to look at me for reassurance. She's gone though, lost in that place where excitement meets terror.

Her attention stalls on something, and I spot a row of Drake sunshine near the back. I wait as those big blue eyes find me next. It's a second that feels eternal. I'm obsessed with making her thrive.

You got this! I mouth and signal Spence to count us in before she can believe the lies her brain screams at her.

The band crashes in with a four-chord progression that shrieks over satin ribbons and obscene flower arrangements. In-your-face alternative angst slides through our veins, pushing us toward Hannah's entry. I glance over and suck in a breath at what I see. She's a woman ready to run, not fly.

Shit.

I gesture behind my back for the band to repeat the intro.

Hannah's attention snaps to me, trance broken. Her lips brush the mic and give me hope.

"Coil of strength wound tight to hide," she leaks out too softly. Her nerves. God, her fear is audible, and I jump in to cover the verse with her. Our eyes meet through our duet, and I smile until she does. Until her gaze brightens with belief.

> "Dirty secrets revealed
> The bed
> I made
> Was never the place
> To trap this broken soul"

Strength suffuses her voice.

> "It's over!"

Adrenaline blasts through me. She's got this.
We're locked in!

> "Stand back, you're gonna want to stand back!"

I ease off the mic and turn the song over to its owner at the chorus. I'm just a backing vocal now. It's *her* show.

Her goth-cut mini-dress wrecks me as she gets lost in the music. Her gritty, airy tone is chaos and beauty, melting my sister's makeup with tears as she moves down the aisle.

I'm making Sophia's dream come true while we break every social convention I hate. Yeah, this moment? Fucking epic, and I pour it all into my harmonies. All I'm missing is a phantom guitar I'm desperate to abuse.

Hannah kills the bridge. Eyes closed, microphone bonded with her fist, she melts into the music with an intoxicating flood I feel in my own soul. Vaguely, I notice all eyes glued to the bombshell owning the moment. My viper, slaying her prey.

She writhes to the beat, unaware of how hypnotic she is.

> "I'm breaking free to strike
> Fangs bared, spring out, out
> Of hell, don't tell
> Me what I am"

She's an artist, owning her song in a private moment. Words curl into adlib runs and variations on the final chorus as some of the guests move to the heavy crunch of a tune that has no business in a scene like this.

I harden at the sight of Hannah coiled around the mic stand—*lying in wait, holding tight, ready to strike.*

When the final chord rings out, I inhale. Look out over the audience and capture the rainbow of expressions coloring them.

Who knew there were so many types of shock? Shocked horror, shocked amusement, shocked wonder, shocked glee, and just your average run-of-the-mill shocked shock of those who can't even process what happened. I recognize many of the faces and love the fact that this will be my legacy.

Against all protocol, a raucous applause erupts, triggered by the bride's rush onstage. She throws her arms around my neck, and I swing her up for tight hug.

"Thank you, thank you. It was perfect!" she says against my shoulder.

I kiss her cheek. "I love you, sis. Congratulations."

Sophia returns to her place between her almost-husband and our father. Dad's reaction... Definitely no tears. His eyes hold a hatred that even I have to admire. My mother's face is a twisted grimace, and I suck in a ragged breath. Then I see it. His nod to security.

Fuck. Really?

The officiant begins his greeting while I spot the men collecting along the perimeter of the room. I squeeze Hannah's hand. She looks up, and her beautiful smile fades.

"I have to go," I whisper. "Remember what you promised." I hate the alarm on her face and give her a quick kiss. "I'll be fine. See you later."

With that I do my best to retreat as discreetly as possible toward the closest member of the advancing security team. I look him straight in the eye as I approach and tilt my head toward the exit. He seems to understand, and I raise my hands slightly in surrender. I can practically feel his breath on my skin as he hovers centimeters away the entire journey from the room. I almost smirk at the thought that most of the guests probably assume they're *my* bodyguards. I can't bear to look back at the reactions of those who know differently.

"This way," he says, grabbing my arm once we're clear of the guests.

I jerk against his grip. "The exit is over there."

"Yeah, you're not leaving," another one says, twisting my other arm behind my back.

"The fuck?" I seethe through clenched teeth.

"You're trespassing. Your father is going to want to talk to you. You can wait for him downstairs."

They shove me along a service hallway and through a fire door. Down a flight of stairs and a few turns later, we're facing a heavy door. The one holding me shoves me into it while another searches me and removes my wallet and phone.

"What the fuck are you doing?" I shout, struggling against them.

"Take it easy. Just—"

I jolt back to free myself and give them an icy look.

"Give my shit back," I grit out. Four-on-one this time, but I still eye each of them slowly.

"We don't want trouble," one says.

Great, so these guys trained at the Bouncer Academy too. Flashbacks of the encounter outside of Harem drain some of the violence from my blood. Wonder if they were classmates?

"Neither do I, so just give me my stuff, and I'm gone."

"Frederick—"

"You know what? You can tell him to fuck off. If he wants to fight he can face me himself."

They exchange a look, and I can see the bouncer training rattling around in their thick skulls.

"Phone, please," I say, interrupting the painful-looking brainstorming session.

"Not gonna happen, guy," one of them decides finally.

"So what? We're just going to stand here staring at each other?"

They don't like my sarcasm, which is unfortunate because I'm already holding back like a champ.

"Fine," I grunt, leaning my back against the wall. I cross my arms and stare directly at them in the most awkward standoff in history. They clearly don't know what to do with me. I see their fists clench and release in a desire to knock me senseless, but I'm not your average party-crasher. No, this dilemma has them way out of their depth. "Can we at least sit?" I point to a stack of chairs.

"Don't move."

I relax into my stance. "What did you think of the processional? Acoustics in the venue could have been better, but a good effort overall. You guys into music?"

"Shut up."

"I'll take that as a no."

I don't stand a chance if I piss them off to the point of violence, but damn, it's so tempting. Being held hostage for crashing my sister's wedding? Kind of a fitting scene, really, and I'm starting to get excited about a confrontation with Dad. Maybe this is the part of the movie where, after a lifetime of opposition, this one moment draws that *good work son* nod of understanding. God, I hope he doesn't try to hug me.

"What's so funny?" Man-Bun growls.

"Nothing. It's not you." *Well, it's kind of you.* I study them again and can't help but think they would have made the perfect boyband twenty years ago. Missed opportunities, man. What can you do? "I heard there'll be an oyster bar at the reception. You pumped for that?" Their glares harden, and I hold up my hands. "Okay, sorry. Not shellfish guys. I get it."

"I thought we told you to stop talking."

"No, I know. You did. I was just so distracted by your suits. Be honest, did you coordinate on purpose?"

I guess they draw the line at fashion because soon I'm slamming into the wall, jaw throbbing. I swallow the pain and reach up to inspect the damage. I know the flavor of blood well, and a few drops stain the concrete floor.

"Did he give instructions to fuck me up too?" I ask through a taunting smile.

"He didn't give instructions *not* to," Shaved Head snarls. So clever, these guys.

"Good news then, gentlemen. I've met with my fair share of hired muscle over the years, and you are easily among the most well-groomed."

I have a harder time shaking off the next blow when it crashes into my sore ribs. Hunched over, I rest my hands on my knees to catch my breath.

"Had enough yet? Ready to shut your mouth?"

I want to. I really do, but these guys say this shit with a straight face. "Yeah, I'm done." I hold up a hand from my bent position. "Just, are the bouncer makeovers part of the training or is there some special salon for that?"

I don't bother fighting back this time. I need my hands more than my face at this point. Protecting your hands with your face —there's a new one. I'm ready for my second blackout in a month when suddenly, it stops.

Coughs rack my body as I fight to draw air into aching lungs. At some point, I should figure out how to keep my mouth shut, but for now my focus is on piecing the swirling hallway back together. That effort becomes easier when I realize I'm no longer the center of attention.

I glance up at the intruder to find the last person on this planet I expected to see.

"This is a private matter," Shaved Head barks at Luke.

He studies the scene with casual interest. "Yeah? Kind of looks like assault to me."

"He was resisting," Man-Bun argues.

"Resisting what exactly?" Luke asks, and even I have to smirk at the innocent trap.

"He was trespassing," Shaved Head says. "Frederick Alton—"

"Frederick Alton authorized a hit on his son at his daughter's wedding? That's going to be a fun headline for him."

The hallway is flooded with concerned looks as the message sinks in. I have no idea what their orders were at this point, but watching them realize they don't understand them either is hilarious.

"Tell you what," Luke says finally. "I happen to know this asshole. I'm willing to bet he'll keep this to himself if you do."

"*And* if you return my shit," I add.

Shaved Head straightens, puffs, and flaunts, but Luke doesn't budge. The dude just looks impatient as he waits for these idiots to make their decision. It takes an eternity for Shaved Head to grunt and nod to Man-Bun, who holds my belongings out to me.

"Not a word," he hisses before letting go.

"Fuck you," I say, and yank them away.

They delay for a few more menacing alpha-struts and disappear up the stairwell.

Luke snickers and drops to the floor beside me. "Dicks."

We stare at the opposite wall in silence as I wipe at the blood on my face with my sleeve.

"Thanks, man," I say. "Were you looking for me?"

"Not my choice, believe me," he mutters.

"Holland?"

"Yep."

"Yeah, you can't say no to Holland."

"Never."

Maybe we both kind of smile at that.

I lean my head against the wall. "Has she done the lip thing yet?"

"Where the bottom one juts out in that cute pout?"

I glance over. "Yeah, that one. It's brutal."

He lets out a breath. "I don't even think she does it on purpose. She's just naturally irresistible."

"Yeah, don't look at her if you want to win. I saved all my non-negotiables for the phone."

"Good tip."

I close my eyes. "She's amazing, man. You got a good one."

"I know. I'm going to do right by her."

I release my clenched fist. *I know.*

"Hannah is waiting outside for you. I'm sure she's freaking out," he says.

"I told her not to follow me."

He laughs. "Dude, she's a Drake."

"How did that happen anyway? Two assholes like us landing two goddesses like them?"

Luke shrugs. "Hell if I know." He stands and reaches out a hand to me. I pause and finally let him pull me to my feet. "Gotta be honest, dude. I don't hate seeing you all fucked up."

SOPHIA INSISTED ON A "SHORT" ceremony, so the guests are filtering from the chapel area to the main ballroom when we make our way upstairs.

I limp along behind Luke, doing my best *I don't look like roadkill* impression. Kind of hard to pull off with welts on your face and giant swatches of blood covering your fancy tux, but whatever. No one wants to risk their own couture wedding attire, so it's a pretty seamless exit. Security Dude at the main door wasn't part of the Fabulous Foursome who took me out, and lets me pass with only a brief wrinkle in his grave security-face. Hannah is another story.

"Oh my... Wes!" she cries, rushing over.

I step back with a wry smile. "Don't ruin your dress."

She wraps her arms around me. "Shut up."

I rest my cheek on her head and finally feel like I can take a full breath. "Yeah, my chat with security didn't go so well."

"Not funny." She pulls back and reaches a tentative hand up to my face. I let her look. This is what she chose for better or for worse. She grabs my hands and lets out a relieved sigh.

"I didn't fight back," I say. "We need those."

She squeezes and brings my fingers to her lips. "It's not right," she whispers, meeting my eyes again.

I shrug. "It's my reality."

Luke hovers nearby on his phone. Probably filling Holland in on the rescue.

And then I see him. Storming forward, face a mask of rage.

"Go back inside," I say to Hannah and step in front of her. I curse to myself when I feel her hand on my back in support. I'd rather her see me beaten by ten dudes than witness a confrontation with my father.

"How dare you?" he growls, stomping toward me, finger extended in impressive outrage.

"She's my sister. Did you really think you could keep me away?"

"She is not your sister because you are not my son! Was this disgusting idea yours or Sophia's? When I find out, so help me..."

"Mine." I swallow the throbbing pain so I can straighten to my full height.

His skin turns purple, veins protruding from his neck and forehead. This can't be good for his arteries.

"You ruined Sophia's wedding. You crossed a line I thought even *you* would never cross."

"I saved her wedding. You heard her. She loved it." I can pull off seething anger too.

"You're lucky I don't have you arrested for trespassing!"

"Go ahead. I'll tell them about the assault while they're here."

He's shaking now. The finger returns to shout what his lips can't. "Stay away from my family."

If I was confused about his words, his eyes leave no doubt. I am not part of that group. I am not an Alton.

Hannah slips an arm around my waist, and I tuck her against my side. Holland has joined Luke, which means she saw it as well. Great. I kiss Hannah's hair while they stare in stunned silence.

I squint after the burning freight train that *was* my father. Dude looks like a troll whose favorite bridge just collapsed as he marches away. "The photographer is gonna have a blast with the family shots," I say.

Hannah laughs and drags me toward the street. "Let's get you home, rockstar."

HANNAH HELPS me into my condo for the second time in recent history. "You could have stayed at the reception with Holland and Luke," I say. "I'm sure Limelight is killing it."

"I'm sure. But I'm more interested in keeping you alive at the moment."

"Aww, she loves me," I tease.

"I need you. You're my meal ticket. Sit." She points to the couch. "And strip."

"Damn. So bossy."

A smile escapes through her resolve, and I gladly play along. But her humor wilts when I shrug out of my shirt.

"I'm fine, Han," I say as her gaze slides from one section of my bruised chest to the next. "A lot of this is still the original injuries. Just a few are new."

"Yeah, well, it's getting *old*," she mutters on her way to gather first aid supplies.

"The price of dating Wes Alton, babe," I call out. I don't earn any points for that, and she seems even more annoyed when she returns.

"You know there are other ways to handle conflict, right? Or did you skip that day of kindergarten."

I flinch at the categorically unsympathetic application of alcohol to a gash on my face.

"Tell that to the assholes who keep insisting on crossing my path."

She's not impressed by my defense. "Strip club bouncers, maybe. But your father's wedding security? Really, Wes?"

"Come on. You saw them," I groan. "Even a nun wouldn't have kept her mouth shut."

There's the hint of my girl's smile—and she's not happy about it.

"A nun would have offered assistance," she says.

"I did. I had all kinds of feedback for them."

She can't resist my crooked grin and snorts. "I'm sure you did." Her gaze softens as she searches my eyes. "Seriously, though, you okay?"

"Of course. This was nothing compared to the Harem thing."

"That's not what I mean." She anchors my face so I can't look away. "Your father had you jumped at your sister's wedding and then disowned you. There has to be something going on in that untouchable badass brain of yours."

"He disowned me years ago."

I smother anything beyond that because that's all that matters. That's part of the frame that will support the next chapter of my life, along with Hannah, music, and a future of proving I'm not a mistake. Yeah, this next one will be pretty damn strong. Strong enough to support Hannah's as she builds her own.

"You should consider pottery," Hannah says. "Or yoga."

I lift the corner of my mouth in thought. "Or MMA?"

29

AUDITION

Viper Rising. Bloody Heart. Proving Scars.

Few things are more frightening for a musician than handing your soul to a jury of label executives. Our panel wants that times three.

"Why three songs? I don't understand," Hannah says, chewing on a nail as her knee vibrates the entire office complex. "They must not be sure about us."

"Will you relax? I doubt this building is rated for this kind of turbulence."

She shoots a fleeting smile and goes back to bouncing.

"I don't know if I can do this."

"Yeah it's too late. You're doing it."

Her gaze is hummingbird-fast all over the conference room. Her brain can't possibly be processing what she sees, and I shake my head with a grin before returning my attention to tuning my guitar. Thanks to the delay of the audition, I can finally play again. Holland still insisted on coming along to the Label's main office, but we lost her to a parade of people she had to greet while we're here.

"I shouldn't have worn this outfit," Hannah mutters through my dissonant twang of the D string.

"You look great." I move on to the G.

"Maybe I should have straightened my hair?"

"Natural is good." *Damn, this thing didn't travel well.* The G is already way out from when I tuned it on arrival.

"Am I wearing too much makeup? Probably not enough actually. I don't look like a rockstar. I should have had Sylvie help me get ready."

The B string is much better. Just a tad flat.

"Makeup is fine."

And finally the E. I'd been tempted to change my strings, but I prefer the richer tone after they're broken-in to the tinny new-string sound.

"What if I forget the words? What if I come in at the wrong time or—"

I grunt and grip her chin. "Han, you are perfect. Your look, your voice—who you are—is perfect. You were born for this. I wouldn't be here with you if I didn't believe that." I place a firm kiss on her lips and return to my guitar.

The tapping moves to her foot. "Okay, but—"

I silence her with a hard stare, and Holland prevents my brain from exploding by bursting into the room. "Good, I didn't miss it!"

"No, we haven't seen them yet," I say, strumming a few test chords.

She nods and drops to a chair beside her sister. "You ready?"

I shake my head with a forceful *stop!* to Holland. She scrunches her nose back at me, and Hannah spins to check what she's missing. She shoves me when she sees my face.

"Well, excuse me for not being a rock god for most of my

life. Some of us have never done this before." She crosses her arms. "I'd like to see you in a courtroom."

I shrug. "Sure. Sounds fun."

One day I'll confess that her vexed-face is ninety percent of what makes it fun to provoke her, but for now I just enjoy the cuteness overload.

A knock on the open conference room door draws our attention. We stand to greet Pam, Raymond, and another man I vaguely recall as Maurice.

"Wes, Holland. Good to see you again," Pam says, shaking our hands. "And you must be Hannah."

Hannah rocks an electric smile as she returns the greeting. "It's great to be here. Thank you for taking the time for us."

"Well, we loved the demo," Raymond says, then introduces the three of them. They take seats at the table, settling in for our performance. Hannah follows me to the stools at the front of the room, and I toss her a wink.

"You ready, babe?" I ask, and my stomach drops at the look on her face. "You got this," I whisper.

She returns an absent nod, eyes huge and glued to the small audience.

Come on, Han.

"This first song is the one from our lunch meeting called 'Viper Rising.' Hannah and I co-wrote it and we performed it at my sister's wedding," I say.

"It was amazing," Holland adds.

I check Hannah one more time but she's completely frozen.

"One sec." I hop off my stool and block their view of her. I bend down to be eye-level. "Hey, babe."

She blinks, and I see the terror on her face.

"Do me a favor. Close your eyes."

Does she even hear me?

"Trust me, Han. Just close your eyes." She does, and I squeeze her fingers. "We're in my condo, okay? On the couch. You're wearing those butt-ugly sweats that still look sexy on you." A slight smile tickles her lips. "So we just finished watching Judge Whatever and now we're going to jam for a bit. You wrote these killer lyrics about a woman who kicks the world's ass. You're fired up and excited and ready to do some ass-kicking of your own." She opens her eyes, and I breathe again at the clarity there. She's back. "You got this." I kiss her cheek and return to my stool.

"'Viper Rising,'" I say, and start the intro.

HANNAH'S VOICE is good as we progress through the song, but not magical like it usually is. The nerves are evident in her tone, which suffers from a slight pitchiness that's uncharacteristic of her raspy vocal. I do my best to cover with harmonies when I can, and honestly, she does pretty damn well for someone as terrified as she is. I've heard and seen a lot worse in these types of situations—you'd never know this was only her second public performance. Still, this isn't a talent show; this is the summit of a musician's climb, and I know in my gut as I read the faces of our small audience that it's not good enough.

I have the lead on "Bloody Heart" so it goes much smoother. Hannah's harmonies are crisp and haunting now that the pressure is off her. She's Hannah again, a beautiful hurting soul on my couch, trying to find her path.

By the time we get to "Proving Scars," we've found our groove. The nerves are past, and when we switch leads at the bridge, Hannah nails it. She even throws in an improvised run I had no idea she could do. Damn, she's a pro. Or could be if these critics give us a shot.

It's impossible to read the final verdict after we wrap. Will they "be in touch" or want to "get us into the studio for a demo"? I've heard both over the course of my career, and I know what Hannah's experiencing right now. She's wired for self-blame, to believe in her inadequacy. I already see the doubt on her face, the guilt for blowing it.

"Thank you," Raymond says with a tight smile. "We have a lot to discuss. We'll be in touch."

Fuck!

"Sounds great," I say. "May I have a word with you before we go?"

They exchange a look.

"Me too," Holland adds, and I shoot her a grateful glance.

Pam checks her watch. "Fine. We have another meeting, so make it quick please."

I smile my appreciation and turn to Hannah. "Hey, babe can you give us a second? We'll be right out."

Tears are already forming in her eyes when she nods. She knows. God, I hate this.

"Thanks for the opportunity," she says with a weak smile as she passes the executives.

"Thank you for coming out," Pam responds.

When we're alone, I take the seat across from them.

"Look, it was a little rough," I say. "But I'm telling you, that woman out there is magic. She's unpolished, sure, but she's raw and authentic, and people are going to love her."

Raymond lets out a long sigh. "We see that, Wes, we do, but her stage presence... Her voice is studio-ready. A rare find, really, but I'm not sure she has what it takes to perform."

I clasp my hands. "I promise you she does. You should have seen her at my sister's wedding. She killed it. Right, Hol?"

Holland nods. "She was phenomenal and that was a very high-stress situation."

I still can't interpret their expressions, but at least they're still in the room.

"I believe in her so much that I would stake my own assets and career on her. You want some kind of guarantee? Give me the paperwork. I'll sign."

And I will. I look each of them in the eye as they consider my offer.

"We're playing Nashville next month," Holland jumps in. "Let them do a showcase and open for us. I believe in them enough to stake my career too."

I stare at her in shock. She returns a smile, and I feel a warmth bubbling in my gut.

Pam hisses in a breath. "I don't know if it's really an acoustic duo crowd, Holland."

"We're not," I say at the same time Holland says "they're not." We exchange a smile.

Holland leans forward. "We backed them up at the wedding with a full band, and I'm telling you, the place was on fire. Hannah and Wes had snooty wedding guests on their feet."

"We'll have a full band together by then," I add. "You've only heard the work tapes really. The final will blow your minds, I promise. Hannah will be ready."

I'm not sure I've breathed in five minutes. I glance over to Holland and guess she hasn't either. We wait while they deliberate with silent looks and motions. And then...

One word siphons air back into the room: "Okay."

THE HALLWAY IS empty when we look for Hannah.

"I'll check the washroom," Holland says, and we move down the corridor. Leaning against the wall, I stare out the window and fight the urge to follow her inside. Was Hannah ready? Did I push her too far? Doubt, man. It sucks. And it's not something I do often or well. When it comes to Hannah, though, I'm learning that every decision takes on a new urgency for me.

I straighten when they emerge from the washroom. I pull Hannah into my arms, and mascara-stained eyes press against my shirt as she burrows into me.

"You did great, babe," I whisper against her hair.

"I blew it."

"No. Didn't Holland tell you? We're getting a showcase."

"I don't want to talk about it. Can we just go?" she replies, and I exchange a concerned look with Holland.

"Yeah. Let's grab some food on the way."

"I'm not hungry."

I sigh and raise her face to me. "I am, and you were amazing, okay?" After a gentle kiss, I sling my arm over her shoulders, grab the handle on my guitar case, and lead her toward the exit.

I ASK Hannah to stay with me for a few days. I'm worried about her being alone with her silence. Her parents were good for her, but the world of artistic rejection is mine. She will punish herself for what she perceives as a disaster of an audition, and I'm the one most equipped to prevent that.

The first few days are rough. The girl is stubborn when it comes to hating herself, and she won't even let me bring up the topic. We don't have time to waste if we're to be ready for the Nashville show, so I start pulling a band together the second we're back in Toronto. I call my buddies Pablo and Josh, killer studio musicians who are between gigs, to see if they're interested in Viper Rising. They jump at the opportunity, and we set up a rehearsal for later that week. After forwarding the work tapes of the songs for them to prepare, it's back to coaxing more magic from our co-lead.

Hannah gives me a brief acknowledgement when I join her on the couch before returning to the TV. Judge Crabby is yelling at someone for doing something stupid.

"We have a rehearsal on Thursday with our new band members, Pablo and Josh."

"Yeah? That will be fun for you," she says, eyes fixed on the screen.

"You too, because you'll be there."

"Uh, no I won't. I told you. I'm not doing this. I'm not good enough."

My jaw clenches as I study her in silence. I don't know if I can be compassionate, but I'm pretty damn sure I can pull off cruel to be kind. I grab the remote from her hand and turn the TV off.

"What the hell?" She lunges for it. "I was watching that!"

I hold it out of her reach. "I'll give it back in a second, but first you're going to listen."

Her eyes narrow. "It's not up for a debate. You were there. I choked. I can't do this."

"Yeah, I *was* there, and I watched you convince a major record label that they wanted to see more of you in a showcase." Her crossed arms don't budge, and I let out a breath. "God, Han. How can you not see? You were given an opportunity most musicians spend their lives trying to get and never do. With no experience, you went in there and impressed them to the point where they're allowing you to open for some of their top talent. Know what they said? Your voice is studio-ready."

Her stance shifts a bit.

"Studio-ready. They don't even say that about me. I'm an

entertainer and a damn good songwriter, but they're not banging down my door for solo records. I'll never be artist *Wes Alton*. I don't *want* to be." I shake my head and grab her hands. "I'm the other half of Viper Rising. That's my future, and if Hannah Drake can't be *Hannah Drake,* then let her be the other half of Viper Rising with me."

I don't know if it's a good speech. But it's my career, my heart, my *life* I'm handing to her in this moment. Her eyes skim over my face, slowly, carefully. This is it, the crossroads to our future. This decision is everything—my bloody heart in her hands—and I hold my breath as I wait.

After way too many seconds for my starved lungs to handle, she squeezes my fingers and smiles. "Why yes, Wesley Alton. I'd be honored to call myself Mrs. Viper Rising."

30

SHOWCASE

Josh fires an absent rhythm on his thigh with his sticks. Pablo bobs his head to a private song in his head. And Hannah... Hannah looks about to vomit.

"There are so many people," she groans, peeking at the audience from backstage.

I lean out and shrug. "Only about ten thousand." For once I wasn't trying to be sarcastic, but she glares at me anyway.

"*Only* ten thousand, he says."

"What? That's a minor-league baseball game. Elementary school bands play those." Maybe not my best encouragement when she shoots me my favorite *vexed-look*. I don't bother trying to stop the grin.

"Han, seriously, you just have to turn your brain off. For twenty-six years you've locked yourself down. It's time to let go." I hold out my fist. "Be my viper, Hannah Drake?"

Her tension melts into a giggle as she taps it with hers. "I'd be honored, Wesley Alton."

"Good." I step back to address everyone. "You all ready to kick some ass? Hannah's wondering what the hold up is."

She's still grinning as we step out into an eruption of cheers. God, I missed this. The energy, the excitement. The anticipation of connecting with your soul on a different level. I check on Hannah and her smile fills the entire stage. She looks like Hannah. She looks like a rockstar.

"Good evening, Nashville!" I shout into the mic over Josh's steady beat on the bass drum. I add a heavy rhythm on the electric guitar while the bass comes in with a sick line you can feel in your blood. "Viper Rising, here," I continue. "Yeah, we're new. Know what that means?" The musical frenzy builds into a frantic plunge toward the intro. "We're about to work extra hard to say hello!"

The crowd roars as I spin back and let the music fly. My body takes over, mind off in that place where freedom meets passion. And there she is. Sharing the front of the stage is a deity from another realm. Long dark hair swaying in time to the jerky movements of a woman caught up in a moment, and I know—I just *know*—this audience is about to receive a gift they will never forget.

Through the lights, the haze, the cacophonous furor of the crowd and the speakers, our smiles connect and fuse a union that began years ago. A purpose neither of us would have dreamed up is now apparent, and ten thousand strangers are enjoying its birth with us.

We are Viper Rising.

> "Coil of strength wound tight to hide. To lie. To
>   wither and writhe. In its prison it cries,
>   'Coil of rage!'"

Hannah's voice slithers over the crowd in a ribbon of sound, teasing, manipulating, controlling every ear it touches. The roar magnifies with each line, each build into the next surprise on this musical journey through her mind. By the time I come in with a harmony on the chorus, I'm having flashbacks to my years on the road. I'm back on the bus, on stage, *living*, because this is life to me. The music. This is the only safe place to let go completely, and it's then that I realize Hannah isn't the only one who needed that lesson. For too long, I've held on to the demons intent on poisoning my world. It's time to cage them in the music. To free my life for people like Hannah. Holland. Sophia, Spence, and a host of others I could love if I can take away the demons' power.

That's it. My "Viper" story. Hannah's is different, but we all have a cage. We all have to fight the demons and find that place where we can fly, driven and untamed. The piece of us that holds the magic.

Yeah, it's on, babe. The world better watch out because the vipers are breaking free.

> Fangs bared, spring out, out
> Of hell, don't tell
> Me what I am
> I'm not, not your pet
> I'm your hidden regret
> So hear me, you should fucking fear me
> As I rise

The end.

EPILOGUE: EFFICIENCY

Giant grins. Open body language. An enthusiastic effort to greet us. Now, I'm smiling too.

I pull Hannah in for a quick kiss on the temple before we greet Pam, Raymond, and Maurice.

"Great show," Raymond says, offering his hand. We shake it, and the radiance on Hannah's face should leave no doubt that they've found a star.

"We were really impressed," Pam says.

"They were amazing," Holland adds because of course she wasn't going to let us go through this meeting alone. She gives her sister a squeeze, and the three of us sit across from them.

"We'd like to get you into the studio and lay down some more demos," Maurice says, expression severe with urgency.

"Absolutely." I reach for Hannah's hand. Her grip tightens on my fingers, and I'd do anything to permanently preserve the smile on her face.

Pam leans forward. "Once we finalize the paperwork, we'd like to look at getting you some shows as soon as possible as well. It would be great for you and Tracing Holland to feed off the relationship while the hype is fresh."

"Why not have them open for us on the fall tour?" Holland suggests.

I've never felt a silence saturated with such a confusion of emotion at once. Shock, awe, excitement, concern, it's all there along with love from the two of us on this side of the table. It's an amazing gesture from Holland, but not nearly as beautiful as watching the sisters share a private moment of mutual adoration.

"That's an interesting idea," Maurice says finally. "We'll definitely discuss the possibility. There are a lot of details to work out before we can commit to something like that, but that would be quite the story to promote."

Holland nods and gives them a stern look. "Well, do your best because I think it would be perfect." She flashes a quick smile at me. "And don't worry about a bus. We have plenty of space on ours."

"SO, how does it feel to be a rockstar?" I ask Hannah as we curl up on the couch in my condo.

"Exhilarating. Terrifying."

I chuckle. "Sounds about right." I pull her against me until every line of our bodies connect. It's addictive how well we fit. "I was thinking. We're going to have a lot of work to do. Writing, rehearsing, planning, all of that. It would be a lot more efficient if you moved in."

She stiffens and twists back to face me. "Are you serious?"

"Yeah, I mean, it's getting old trying to think of excuses to keep you here."

Her face scrunches into that expression I just have to kiss

off. She softens under me as I shift and move in for the kill. This woman. I'll never get enough. My need intensifies with each reaction of her body to mine.

"So this invitation is purely out of convenience," she breathes against my mouth.

"Purely." I assert my attention on her neck. She arches as I tickle the sensitive skin with kisses down to her collarbone. Her hands fight with my shirt until I straighten and rip it over my head.

"My god," she whispers, gaze running over me in wonder—then humor. "You are *such* an alpha."

I smirk. "And?"

FOR UPDATES AND ANNOUNCEMENTS, subscribe to Aly's newsletter.

EXPERIENCE the original song "Greetings from the Inside," along with the rest of Aly's music, wherever you stream music.
Spotify
Apple Music
Amazon Music

MORE FROM ALY

From angsty and dark to snort-laugh funny, Aly writes romance from
her soul to yours.

THE SAVE ME SERIES

RISING WEST (available on audiobook)

FALLING NORTH

BREAKING SOUTH

CRASHING EAST

GUARDING SHADOWS

CHASING RIPTIDES

THE WRECK ME SERIES

ASHTON MORGAN: Apartment 17B

CAMDEN WALKER: Apartment 8C

TRISTAN & ISABEL: Apartment 11F

THE HOLD ME SERIES

Available on audiobook.

NIGHT SHIFTS BLACK

TRACING HOLLAND

VIPER

LIMELIGHT

AN NSB WEDDING

SMARTYPANTS ROMANCE
STREET SMART
PLAY SMART
LOOK SMART

STANDALONES
YOUNG LOVE

PARANORMAL/SUSPENSE
GIFTED (Gifted, Vol 1)
CURSED (Gifted, Vol 2)
SÖREN (Gifted, Vol 3)
HAUNTED MELODY
TRAITOR

STAY IN TOUCH

Thank you for taking this journey with me. I would love to hear from you! For updates, reveals, and more subscribe to my newsletter and join my fun, laidback reader group on Facebook: Aly's Breakfast Club.

You can also follow Aly's original music wherever you stream music:

Spotify
Apple Music
Amazon Music

Find Aly here:

Amazon
Facebook Reader Group – Aly's Breakfast Club
Newsletter
BookBub
Spotify
Apple Music
Facebook Page – Author Aly Stiles

Goodreads
Website
Instagram
YouTube
Blogger sign-up for notifications about future releases
Pinterest

Aly Stiles
PO Box 577
Trexlertown, PA 18087-0577

NOTE FROM ALY

Depression is a serious illness that can go unrecognized by the victim and surrounding loved ones.

If you, or anyone you know, have plans to harm yourself, or you just need someone to talk to, help is available. Dial 988 for the Suicide and Crisis Lifeline, which is a 24-hour, toll-free hotline available to anyone in suicidal crisis or emotional distress.

Please know you are not alone, you are important, and you are loved.

Sincerely,

Aly

www.ingramcontent.com/pod-product-compliance
Lightning Source LLC
Chambersburg PA
CBHW072129250626
47159CB00007B/2619